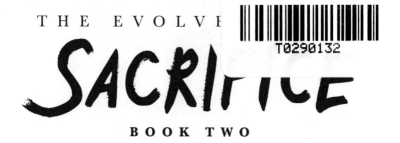

THE EVOLVED

SACRIFICE

BOOK TWO

NATASHA OLIVER

Marshall Cavendish
Editions

With the support of

NATIONAL ARTS COUNCIL
SINGAPORE

Published by Marshall Cavendish Editions
An imprint of Marshall Cavendish International

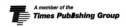

A member of the
Times Publishing Group

Other Marshall Cavendish Offices:
Marshall Cavendish Corporation, 800 Westchester Ave, Suite N-641, Rye Brook, NY 10573, USA • Marshall Cavendish International (Thailand) Co Ltd, 253 Asoke, 16th Floor, Sukhumvit 21 Road, Klongtoey Nua, Wattana, Bangkok 10110, Thailand • Marshall Cavendish (Malaysia) Sdn Bhd, Times Subang, Lot 46, Subang Hi-Tech Industrial Park, Batu Tiga, 40000 Shah Alam, Selangor Darul Ehsan, Malaysia

Marshall Cavendish is a registered trademark of Times Publishing Limited

National Library Board, Singapore Cataloguing in Publication Data

Name(s): Oliver, Natasha, 1974-.
Title: The evolved ones. Book two : sacrifice / Natasha Oliver.
Description: Singapore : Marshall Cavendish Editions, [2020] | "With the support of National Arts Council Singapore."--Title page verso.
Identifier(s): OCN 1155613611 | ISBN 978-981-48-9311-4 (paperback)
Subject(s): LCSH: Fantasy fiction.
Classification: DDC S823--dc23

Printed in Singapore

Cover design by Kelley Lim

To Mom and Dad.
Thank you for your unwavering love and support
as I hopped from here to there and everywhere.

Oh, and Mom, I spilled nail polish remover on your
brand new Queen Anne coffee table when we were
living in the apartments in Maplewood. I used all
of my pocket money to pay a furniture repairman
to fix it before you came home from work.

And Dad, you should know that was the only mistake
I ever made and I still remain your perfect little angel.

I love you both, more.

CHAPTER ONE

~

Distracted

August 1st, 3:30pm
Washington State, USA

"Well, I have to admit I wasn't expecting this," Josh said.

Neither was Sam. Shards of broken glass were scattered across the floor like caltrops. A painting that could only be described as a novice's failed attempt of a forest at dusk was lying on its side, its frame cracked. The sofa was on its back with a leg broken off, and two very nice end tables were turned upside down in the middle of the entranceway.

"Notify Meita," Sam said.

Josh's boots crunched on the shattered remains of a lamp lying at the base of the stairs, its shade wedged in the corner behind the front door. "Your phone works too."

Tyson Li owned one of the more modest homes in the popular Queen Anne area of Seattle, and from the looks of things, it had seen better days. The living room appeared as if a small demolition crew had swept through it.

The kitchen and dining room had fared better: the refrigerator remained upright and the table still had all four of its legs. Three chairs had been pulled out and were turned to face a single one that had its back pushed up against the wall. A tangled rope hung around both its armrests as well as the chair's two front legs.

This did not bode well for Tyson, and even less so for Miles, Tyson's younger brother.

This place was only hours away from turning into an active crime scene.

"Don't touch anything," Sam shouted.

"What?"

Sam stepped over a bookcase and its contents as he made his way to the bottom of the stairs. "Gloves. Wear them."

Josh wrapped his fingers around the banister and leaned over the railing. "They're in the glove compartment."

Sam pinched the space between his eyes. "Wipe down anything you touch."

He had hoped locating Miles would have been a lot easier than this. The teenager had been missing for twenty-four hours before anyone at Halo noticed. But in everyone's defense, the boy was a recluse. He hadn't wanted to socialize with any of them, but neither had he wanted to return home to his parents after he and Rox escaped from Wonderland. In fact, in the last ten months, Miles had only participated in half a dozen of their training sessions. He managed to skip almost all of his psychological assessments with Bethany, their in-house doctor, and now he was missing. His disappearance kickstarted a wild goose chase that led across the country to his older brother's house where, if the state of the living room was anything to go by, his brother had one hell of a fight with someone … probably someone*s*.

Sam would have preferred to spend his time helping evolved ones who actually *wanted* help, but Walter refused to turn the boy away.

His father was right, of course. New abilities, raging hormones, and let's not forget post-traumatic stress from being held and experimented on, meant it was also possible that Miles could be the *someone* that Tyson had that "hell of a fight" with.

If Sam was right in his latter assumption, Miles needed the kind of help Halo wasn't equipped to provide. Halo created new identities, relocated families, helped individuals start over with just enough funds to make a go at a second life without the threat of being discovered. Miles needed help not from a relocation provider, but from a psychiatrist, someone dedicated to him and his recovery.

Sam used the toe of his boot to spread out some papers that had been thrown on the floor, but all of it was useless. A few bills and some kind of homeowner insurance letter. Nothing that could help him locate Miles … or Tyson for that matter. Whoever turned this place over had a good head start on them.

Why did Miles run? He was clearly safer with them than off on his own. Could his disappearance and the current state of his brother's house be nothing more than a coincidence?

"Yo," Josh yelled from over the banister. "You got the gloves?"

Sam stood up and kicked at the papers. He stepped over the foam from the inside of a cushion and struggled to open the front door because of the lampshade. He shoved his boot into its largest opening and slowly pivoted on one foot so he could swing it into the living room with the rest of the overturned furniture.

The air was surprisingly humid for Seattle. He hadn't spent much time in the Pacific Northwest, but he didn't think it ever got this hot in this part of the country. The front garden was lush with greenery and colorful plants. Wherever Tyson had gone – more than likely *carted off* – he hadn't been missing for long. The plants looked well-watered, but then again, it could have rained recently.

Sam made a mental note to check the weather reports.

A crow almost the size of a raven announced its presence as it flew across the yard, drawing Sam's attention from the yellow and purple flowers lining the narrow path. Nothing about the man standing just outside of Tyson's front gate was out of place. His clothes said he was someone out for a run, but it was the way he stilled when their eyes met that alerted Sam something was off. The runner held his hand steady over the latch, like he was frozen in indecision, and then he turned and took off at a full sprint.

"Josh!" Sam shouted as he gave chase.

It was late afternoon and the roads were about an hour from getting busy. The sidewalks were somewhat slippery, which told Sam it *had* rained recently, which meant they were no closer to knowing when Tyson's place had been ransacked.

The runner was about a good hundred yards ahead of him, but Sam wasn't worried. Very few people ran as long and as often as he did. The key was not to do a full-out sprint, but to keep pace, because eventually, everyone tired.

The runner turned left up a side street, disappearing around the corner for a few brief seconds until Sam rounded after him.

Where are you?

Regardless of how much they had trained together in the past ten months, Sam still struggled with Josh's presence inside his head.

Why are you running? Ohhh … stay connected and I'll bring the car.

As if Sam had a choice. Rox was the only one who could stop Josh from invading her thoughts, and no one had spoken to her since she reconnected with her family.

Perhaps it was a good thing Miles disappeared. Sam hadn't realized just how much pent-up energy he had until his gait widened and the distance between him and his prey lessened.

In training, Sam was always aware of the differences between him and Josh. While Josh had natural talent, plus years of ad hoc training, he lacked formal experience. Meita was the closest to giving Sam a real fight, but it was simply a matter of physics with her; he had more mass to throw around. But where he had strength, she had precision. She hadn't survived as long as she had without knowing when to strike, and when to evade.

Meita bint Tariq al-Shaikh was the best information specialist he had ever met – and that was saying something because Sam knew his way around a firewall. In fact, Meita was the reason they all still lived. Her and Josh's timely appearance at Watership Down had saved all of them. Then she saved them again by getting them the backup they needed to get Rox out of Wonderland. However, it was that second dose of help that had changed everything because she didn't offer it without conditions. One of them was that Sam, Josh, and Rox work for the Global Frontiers Organization (GFO), a non-profit that aided in the advancement of evolved ones. Technically, GFO didn't exist. They were just an invisible line item on a black-ops budget spreadsheet that lacked oversight or a true mission statement. Whoever was in charge of GFO – right now that was Katherine Louise Cheung – set the objectives and decided to what extent they would "advance" evolved ones.

The runner looked over his shoulder and stumbled. Sam mentally flicked through the different ways he would subdue him once he caught up, but then the runner hooked another left onto Queen Anne Avenue.

Sam relayed his new direction to Josh.

I know. I can see where you are.

The runner made a sharp right across the main artery and down a side street, causing Sam to shorten his stride to let a passing car go by.

A dog barking alerted Sam that the runner was crossing to the opposite side of the street. Sam was debating whether to use his ability when a horn blared. The runner had cut in front of a car coming out of its parking space. The driver lowered his window to toss out a few words before speeding off.

The distance between them closed and it would have been a textbook tackle, but the runner lost his footing when he glanced back. Sam came in too high and slammed into the runner's shoulder. His weight and the momentum of the collision bruised two of his ribs. Both men cried out, but Sam had the advantage of practice. He rolled with the pain, bringing the runner with him.

The sound of tires squealing lifted Sam's head. Daytime running lights were positioned at eye level, and all Sam could focus on was the absence of her energy pulses, but then nails scratched the back of his neck as a hand yanked him out of the path of the skidding car.

Free from the weight of Sam on top of him, the runner lifted his head at precisely the wrong moment and the front bumper came to a full stop mere millimeters too late.

The runner's nose received the brunt of the impact, and whatever injury he had suffered from the fall was insignificant compared to this new one.

Sam was sure the runner was paralyzed. It was the way his cheek rested on the bumper, the rest of his body completely motionless. But then his eyes started to blink. It meant he was alive, but something was terribly wrong because no one blinked that rapidly or that frequently. Then his mouth fell open and blood poured out.

Sam was about to tell him to remain still, but the runner's limbs began trembling as he pushed away from the car. It took him a few tries, but he managed to get to his feet even though he swayed like his brain was struggling to catch up with his body's movements.

"Well, as far as being hit by a car goes, it's not *that* bad," Josh said.

The runner used the hood for balance as he attempted to take his first step.

"I'm no doctor, but I'm thinking concussion," Josh said. "Definite cranial damage."

"Then connect with him before he passes out," Sam whispered.

His thoughts are gonna be a jumbled mess.

"Oh my God!" The man who had been driving the car climbed out. "Are you alright?"

I'm gonna go ahead and answer on his behalf—

"*Josh!*"

"What were you guys doing?" the driver said. "Running in the street like that is dangerous!"

Sam was still on the ground, his knees bent with his elbows resting on top. In hindsight, he should have used his ability to stop the chase before it began, but it felt good to run flat out like that.

Josh reached for his mobile to phone Meita. She would need to know that their only lead for locating Miles was missing and his home had been ransacked.

"Did you hear me?" the driver said. "What were you guys doing running into the road like that? This wasn't my fault!"

Sam pushed to his feet with the feeling that things were snowballing downhill rapidly. Luckily, the runner hadn't gotten far. He looked as if he were stuck in a mental loop, contemplating the mechanics of walking. Sam sent a thought to Josh that they should get what they could from the runner before the paramedics arrived.

"This was not my fault," the driver shouted again. "I have a camera in my car."

Josh stopped mid-sentence with Meita and ended the call. *I'll take care of him, you sort out the camera.* He turned to the driver. "Help me check him over," Josh said as he directed him to the front of the car.

"You a doctor?" the driver asked.

Sam lowered himself into the driver's seat slowly, knowing that once the adrenaline wore off, pain would rapidly set in. The camera was fixed to the windshield just below the rearview mirror and looked to be one of the older models. It was a long cylindrical tube with a black button that ran the entire length on the right side and a shorter button on the left, just beside a narrow slit that housed the SD card.

"Check SD card," the camera announced when Sam pressed the eject button.

Two heads appeared over the front of the car.

"Check SD card."

Sam hit the start/stop engine button.

"Check SD card," the camera continued.

Pull the power cable!

"What are you doing in my car?" the driver asked, making his way to the driver's side. Sam switched on the hazard lights with one hand and pulled the power connector from the camera with his other hand.

Sam wasn't exceptionally tall or overly muscular. He was more lithe than thick, and was dressed in black cargo pants and a long-sleeved black shirt designed for performance. But it was the way he crossed his arms over his chest as he climbed out of the car that made the driver step back. "Trouble finding the hazard lights."

"I-I don't want no trouble," the driver said.

"Think you can call 9-1-1 for us?" Sam asked.

The driver looked confused, but then slowly nodded as he sidestepped Sam to reach in the car for his phone.

Got anything? Sam asked as he came to the front of the car where the runner was now seated and struggling to remain conscious.

Josh reached up and grabbed Sam's wrist to create a three-way connection.

Nausea churned in Sam's stomach as Josh struggled to find a single coherent thread inside the runner's thoughts that could lead them to the information they needed.

Where is Tyson?

Sam felt the runner try to resist, but just asking the question brought about unsequenced memories of Tyson and his home.

Images of the runner and two other men breaking into the house briefly took form. A glimpse of a bleeding Tyson tied to one of the dining room chairs, followed by questions and feelings of euphoria at Tyson's pain when he couldn't tell them where his little brother, Miles, was located.

What did you do with him? Sam asked through Josh.

The runner groaned, but a memory of him driving a car into Tyson's garage and his two buddies loading an inert body into the trunk told Sam everything he needed to know. They had strangled Tyson, and one of the other two men had gotten rid of the body.

That would explain the lack of blood back at his place, Sam said.

What do you want with Miles? Josh asked.

"Hey!" the driver cut in as if this wasn't his first time trying to get their attention. "The paramedics are on their way." Then he pointed to the runner. "He alright? He's starting to lose color, man."

"Joder," Josh said and tried to regain his connection, but all Sam felt was silence. A sad kind of nothingness. No peace, no darkness. Only silence, and the growing sounds of sirens.

"You got something, right?" Sam asked.

Only what you saw.

Sam swore. *What did Meita say?*

To go with the locals. She doesn't want us causing a scene. Katherine will make a few calls to get us out.

That could take hours.

It will *take hours. Meita will look into Tyson. I get the impression he's not been dead long.* Josh explained that the images from the runner were too vivid to have happened more than a day or two ago.

Meita say what our story should be? Sam asked.

She said you'd think of something.

Right now all Sam could think of was a warm shower and a bed. His left side was beginning to throb, so he leaned against another car parked on the street. He pinched the space between his eyes and tried to ease the tension that was bringing a headache with each siren's wail.

They're here, Josh said in a sing-song tone.

Sam shifted to his feet and took a deep breath. "We go with the truth."

That on our search for our empathic friend, we stumbled across our friend's brother's killer who confessed to me telepathically—

"I meant—" Sam took a deep breath as he realized the truth was probably not a good idea. "—we go with something as close to the truth as possible."

By saying ...

"We came to Seattle to meet Miles at his brother's house, but when we got there it was ransacked. We saw him," Sam pointed to the runner, "walking up the pathway, and he ran before we could ask him any questions."

And that doesn't seem odd to you?

"Well, yeah. That's why I ran after him."

I'm talking about the fact that me, a handsome, 30-something male, and you, just shy of a mid-life crisis, would be friends with a seventeen-year-old boy?

Sam swore under his breath. He looked at the driver, the runner who was now lying unconscious on his side, and the female police officer who was stepping out of her vehicle. "I'll think of something."

~

Dominoes

August 1st, 7:42pm
New Jersey, USA

"We've located the empath," Harry said.

"Did your guys get 'em?" Tusk asked.

"No. We think he's left the country."

"What?"

"We think he used his brother's passport and booked a flight to Singapore."

"Singapore?" Tusk asked. Why would he go there?

"I had his records checked, and he's not from Singapore. At first, I thought he was running to his family overseas or something, but he's an American of Taiwanese descent. His folks moved here before he and his brother were born, so there's no obvious connection. I'm having my people look at old girlfriends or past acquaintances, but the kid's just seventeen. I'm thinking family friend perhaps."

Tusk wasn't sure what to think. His main interest in the boy was his link to Tara. Tusk hadn't been able to uncover how their paths crossed, but his Wonderland surveillance footage showed she risked her own escape to save him. The kid had to be the key to finding her.

"Where is the empath?" Leona asked, interrupting Tusk from his thoughts and his call.

He had forgotten she was there, which was normally very difficult to do. Tusk didn't particularly care for Leona. She was tedious and had far too much hubris for one so short on experience. But the girl had money – tons of it. She was evolved, but he couldn't quite figure out her ability, and she wasn't keen on sharing. The one wise thing about her was that she didn't trust easily. She said she was interested in funding his research for personal reasons, and she had transferred enough cash into his account to convince him she was worth going against his own instincts.

"We think Singapore," he said to her.

Losing Watership Down and Wonderland in such close succession had hurt. He'd also lost his assistant, Nancy, who had been with him from the beginning. She died shortly after being taken into custody, as per the protocol.

"One of my guys got picked up in Seattle at the brother's house," Harry said.

"How?"

"We've been watching the empath's family just to see what surfaces, and what'd you know, Major Watts and Josh Mendez show up. I haven't been able to access any satellite footage over that area since then – probably Katherine's doing – but when I do, I'm hoping it'll show me what their abilities are. My guy was good, so it stands to reason that those two might have active abilities."

"Will he talk?" Tusk asked.

"Did Nancy talk?" There was a moment of silence before Harry continued. "Sam showing up means that Halo's still in operation."

"Halo? That group you said your old military contact started? That's a mickey mouse operation hardly worth our time—"

"Let's not forget that it was that same mickey mouse operation that infiltrated your Dominican facility despite me giving you the head's up they were coming."

"They had the healer. They had Tara."

"Being able to heal yourself is impressive, but that's not enough to explain her escape from either facility, Cliff," Harry said.

"Yes, but I'm certain that she's able to … I don't know, harm other people as well." Tusk couldn't exactly explain it, but somehow her ability enabled her to incapacitate people – the man at the helicopter when they were exchanging Josh's son, the guard inside of Miles' room, and then Nancy. No one got the drop on Nancy. Ever.

"You really think she's that powerful?"

"Harry, look, we pumped her full of sedatives, and I'm not talking horse tranquilizers, I'm talking enough to knock out a damn elephant. And she kept waking up. Every blood sample, DNA, bone marrow, you name it, they always degrade. It's like the sample begins to rapidly deteriorate after being extracted in just a matter of hours." Did anyone understand how hard it was to work under those conditions?

"You think you can replicate it?" Harry asked.

"I don't know what I can do, but I've literally set her on fire, and within a matter of hours, there wasn't a single burn scar remaining. Her cells die off just like everyone else's, but when they replicate, they do so with one-hundred-percent precision. Listen, Harry, all of our cells deteriorate, our bodies are programmed to die – you know this – but it's like at some point, her cells simply stopped … I don't know … aging!"

"Is she getting younger?"

"No. As far as I can tell, she's in some sort of perfect stasis." Tusk took a breath to steady his voice. This was the first time he was telling Harry about the extent of the experiments he conducted on Tara. He trusted Harry – they had worked on far too many projects and had too much evidence against the other to do anything but operate on complete trust. Still, Tusk hated sharing his work until he had a better handle on things, and he was far from understanding Tara.

"I've killed her, Harry."

"You killed her?" He repeated it like he was unsure he heard correctly. "Cliff, what does that even mean you 'killed her'?"

"She's capable of dying. Her heart stops, respiratory functions cease, her brain literally dies, Harry. But then …"

There was a soft chuckle on the other end of the phone, and Tusk knew it for what it was: Harry struggling to make sense of the inexplicable. Tusk remained silent and let his friend adjust to the new information.

Dr Clifford Tusk and Harry Carter had been roommates at university and had developed a friendship that lasted long after graduation. Harry went into the family business of politics while Tusk went into genetic engineering. Tusk accepted a long time ago he would never have money like Harry, but it had never been about the money. They were both pretty much after the same thing – legacy.

"So, let me get this straight. We had in our possession a woman who can not only heal herself, but we suspect can harm others, and then if that's not enough, she can actually come back to life after death? And we let her get away?"

It was Tusk's turn to chuckle. "I think 'let' isn't the fairest of descriptions. But that's all moot. What we need to focus on is how to get her back, because if I can figure out how her body does what it does, think of the implications."

All Tusk could hear was the slight increase in Harry's breathing. "You think this kid, Miles, is the key to finding her?"

"Why else risk your escape? She had Nancy's access card; that gave her carte blanche to the entire facility."

"Alright. Then Tara is the priority. Hell, Cliff, why are you just sharing this with me? I could've sent more men to Wonderland."

That was the difference between Tusk and his best friend. Harry thought his title and family name meant men were loyal to him and would follow him into the halls of death if he commanded. But Tusk understood men at a more fundamental – some might even say *biological* – level. He understood most people were decent, had their conscious line in the sand, and lived their lives so they rarely had to approach it. But working at the forefront of science meant you erased your line because there was no point at which you would stop. There couldn't be. Very few people could live like that, and so the more people who knew about their work, the greater the risk they ran of being exposed. Someone would inevitably crack.

"What's important is that I'm telling you now," Tusk said.

"No more secrets like that, got it? You think you're on to something, you let me know right away. I can't do my job if you're not upfront with me."

"Yep. Lesson learned. I thought I had more time, Harry." He knew that Josh would be looking for her, but he had no idea that he would actually find her.

"How's the new girl?" Harry asked.

Tusk glanced at Leona. "Fine. I guess."

"Yeah, I did some digging. She's got deep pockets, and the money's legit."

"You say that like being legit is a bad thing?"

"It is," Harry said, "so tread carefully. She's got property all over the world and she pays her taxes."

Tusk hesitated. "How's that relevant?"

"It's relevant because she's got enough money that paying taxes is the equivalent of a charity donation to her. And secondly, it means she's smart enough to avoid tax evasion. That's how most of her kind go down."

Tusk began to take on a new respect for the wealthy who paid their taxes.

"Anyone not motivated by money is someone you definitely shouldn't trust," Harry said.

"You're not."

"Yeah, but I don't pay taxes." Harry chuckled. "Listen, I'm going to keep digging, but keep me posted on how things go at the border. When are you leaving?"

"Midnight," Tusk said.

"It's been far too long since I've been there. Safe travels."

Tusk looked over his shoulder at Leona, who was on her laptop, after he hung up. They had been working out of one of her apartment buildings just over the bridge from Manhattan. He would have never thought to secure himself in such a place – it lacked anything remotely resembling the equipment he needed to continue his work – but that's why Leona said it would work.

Tusk looked at the river below as the day's fading colors created a bonfire on the water's surface. He supposed he'd stayed in worse accommodations. The high ceilings and wooden beams would be a yuppie's wet dream. The views from the expansive windows were enough to entice anyone hoping to make a better life for themselves. Sad thing about it was it was a trap. An elaborate one, but a cage of working on someone else's schedule while actually never achieving anything of true meaning or lasting value.

"Everything OK?" Leona asked.

"No," Tusk said. "We've lost Miles. Harry thinks he might be in Singapore."

Leona nodded and ran her thumb across her fingertips. "He's looking for something." Her eyes narrowed as if she were trying to see something that wasn't there.

"Why do you think that?" he asked.

Her chair swiveled around so she was fully facing him, and Tusk had to admit she was gorgeous. He wasn't sure if it was her confidence or if it was the way she braided her hair to the side and wore it over her shoulder. He didn't want to look at her that way, but a beautiful, young woman was hard to ignore.

"Well, you said you've been looking for him and the healer for months, yet nothing. Now, out of the blue, he surfaces, heads to his brother's, and ends up in Singapore? Ergo, he's looking for something."

"And does your ability give you any insight into what he might be searching for?"

Leona rubbed her thumb over her fingertips again. "Does it matter? We find him, and we'll find what he's looking for, and then both will be ours."

"You confident whatever he's searching for has value?"

Leona held his stare. "Logic dictates that a man on the run would only leave a secure location when he's after something more valuable than his own safety. And what's greater than that?"

"You think he knows where the healer is?"

Leona shrugged. "No idea. But whatever he's looking for is worth risking his own life. So that makes me interested. Very interested."

CHAPTER TWO

~

Home

3rd August, 5:38pm
Siglap, Singapore

Rox came around the corner too fast, slipped on the metal grate that covered the sewer drain, and lost her footing. She went down on her side, but recovered with the determination of someone with something to prove. The sky crackled white, and a few seconds later, thunder drowned out the sounds of her heavy breathing. The clouds finally released their hold on the moisture they had been accumulating for over a month, and rain fell in deafening drops around her, washing away the fatigue that had settled in her muscles.

She was about six hundred meters from home. *Home.* Her stomach still contracted whenever she thought about it. She pulled on the kinetic energy from the storm and shortened her stride. She pumped her arms and sprinted up the hill towards belonging. She was grateful for the rain because even though it made the road slippery, it was a reprieve from Singapore's oppressive heat. At 20 to 6 in the evening, it was still suffocating. But it beat itchy blankets and the cold floorspace of the random buildings she had been forced to seek shelter in during the winter months back in the US.

The rain was too loud for her to make out the neighbor's barking dog as it ran alongside her behind its fence. Shaira would never let something as pedestrian as a gate stop her from giving chase.

Rox was surprised how often her mind wandered to the wolf. She hadn't seen her since they were forced to separate back at Watership, and Rox wondered how she was getting on. Probably fine. She was an animal after all. She had more than likely forgotten all about Rox, especially now they had Val, Sam's sister, back home.

Sam. That was another name that often captured her attention despite her best efforts to focus on the here and now. The comfort of his embrace and the images of him bursting into Miles' room to rescue her accompanied her to sleep each night. He was the promise of what she could have had, of what she had sacrificed to return to her family.

Rox wiped her eyes as she turned left through the open gate that enclosed Michael's property. MJ sat in the doorway with his stopwatch in hand, the wraparound porch protecting him from the rain. He jumped up and pressed the stop button when her foot hit the first step.

He looked down at the stopwatch with the expectation of a child, but then his smile slipped, just a little. "It started raining," he said, offering her an excuse for not setting a personal best.

A combination of intense joy and guilt brought tears to her eyes as she realized she would never receive more love from another human.

"I slipped and fell," she said, hoping that her son hadn't noticed the catch in her voice.

"Ugh, you're wet and sweaty," he said as she pulled him in for a hug, but he wrapped his arms around her anyway.

It was almost five years ago that everything changed for Rox – or perhaps *began* would be more accurate. She awoke without memory and discovered she had the involuntary ability to heal. If that wasn't enough to come to grips with, she didn't wake up in Singapore with her family, but instead in the US with Josh, a stranger and a master manipulator.

The only reason she made it back home was because she agreed to work for GFO. It hadn't been an amicable arrangement. They had dangled information about her true identity in front of her with the caveat she work for them, on their terms. It was an easy *no thank you* until she realized they were her best chance at not only finding her family, but also protecting them from people like Dr Tusk.

"You and Dad still going out?" MJ asked.

She had forgotten about that. "Think so," she said. "Where is he?"

"Call," MJ said, which meant Michael, her husband, was in the room off to the left of the kitchen that served as his home office, more than likely with the door closed and his headset on so he wouldn't be disturbed.

MJ sat in front of the television and resumed playing his video game. Rox would have followed him, but the floors were marble so she walked along the side of the house to her quarters at the back.

It was the nicest place she'd stayed in since leaving Josh. The walls were a pale yellow with an off-white border, and when she first arrived, smelled as if it had been recently painted. The furniture was new and looked like it belonged on the cover of a high-end magazine for beachfront property. A few family photos were spread throughout her single room, which made it feel warm, almost inviting, and although it was on the outside of the main house, it had become her sanctuary.

Rox pulled off her wet running clothes and dropped them into the bathroom sink. If she left them there, they would disappear and reappear a day later, laundered, pressed, and folded in the drawer designated for her workout gear. She shook her head at the drastic turn her life had taken.

Rox flipped the switch for the hot-water heater and wrapped a towel around herself. Working for GFO meant she had a legitimate job and a real paycheck, but she didn't make enough to afford the dresses that hung in her closet. Those were gifts from Michael when she had returned with only a single change of clothing.

Reuniting with her family had been exhilarating, at first. There was so much to learn, and she wanted to hear everything, no matter how small the detail. She also wanted to tell them everything, how Josh had found her and then how he trained her and taught her to defend herself. But to share that meant she'd have to explain her personal relationship with him. She didn't know how to explain that they had been lovers, and then at one point she had considered him her enemy, but now, after all that happened, in those quiet moments when she was honest with herself, he was her family.

Rox glanced at the clock. She had forty minutes to get ready; that was more than enough time. She'd simply tuck her curls back at the sides with a few hair clips she had picked up from Chinatown. They were far from expensive, but living on the street had taught her not everything worthwhile came with a high price tag – which was the opposite of her new life here where people had the attitude of "you got what you paid for". Everything in Singapore felt grand, even down to the hawker centers that served her morning coffee for under a dollar.

By the time Rox was showered, her hair washed and styled, and in her evening dress, she had twelve minutes before they had to leave. She decided to put on a little make-up and grab a clutch from the box of Tara's designer handbags that Michael had stored away for Ruby and Emma when they got older.

Ever since returning "home", her life had become a series of repetitive moments. There were school drop-offs, pick-ups, homework, tuition classes, tutors, co-curricular activities, birthday parties, and a never-ending stream of exams. In between that, she attended two weekly briefings with Meita and had a workout schedule that consisted of three, two-hour sessions per day – once before the sun rose, another before lunch, and the last one was before dinner (or after, depending).

Tears blurred her vision when she accidentally poked herself in the eye with the mascara brush. She never took this much pain with her appearance even when she was with Josh. Maybe some lipstick and blush. But since arriving in Singapore, she felt the need to fit in with the other mothers. They were beautiful, salon-finished, educated housewives who sacrificed their careers for playdates and calendar-overload. The few mom-friends she reconnected with were well-traveled, held advanced degrees, and had never spent a day worrying about where their next meal would come from. They spoke about their lives before children or their travels abroad. Some even talked about the businesses they recently started now their kids were old enough. They remembered things about her that left her feeling inadequate and altogether a lesser version of her former self. When she was with Josh, they had dined at some of the best restaurants, but never did she feel like a fraud.

Rox knew how to run. She knew the importance of a good hiding space and how to go unseen. She knew how to take a hit and get back up. She knew that not all smiles were friendly and that everyone wanted something. She also knew that outside of this gilded bubble she had entered, there was a world where her kind were being kidnapped and experimented on by people who would stop at nothing to uncover how evolved ones got their ability. But she didn't know how to slip that into the conversation when everyone was talking about how their children had grown or the worry that consumed them when their kids were challenged.

Rox had just met her children. She didn't know their likes any more than she did their challenges. She had no idea what they were like as toddlers so she couldn't say things like *she's finally come out of her shell* or *her reading's improved wonders. Remember when* ... Remember when what? When they were taking their first steps? When they said their first words? First day of school? Hell, the memory of their *last* day of school would have been an improvement.

She placed the applicator back in the tube. Who could tell if she had on mascara anyway? Michael's award ceremony was in one of the most expensive hotels. She couldn't remember the name, but she knew the room would be dark, or dark*ish* at least. People weren't there to see her anyway. She was just a bit of the candy on the side, the missing (and then found) wife of a very successful businessman, the mother of his three children – one of whom wished she had never returned. She put the make-up back in its bag and looked at the stranger staring back at her in the mirror. There were some things even a high-end concealer couldn't hide.

The rain had stopped by the time Rox entered the main house through the kitchen door. Michael was in the living room chatting with their eldest, Ruby, who had made it quite clear that Rox was not the same woman who had given birth to her.

It was obvious that buried underneath all of Ruby's anger was a chasm of pain. She had grieved the death of her mother, and for Rox to return was reopening a wound that had probably never truly healed.

"You look pretty," MJ said as he leaned over the back of the sofa when she came in.

Rox blushed. "Thank you."

"I'll be in my room," Ruby said, rolling her eyes.

Michael sighed and waited until his eldest disappeared up the stairs. "I keep telling myself it's just a phase."

"She'll come around sooner or later."

"More like never," MJ mumbled as he returned to his video game.

"He's right, though," Michael said. "You do look beautiful."

The dress was designed by someone whose name she was sure at one time she was able to pronounce. It was a deep shade of maroon with a sheer overlay that flowed with her movements. She grabbed a pale pink shawl to wear over her shoulders because despite the obvious beauty of the dress, it was wholly impractical for indoor affairs where the air conditioning would be set to arctic.

Rox went over to the shoe cupboard and took out a pair of heels. The hem of the dress brushed along her ankles, allowing the design of the shoes to be visible. They, too, were impractical. She would never be able to run in them if the situation arose. Go unseen? Not likely with the noise they would make with each stride across the marble floor.

"That workout routine has your arms toned."

That workout routine still made her nauseous. Mika, her personal trainer provided by GFO, took it as his life's mission to find new ways to torture her. She swore he took pride every time she had to crawl off to the side and dry heave – second lesson in training with Mika, never arrive with a full stomach.

First lesson: never train with Mika.

Sam probably wouldn't recognize her now. Not with all the make-up and fancy attire. She was sure the image he had of her was one of bloodstained clothes and matted hair. That was if he even thought about her at all. She could have easily been nothing more to him than a means to rescue his sister. She hadn't heard from any of them, except Josh. He couldn't project his thoughts into her mind because of the distance, but they had a way of knowing when it was time to reach out, and she wondered if that meant something. If they had a special connection that she would never have with Michael, or anyone else for that matter.

Rox was surprised at the change in their relationship. Josh had become the support she needed as she tried to adjust to her new life here. She looked forward to their catch-ups, even if they were handwritten and sent by snail mail. And she missed his son, Jay, who always included a separate letter in with Josh's. She was grateful he was adjusting to his new school and his home life at Halo where he and Josh now lived. MJ reminded her a lot of Jay. It was the way they looked at her, like her best would always be good enough.

"Tara?"

"Oh, sorry, yes. I'm ready to go." It had taken more time than she thought it would adjusting to her new – *old* – name. People often had to call her a few times before she realized someone was speaking to her.

Michael held the car door open for her until she was seated with her dress tucked safely inside. He had two cars and one Ducati he only took out on the weekends.

When Rox found out the price of a car in Singapore, she almost had a heart attack. When she discovered the amount he had paid for this two-seater, she thought the man had more money than sense. For that amount, she could have hired Meita herself to find her family *and* still have some left over for the children's college funds.

Michael put the car in gear and slipped his hand over hers. "You're quiet. How was your run?"

"Sorry. Just a bit distracted. How was your day?"

"Good. Productive. Finally figured out what we're doing for V-R's five-year anniversary next year."

Michael had built a virtual reality social media platform that allowed users to interact in real time as either themselves or an avatar they custom built. It was lauded as one of the most revolutionary pieces of technology of its time, and he was being given an award from the Chairman of the American Chamber of Commerce in Singapore. It wasn't a particularly prestigious award, but it was a way for him to pay homage to his national roots given he wouldn't move the company's headquarters to the US despite some tempting offers.

Michael chose to remain an American citizen, but had lived in Singapore for the past twenty years, and he and his family had become permanent residents. His company was registered in Singapore, so it brought in a lot of revenue and jobs to the small island-state. Not that the country was hurting for money. Never had Rox seen such opulence from a government – though to be fair, Rox's memories only covered the last five years. Every time they drove from his home in Siglap into the Central Business District, she was struck by the pristine skyline and bright lights. Even on a cloudy day, the skyscrapers visible from the East Coast Parkway were impressive.

He ran his fingers up her arm to give her muscles a squeeze. "I'm gonna become afraid of you if you keep this workout routine up."

"It's torture. Absolute torture. I'm perpetually sore."

"I could give you a massage later."

The offer was so unexpected she stared at him for a moment. They had tried to be intimate a few times since her return, but it always ended in awkward laughs and the agreement to give it more time. They were still working on getting to know one another, she reasoned, which was surprisingly difficult with their schedules. Michael traveled a lot between China, India, and the US. It was no secret he loved what he did by the number of hours he dedicated to his work.

"I can always have someone come by and give you one if—"

"No, it's not that. I mean, sure. Thanks. I haven't had one in a long while." Rox looked out the window and wondered, not for the first time, if this were real or if she were still trapped in some tank in Wonderland, creating this fantasy to cope with whatever new experiment Tusk was running on her.

"I was thinking, once we've gotten through the anniversary planning, maybe we can have a family holiday.

Term break's coming up in a week or two. Why don't we go to Bali or Koh Samui? I should be able to get away for a few days."

She chuckled. "You know, a year ago this time, I remember sifting through the dumpster of a Dairy Queen."

He frowned, and Rox wasn't sure if she had upset him or if he was simply concentrating. "I would have never stopped looking for you had I known you were still alive."

"No, no it's not that. It's just … " she thought about all she had gone through to get to this moment, here, in his car, on this road and driving to his award ceremony. "It's been a long journey, and sometimes it's hard to believe that I'm actually here."

"If you ever want to talk more about it … I mean I know you've told me a little bit, but … "

It wasn't the first time he had offered to listen to her story, but she wasn't even sure where to begin. She had told him about her complicated relationship with Josh, the training he put her through, and her life on the run. But she hadn't mentioned anything about his abilities or the fact that she was evolved. In hindsight, she guessed she wanted Tara's life to remain unsullied by Rox's.

She also hadn't told Michael about Sam. Or Watership Down or Wonderland. The timing never seemed right. Those days were dark, filled with pain and suffering. Finding her family on this literal tropical island was like a fresh start, an opportunity to leave all the bad things in the past behind.

"Alright, how about this: I accept this award, I do thirty minutes of obligatory mingling, and then we head up to some rooftop bar somewhere and see where the night takes us."

Rox settled back into the soft leather seats and smiled. She liked Michael. He wasn't perfect. He could be curt and dismissive when he was working on something, which was always, and she was convinced he thought he was the smartest person in the room. But her real reservation about him was that she wished she *felt* something when she was around him. Some kind of connection – something that pulled her to him. If not a memory, then a feeling.

But maybe it didn't work like that. Maybe real love, the kind that lasts, simply took time. Maybe she was asking for too much too soon. She had only been back for ten months, and in the grand scheme of things, that was just the blink of an eye. Could she really fill six years in just ten short months? Maybe what she was hoping to feel for him would come in time. She just needed to be patient.

"That sounds like a nice idea. I like the view of this city from high up," she said and took a deep breath. She could wait.

~

Instincts

3rd August, 8:45pm
Bayfront, Singapore

"So, you're staying here and hiding in the room?" Josh asked.

"Leave him," Meita said as she stood up and smoothed

out the length of her dress. Her tone was that of a mother warning her children on the brink of an argument that it was in everyone's best interest to return to their respective corners.

"I need to catch up with Mika," Sam said.

"You get reports from him like every day," Josh said. "You're avoiding her. That's what this is about."

Sam closed his eyes and fought the urge to reach for a drink, but he had made a promise to his father.

"Leave it, Josh," Meita said again, this time with a little more bite.

She was dressed in an evening gown that did little to hide her natural beauty despite its obvious efforts. Its color was the shade of gray that looked good on a sweater or one's favorite woolen pajamas, but an unlikely fit for such an occasion as she and Josh were attending. Her hair was pulled back in a bun, not a single hair clip or bobby pin to be seen, and her shoes resembled simple ballet slippers with a pompom attached at the toe.

Sam got the impression her choice of outfit was intentional. They weren't here to mingle or to socialize. They had an objective. Michael's award ceremony was just the most logical – and safest – place to make contact. But regardless of Meita's efforts to blend in, she was beautiful, and there was no hiding that. It was a combination of her natural skin tone and the way she carried herself with an aura of confidence and sophistication. No one would guess by looking at her that she had just set up a decryption program to gain read-access to one of Singapore's government satellites. It would have taken him months of planning and an equal amount of time to execute something like that. Meita? Just over forty-eight hours.

Sam told her it wasn't necessary to hack into anything. He could ask Mika, who would supply them with copies of the images and information they needed. But Meita said she didn't want to waste time waiting for Mika to climb the bureaucratic chain of command. Besides, her motto was why ask when you can take.

"I'll see what type of access Mika can get us," Sam said, ignoring Josh's earlier comment.

"Good, and don't tell him about my … " she nodded towards her laptop on the dining table, "side project. I know he's your brother, but we need to be careful."

"He trains Rox every day," Sam said. "I think we can trust him."

Meita sighed like they had been over this already. "That was a private arrangement you worked out and I approved. Sam, I'm not asking you to lie to your brother. I'm just reminding you that you don't need to share everything with him. Not yet. Let Katherine convince Singapore to sign the petition for Article 31 first, and then I'll be happy to bring him onboard. But telling him anything prematurely just presents *him* with a potential conflict of interest."

The petition for Article 31 was designed to put pressure on the UN Human Rights Council to add another article to their Universal Declaration of Human Rights. It was aimed at protecting the rights and lives of evolved humans around the world, making it an explicit crime against humanity to experiment on them. The idea, as well as the petition, was still very much in its infancy, but Katherine was working behind the scenes to enlist more governments. So far, she said the big four had signed on, but Singapore was still undecided. Katherine was arriving tomorrow to have meetings with officials known to be sympathetic to the EO cause.

Sam pinched the space between his eyes and inhaled. Meita was right. He knew it, but he hadn't seen his younger brother in far too long, and Sam's need to reconnect with him was something he couldn't readily explain. Perhaps it was because they had only recently gotten Val back. Perhaps he just needed someone else to talk to. Someone who couldn't read his thoughts.

"You can always take my place and I can get that update from Mika," Josh offered, but the look on his face indicated his lack of sincerity.

Where Meita dressed to go unnoticed, Josh looked like he was eager to impress. It wasn't that he wore anything grand; instead, it was the attention he paid to the smaller details. Like the turquoise silk handkerchief, casually yet stylishly placed in the breast pocket of his navy blue suit. The color of the handkerchief was an exact match to his socks as well as his shirt. Josh had even taken the time to visit the hotel's barber and got a proper wet shave, making his already flawless skin smooth and shiny.

I'm so glad you approve.

Sam rarely lost control, but there was something about Josh that always pushed him over the edge. If it weren't for Meita's hand gently but firmly pressing him down in his seat, he had a feeling he would have done something they would all come to regret.

He wasn't ready for this. He thought he had another couple of months to work out his feelings towards her. And when he did see her, it would have been on his turf. Not here, with her family, at her very successful and very rich husband's award ceremony.

Cry me a river.

Meita must have felt his muscles tense because she spun around in front of him, her dress swirling, essentially providing its own barricade between him and Josh.

"Why don't you go ahead downstairs, Josh. Make sure the ceremony is over." Her tone was just a little too eager. "See if you can spot her."

Josh slipped his hands into the front pockets of his trousers, and for the first time since he had stepped out of his room looking like an international playboy, his smile slipped.

Look, I know what you're going through. But sitting in here hiding ain't gonna make any of it go away.

Sam hated Josh hearing those thoughts he would rather have kept private, but Sam had come to learn that the more anyone complained, the deeper Josh probed.

Meita waited until the door closed before she released Sam and gave him a genuine look of concern. "You going to be alright?"

He nodded.

"Wanna talk about it?"

No, he didn't want to talk about it. What he wanted was a drink. "Go, I'm fine."

She hesitated like she knew he hadn't meant his tone

to be so rough, but then she patted his arm and followed after Josh.

The door slid shut without the usual clank when the lock engaged like most hotel doors. Sam laid down on the sofa and stared at the ceiling. A chandelier with far too much chrome and crystal for his liking interrupted the steady flow of light, and he sat back up and laid down the other way.

This wasn't his first time in a suite, but this was definitely outside of his budget. The small but well-equipped kitchen was more modern than anything Halo could afford. The brass coffee table, matching dining table and chairs, and en suite for every room made him feel like an imposter. It's not that he didn't like it – who wouldn't appreciate such refinement – it was just … uncomfortable.

Sam sat up in one fluid motion and hopped to his feet. He needed a drink. He lifted his right hand to see if it shook. It was steady, well, steady enough. He closed it into a fist as he walked to the bar. He slowed as he contemplated the burn from that first sip. He reached for the bottle and noticed the slight tremor.

"Dammit," he muttered, and allowed his feet to take him in the direction of the shower.

Afterwards, he read through the file they had compiled on Miles. There wasn't much. The kid was seventeen. A runaway and reported missing two years ago. Didn't have any kind of record, not even a juvie one, but had been in and out of therapy. Most of the doctors agreed he was an anxious kid having trouble processing his emotions. He had been on a few antidepressants and a few anti-anxiety meds, and one doctor suspected he had been the target of school bullying while another noted he may have an unhealthy "admiration" of the popular kids in his class. No one had considered that Miles might be evolved, but then again, why would they? When it became obvious that EOs weren't going to take to the skies or fight crime in matching outfits, the public quickly lost interest, which allowed doctors like Tusk to slip beneath the radar with their illegal experiments.

Nobody had really helped the kid, not in the way that he needed. Who knew how genuine the doctors had been. Their notes were thorough enough, but it just illustrated the lack of support EOs had when dealing with their abilities. Neither Miles' parents nor his brother, Tyson, were evolved, which meant they had assumed something else was wrong with the kid.

But why come here? It was one hell of a coincidence to come to Singapore if he wasn't looking for Rox.

Sam leaned back on the sofa and closed his eyes. Miles had mentioned that Rox affected him, that she calmed things for him.

Sam chuckled. "Join the club, kid."

After they had rescued Rox from Wonderland, Sam had been feeling … fractured. He was in denial about the emotions he wouldn't allow himself to fully admit he had for a woman he barely knew. Then there was the guilt that kept him up at night. Halo was about helping EOs and they had used Rox like she were nothing more than a means to an end. She had died because of it. Twice that he had witnessed and countless other times when she had traded herself for Josh's son.

When Sam had finally sobered up enough to read the reports of her imprisonment at Wonderland, he wanted nothing more than to reach out to her and apologize. If they had just helped her and done what Halo was designed to do, there would have been no reason for her to die in the first place. But then they would also not have saved his sister.

Val had been missing for eight months when Rox stumbled onto their property asking for help. Her timing was impeccable, and Sam and his father couldn't ignore the advantage of having someone with her abilities accompany them to rescue his sister. They had never before negotiated with an EO who needed their help, and they had never turned their back on one either, but that was what they had threatened to do if she didn't help them. Rox had been lost, running scared, and operating with only four years' worth of memories, and they had used her like she were common currency.

No wonder she hadn't reached out to him. To any of them. Why would she? In the end, it had been Katherine who had found her identity and the family she was searching for.

Sam collected the notes he had scattered across the coffee table and put them back in the folder. Halo wasn't equipped to help someone like Miles. The boy had been happy to sequester himself in the room they gave him, and Sam was happy to leave him there. But if Miles were here looking for Rox, then it made sense that whoever was looking for Miles was also probably here.

There was a knock at the door, and Sam opened it to the smiling face of his younger brother.

"Kor-kor," Mika said as he pulled Sam in for an affectionate hug.

A few years after Sam's mother had died, his father remarried. Marissa was a feisty Chinese Singaporean woman with a heart of gold. She had accepted Sam as if he were her own and never played favorites among the three of them. Mika was Val's older brother by a minute, and the slight dusting of freckles around his nose reminded Sam of their baby sister.

The two brothers didn't share the same features, but that changed nothing about the love they had for one another. Growing up, Sam had spent a few summers in Singapore and often envied Mika and Val for having two separate cultures.

"Nice to see you putting back on a lil' more muscle," Mika said.

The two of them didn't see one another as often as Sam would have liked. A few years after Mika finished university, he chose to move to Singapore and explore the other side of his heritage.

"I was starting to worry you were letting yourself go," Mika said.

He *had been* letting himself go. "You pumping iron?"

"Nah, just using my own body weight as resistance." He stepped around Sam and whistled as he looked inside the suite. "Whoever you signed up with has got deep pockets. No wonder I had a hard time getting up here. Bro, you said you were staying in a suite, this is one of their rental apartments. I had to flash my credentials."

"Suite. Apartment." Sam shrugged. "G and T?"

"You know it. So what brings you to the little red dot?" Mika asked. "You worried about your lady friend? She's showing progress. I didn't think she had it in her, but the good news is she's stopped vomiting. Mostly."

Sam smiled. He had told Mika not to take it easy on her, but to prepare her like he would anyone who would find themselves in live combat someday.

"You said that in your report." Sam passed his brother his favorite drink.

"Yeah. She was just out of shape is all. Once we got her cardio up, you could tell she used to be fit." Mika took a sip and sighed. "So what's her story?"

Sam poured himself a glass of whiskey, but left it on the coffee table as he took a seat opposite Mika. "I owe her. In fact, Halo owes her."

"Alright ... " Mika said and waited for Sam to continue.

"She's the one who found Val."

Mika's glass stopped before it reached his mouth. "Come again?"

Sam leaned back into the sofa and sighed. It was a long story, and he didn't know how to shorten it *and* leave out the bits about GFO. Or Meita. Or Josh or Tusk or his feelings for Rox, so he sat back up and shook his head. "Another time. That's not why I'm here. Anything out of the ordinary with EOs on this side of the world?"

Mika took a slow sip from his glass and made a soft hissing sound like the tonic had gone down differently than the gin, but then he shrugged his shoulders. "Rumor has it that some big player's trying to reopen a research facility. Don't have enough intel yet to know if it's in Myanmar or Laos."

"Any idea who?"

"I emailed you the list of suspects just before I left the office. It's surprisingly long. There's like ten names there."

"Any proof?" Sam asked.

"Nothing we can use legally. A few meetings and a land purchase by known players in the EO trade, but none of that's illegal."

That wasn't much for Sam to work with, but perhaps Meita could make something of it.

"Why the sudden interest in the Southeast Asian EO trade? Halo only covers North America."

Sam opened the file and showed Mika a picture of Miles. "He's gone missing and we think he's here. Or, well, we know he came here, but not sure if he's *still* here."

"Singaporean?" Mika asked.

"No, American. Taiwanese descent."

"What's he doing here then? I take it it's not for the Night Safari?"

Sam chuckled. He forgot how much Mika's humor was like their father's – dry, filled with sarcasm, and always delivered at precisely the most uncomfortable moment.

"I think he's looking for Rox," Sam said.

Mika's glass stopped shy of his lips again. "Your Rox? The woman I'm training?"

Sam nodded.

Mika sat silently for a moment as he processed the implications. "Hostile or friendly?"

"Not sure. But my guess is friendly. He's got some kind of ability. We think empathic. Kid says there's something about Rox that helps him manage the emotions."

"I get that. Whatever her ability, it's a calming one. When I'm training her, it's like she brings me down to her level, but like in a Zen sort of way. Bro, her scent, it's like nothing I've ever encountered."

Sam reached for his drink, but sat back. "What do you mean, 'her scent'?"

"I don't know. It's kinda hard to describe, but it's like she speaks to the animal side in me. Like, I know she doesn't mean me any harm. In fact, it's like I get this sense of peace when I'm around her."

"Do you feel anything else? Like a … like a *wave* of peace?"

"You mean physically? No. Just a sense."

Sam's shoulders relaxed, and it surprised him how much he had tensed from the possibility of someone else experiencing the same energy pulses as he had.

"You gonna tell me what her ability is or am I going to have to guess?"

Sam wanted nothing more than to open up and tell his brother everything.

"Classified?" Mika asked.

Sam reached for his glass once again, and once again stopped.

"Val called and asked me to keep an eye on you," Mika said. "Said she was worried. Rox have anything to do with why she's worried?"

Val didn't have abilities, but she didn't need them to know her brothers. Despite being the youngest, she ruled over the both of them in the way only a younger sister could. If she told Mika to watch over him, then Mika would know Sam was hiding something.

Sam leaned his head back on the sofa and groaned in frustration. He knew Meita's orders were the right ones. Information was always best disseminated on a need-to-know basis, and the truth was, Mika didn't need to know. But Mika was his kid brother and would have his back in ways that no one else ever would.

"Bro?" Mika sniffed the air like he had caught the scent of something. "Talk to me."

Sam ran his hand down his face like he was exhausted. He *was* exhausted. He had only caught a few hours of sleep on the flight.

He glanced at his watch. It was just after nine in the morning back home. His dad would be taking Shaira out for her morning run. Not that anyone needed to take Shaira anywhere; she went out when she wanted.

Mika got up and made himself a drink, then poured Sam's whiskey down the sink before sitting back down. There was genuine concern in his eyes when Sam looked at him, so he followed his instincts and told his baby brother everything.

~

Secrets

3rd August, 9:03pm
Bayfront, Singapore

Rox realized a few years back that drinking had an interesting effect on her. While she could get drunk, her body processed the alcohol too quickly for her to remain inebriated. Then there was the unwanted side effect of how often she had to use the bathroom, which meant she spent most of her evenings standing in line for the lady's room. She had learned early on to keep her alcohol consumption low, but tonight, she felt like indulging.

She sat at the center table nearest the front with a glass of champagne feeling satiated. The room was decorated in the same bright, sunshine yellow as Michael's corporate color. Even the china had a fine gold trim around its edges to match. Each table held a yellow-gold vase holding a fresh bouquet of white roses. It was a nice touch, and it explained the high ticket price for attendance.

Michael was captivating when he gave his acceptance speech. He struck the right balance between sobriety and humor. Now, he was mingling around the room, giving the people what they wanted. His time. His thoughts. His attention.

The lights brightened softly, signaling that the ceremony was coming to an end, so she glanced over at Michael where he was circled by a crowd of people. He was handsome in his tailored suit, going for a type of formal-casual look that only few could pull off. He had left the top two buttons of his yellow shirt undone, which showed off the promise of a smooth, hard chest. For a man his age, he looked good. He wasn't as fit as Sam, but then again, Sam had a different lifestyle.

Sam ran Halo, which was more of a physical job than a programming one like Michael had. A smile crossed her face – Sam jumped out of helicopters over large bodies of water during tropical thunderstorms. He infiltrated research facilities as a pastime; he needed to be more physically fit. It wasn't that he looked like your typical weightlifter or some bodybuilder type, but he had a way of spreading his arms over his chest that made him appear larger than he actually was.

Really?

Rox choked on her champagne, and the few people still seated at her table looked at her in concern. For a moment, she couldn't breathe and fought the temptation to look around. Instead, she covered her mouth with her cloth napkin and waved she was alright.

Josh?

The one and only, mi amor.

What are you doing here? Excitement raced up her back, and she again had to fight the temptation to look for him in the crowd.

Are you happy to see me?

Rox blushed.

What's the matter, domestic life not doing it for you?

She laughed behind her napkin. *No, it's not that, it's just … wait, what are you doing here?*

Watching the man you're not *thinking about be just about as bored as you are.*

Get out of my thoughts.

I thought you'd never ask.

What?

There was only silence.

Josh?

The empty chair next to her was pulled back, and Josh sat down.

Rox couldn't hide the joy she felt at seeing him, and he knew it because he was reading her thoughts.

"I've missed you, too," he said.

"What are you doing here?"

"You look beautiful."

"Thank you, but for like the eleventh time, why are you here?"

Josh tilted his head to the side and then smiled. "That's not what you really want to ask me."

"I thought I had a year. You're two months too early."

"We're not here to take you back. And that's not what you were thinking about. That just popped into your head." He leaned towards her and inhaled. "Is that perfume? When did you start wearing perfume? You didn't like to when we were together."

Rox's eyes grew large as she turned to make sure no one at her table overheard. "What are you trying to do?"

Josh smiled and tugged on one of the curls that escaped from her combs. "I've missed you, and you can't blame me for having a little fun."

She didn't. She stood up and he followed suit as she wrapped her arms around him. She hadn't realized just how much she missed him until that moment. They had a complicated past, but he was the first person she remembered.

"Tara?" Michael asked.

Rox stepped out of Josh's embrace. "Oh, hey, Michael. This is my … um, this is—"

"Josh." Josh extended his hand.

Michael hesitated, but then reached out. "Michael."

"Congratulations on your award," Josh said.

"Thanks."

He's got a firm grip. Works out does he?

Stop it!

"You found her!"

Rox turned at the sound of another familiar voice. "Meita!" she said, with a little too much enthusiasm.

Rox fumbled through a slightly better introduction as she purposefully positioned herself closer to Michael.

"I'm sorry to interrupt, but is there somewhere we can speak privately?" Meita asked.

Rox felt Michael's hand slip over hers and the move surprised her.

"I got us one of the apartment suites," Michael said as he turned to Rox. "I was thinking we could bring the kids over tomorrow and we could all see a show and then stay the night."

Things were quickly spiraling out of Rox's comfort zone.

"If you need to talk, we can go up to the room," Michael said to Meita. "I'm done here anyway. They've just turned on the lights."

"Maybe we could just get a corner table at the bar or something?" Rox wasn't ready for her two worlds to collide. She thought she had more time.

Meita shook her head. "Uh … "

"C'mon," Michael said. "We can use our room."

Rox wasn't sure why she was feeling so nervous. She had told Michael about her relationship with Josh, albeit leaving out the bits about him being a mind-melding EO. In fact, thinking about it now, her summation seemed awfully light on details, which was much like everything else she had shared with him. Her plan had always been to tell him everything, but when she arrived, everyone was more interested in telling her about who she used to be – when she was Tara – than hearing about what she had gone through and who she was now. Then one month turned into two and it never felt like the right time.

The elevator ride up to their apartment suite was quiet as another couple joined them just before the doors closed. They were staying on the same floor, but luckily the man and his wife turned right when they exited.

Rox took one step in the hallway and struggled to exhale her next breath. The energy pulse running through her was sweet agony, and she had to reach for the wall to stop from falling.

"Tara?" Michael asked.

Another one hit her and it was like she was back in the woods at Halo, but this time she had different things to fear.

She cleared her throat. "Champagne plus heels this high aren't a good combination."

She didn't want to think it because Josh would know, but it was the only thought that would form. Rox looked up at Meita who was wearing a look of sympathy, like she understood what was happening.

Why isn't he here? Rox asked.

He thought it best to stay in the room. Josh's tone held a note of sympathy she wasn't expecting.

The lighting in the hallway suddenly seemed too bright.

Michael reached to take her hand just as she noticed the softness of the wallpaper. It was velour or maybe some kind of velvet. Everything had an air of perfection, an atmosphere of luxury.

The hallway came alive with energy and the lights flickered when another pulse hit her as they passed a door where the vibrations were more intense.

Rox had spent hours dreaming about their next encounter. She would go back and forth wondering if the feelings they had for one another were too intense to be long-term.

Is he … alright? she asked.

Rox felt Josh's surprise at her question. They were doing that awkward thing where they just stared at one another, but she didn't care. The pulses were coming too frequently now, and for the life of her she didn't understand why she didn't ring his doorbell.

I have a feeling, Josh began, his thoughts flowing slowly like he was careful of not thinking the wrong thing, *he's a bit like you.*

"Two doors down on the right, and then you can take your shoes off," Michael said, his voice bringing her out of the trance.

They stepped inside the suite and the silence hung there like an empty room. Meita stepped in the center and spoke first. "Have you heard from Miles?"

Rox leaned against the wall and began to loosen the straps on her heels. "The kid from Wonderland?"

"Who's Miles?" Michael asked.

Meita and Josh looked at Michael and then back at Rox.

How much have you told him?

Rox lowered her head. *Not enough.*

Another pulse swept through Rox and she leaned forward, resting her hands on her knees.

"Did you really have that much to drink?" Michael asked. "They can come back another time if you're feeling unwell."

You can feel him in here, can't you?

Rox stood up and went to the bar. "I'm alright, Michael. These are the people who helped me find you, and they wouldn't be here if it weren't important."

How was she even to begin to explain everything to him? That was the problem she had since returning. How was she meant to slip the complicated, convoluted, and downright confusing last four years into everyday conversations? Michael had been trying so hard to accept her back into their lives, and she wanted to be the wife and mother they all clearly missed, but she was afraid to tell them about her last four years. What if they rejected her because of it?

Just tell him. Katherine's already got him clearance.

Rox passed Josh his drink. The moment their fingers touched, she realized just how telling her actions were. She hadn't even asked him if he wanted anything, let alone *what* he wanted.

Er … so he'll have a cognac, neat, and Meita always drinks tea. Doesn't matter the kind.

Rox glanced at Michael as he removed his jacket and laid it on the back of the sofa. He was studying them, looking between her, Josh, and Meita like it was three

The Evolved Ones: *SACRIFICE* 57

against one. That hurt, but she understood his feelings. She hadn't been forthright or forthcoming about her past. It was difficult to explain who she was when she was still trying to figure out who she wanted to be.

Rox cleared her throat as she filled the kettle with water and turned to face Michael. "I was held captive at a facility called Wonderland," Rox began. "They do experiments—"

"They *did* experiments," Josh said.

For a moment her breath caught, and she wasn't sure if it was from one of Sam's pulses or from understanding what Josh's use of the past tense meant.

"They 'did' experiments on people, certain kinds of people. Miles was one of the kids they were experimenting on."

"What kind of experiments?" Michael asked.

"Awful ones," Meita said. "Your wife, R— Tara, was one of the many unfortunate to be held there against her will. She managed to break free and on her escape, she helped a teenaged boy named Miles. He's gone missing and we need to know if she's seen him."

"Is he alright?" Rox asked. "I haven't seen him since I was taken to the hospital." She hadn't seen Sam since then either.

"We think he's looking for you," Josh said.

"Me? Why?" How did he even know where to find her? "I thought my location was classified."

"Classified?" Michael interrupted.

"It is. That's one of the reasons why we need to find him," Meita said.

"Why would your location be classified? *How* could it be classified?"

Any of the thousands of moments before now seemed like a better one to explain her past to him. She was supposed to have more time.

"Are the kids in some kind of danger?" Michael asked.

Rox swore under her breath and reached down to massage the pain in her pinky toe. She hated heels. Her feet were too wide, and there was absolutely no way to run in them.

"No." Rox handed Michael his cognac and poured the hot water into a pot of fruit tea for Meita. "I have agreed to help the Global Frontiers Organization build more peaceful relations with … " she took a deep breath, "evolved ones."

He stared at her like she were someone he didn't know, which in truth was exactly what she was, a stranger. She could see from his body language he was closing himself off to her, and the irony that tonight she had been considering telling him everything wasn't lost on her.

The silence stretched, and that made it more awkward. She heard Meita take a sip of tea, and Josh just stood there, watching her watch Michael, who looked hurt and confused, like a boxer with his guard up waiting for the blow he knew was to come.

Give him time. I can tell he cares for you. Right now, he's feeling a bit outnumbered. His pride and his need to know what's going on are competing.

Is he angry at me?

Josh tilted his head to the side and then gave a nod. *But if it's any consolation, he's not a fan of me either.*

Rox smiled.

And for the record, there's never a right time. Trust me.

Rox thought back to the secrets Josh had kept from her. For the first time, she understood why he hadn't told her everything. He, too, had been waiting for the right moment. But the truth didn't need the right moment. It only needed to be spoken.

I love you, Rox said. It was a deep and complicated love born out of a jagged history. No one knew her as well as Josh. No one had been inside her head and seen into her heart.

Mi amor, no hay ninguna otra para mí.

She felt the truth in his words and cleared her throat as she turned her attention back to her husband. "In two months, I have to return to work. I've not been told where I'll be posted or what I'm supposed to do for that matter, but I was given a year." Rox lifted her glass and swallowed the alcohol much too fast. It burned as it went down, but it was only temporary. She was learning that everything was.

"And Miles? Is he a threat?" Michael asked, his tone lacking his earlier concern.

"As far as we can tell, no," Meita answered. "Rox has a special ability that seems to affect the boy. Maybe it helps him, we don't know. But we think he might be troubled, and if so, we want to get to him before someone else does."

Michael nodded like he understood, but Rox knew he didn't. He slipped one hand into his pocket, while the other held his glass. "I wasn't actually sure if 'evolved ones' really existed. I mean, I've heard the stories, read the reports, but," he snorted. "It's not like you guys have an effective marketing campaign."

"It's in our best interest to be discreet," Josh said.

"Being evolved was the only thing to talk about ten years ago. But when it seemed all anyone could do was basic stuff like synesthesia, I have to admit, even I lost interest," Michael said.

"When you left," Josh said to Rox, "Miles said something about you helping him to manage the emotions. Did he say anything like that to you when you guys were trapped together?"

Rox shook her head. "We didn't really talk." Memories she failed to suppress rose to the surface. She rubbed the back of her neck as she walked over to the sofa. She thought about sitting down, but changed her mind. "They had increased my dosage. The sedatives were stronger and I, I was so hungry. I didn't get sleep there – well, not real sleep – and they hadn't fed me in days." And they tortured me. *They still torture me.*

Josh shifted the weight from one foot to the next like he wanted to go to her, but decided against it.

"We think he might have an ability that impacts how he processes emotions," Meita said.

"Like someone on the spectrum?" Michael asked.

"No, like someone who can feel emotions," Josh answered. "Perhaps ones that aren't his own."

The wrinkling of Michael's brow indicated he hadn't been expecting that kind of response. He turned to Rox. "She said you had a special ability. Does that make you evolved, too?"

"Yes."

He nodded again like he understood, but she had learned in the last ten months that only meant he was processing. He turned away from her and then spun back around to face her. "You could have told me."

There were over a thousand solid reasons why she hadn't, but none of them seemed good enough anymore. "I'm sorry."

"And the kids? Is it hereditary? Are they going to evolve as well?"

"The research thus far is inconclusive," Meita said. "There are just not enough of the evolved to make any meaningful inferences about the population as a whole. There are evolved families as well as families with only a single evolved member."

"Do they all lose their memories, like Tara?" Michael asked.

"No." They answered him in unison.

He smirked and then crossed his arms over his chest. "Does it hurt? I mean if the kids do evolve, will it be painful for them?"

Rox was silent because her memories only spanned about five years back; therefore, she had no clue if there was pain involved.

"No," Josh answered for her. "When I evolved, it was like a switch flipping. One day I was normal, and the next I simply had this ability I didn't have before. No pain. Just a helluva lot of questions."

"And what is your ability?"

"I'm afraid he's not at liberty to share that," Meita

jumped in. "But I can assure you he means you and your family no harm."

Oh, he's pissed now. It'd be better if I just told him.

Rox thought about that for a moment. *No, Meita's right. Michael's a good, honest man who works incredibly hard. But if he knew at this moment you could read his thoughts, I don't know him well enough to predict how he'd react.*

"What's your ability?" Michael turned to Rox, but then held out his arms in a defensive stance. "Sorry, are you at liberty to share?"

Rox swallowed the lump forming in her throat and gave him a soft smile. "Of course. I'm a healer."

He blinked like he wasn't sure he'd heard her correctly, but then laughed. "So what? You can heal everyone else but yourself. Is that it?"

There was a tense moment of silence as Rox wondered what he meant by that comment.

Josh crossed in front of her, breaking their eye contact and slammed his glass down on the counter. He yanked open the drawer underneath the bar and pulled out the wine bottle opener. He released the foil cutter and stabbed it into the center of his palm with the ease of someone simply opening a bottle of red.

"Josh—" Rox cried, but his purpose became clear. The pull on her was instantaneous. Energy slipped along invisible tentacles to wrap around Josh's hand. The blood dripping down his arm and into the sleeve of his suit jacket slowed and then stopped. He must have felt her healing him because he reached for the handkerchief in his breast pocket to wipe away the blood. He held his palm up so that Michael could see it.

For the record, the only reason my bloody fist isn't smashed into his face is because I know you care for him.

Michael lifted his drink to his mouth, but Rox noticed the tremor in his hand. The tension broke when he cleared his throat and asked, "Can you heal anything?"

"I can heal *almost* anything. Depending on the illness. But the effects may not last." Rox said. "Some things just keep coming back."

"Can you resurrect the dead?"

Rox looked stunned. "No. Death can't be healed." Unless it were her own.

"And the people who took you? Who held you captive, they knew this?"

Rox nodded.

"They won't stop looking for you," he said as he went to the bar and poured himself a double. "That ability is simply too extraordinary not to explore, you know, on a scientific level."

"I know. And that's why the best thing I can do is work with people who can help to keep me safe. And they'll keep you and the kids safe as well."

An energy pulse slipped through her that was more intense than the ones before. Rox glanced over her shoulder at the door.

Sam wants to knows if you're alright.

It was in that moment she knew that what she and Sam felt wasn't a passing fancy. The proof was tangible. It coursed up her spine and sat in her gut like it belonged there.

"Tara?" Michael said.

Tell him I'm fine. She turned back to Michael. "Sorry," she said. She wasn't ready to explain Sam. "So, you guys think Miles is in Singapore?"

"Yes, and we're here until we can find him or find reliable information that he's gone somewhere else," Josh said, helping her change the subject.

"Sorry again for the interruption," Meita added. "But we had to check in with you. If you see him, contact us and try to stall him until we get there."

"Is he likely to hurt her?" Michael asked.

Josh chuckled. "Rox is more than capable of taking care of herself."

"Her name is Tara."

Mcita placed her teacup on the bar. She gave Rox an awkward smile. "I'm hoping to have more information for you tomorrow. Josh, shall we?"

Meita was already at the door when Josh leaned over and kissed Rox on the forehead. She hadn't seen it coming or she might have moved out of the way, but she smiled up at him and mouthed a thank you.

Never let them take your name.

Rox rolled her eyes. *My real name is Tara.*

I've got a birth certificate that says otherwise.

A forgery you created!

"Enjoy your evening," he said to her as he closed the door.

She looked over at Michael, but for the life of her, she couldn't guess what he was thinking.

~

Lies

3rd August, 10:00pm
Bayfront, Singapore

All they did for a long while was sit in silence with their separate thoughts. Rox opened her mouth a few times to apologize or to say something, anything, but nothing that came to mind seemed good enough.

"Why didn't you just tell me?" Michael eventually asked.

"I don't know. Each time I thought about it, it just didn't seem like the right time."

"And now, in front of your ex-boyfriend seemed like a better one?"

If she had known Josh and Meita were going to show up, unannounced, then she would have handled things differently. "No, now I wish I had picked any of the other times that seemed wrong to tell you. Trust me, I didn't want you to find out this way."

He stood up, and Rox thought he was leaving, but then he went over to the balcony. Their room had a view of the downtown skyline. It was unobstructed, and at this hour, all the office buildings were lit in a myriad of colors.

A rush of warm air entered when he opened the door. The clouds had moved on, leaving the sky clear and intoxicating. Up this high, the traffic below was silenced, but the night still held its own sounds.

An energy pulse slipped through her and she grabbed the arm of the sofa. They were rhythmic now, like the adrenaline and excitement of being near one another had worn off. In an odd way, it was comforting knowing he was so close, even if the circumstances were less than ideal.

Rox noticed a bucket resting on a pedestal with a bottle of champagne sticking out, the ice well on its way to melting. She hadn't meant to hurt Michael. She meant it when she said he was a good man. He didn't deserve this.

"Do you still have feelings for him?"

His question surprised her, and it took her a moment to realize he was speaking of Josh. She was sure they had looked uncomfortably familiar together.

"Yes, but not in the way I think you're thinking," she said.

Josh had told her there was no right time, so she waited for Sam's ripple to fade and decided that now was as good as any time to be honest with Michael.

"He came for me," Rox said. "When I was ready to give up, he wouldn't let me."

She walked over to the bar, made Michael another drink and then she sat down across from him. She waited for him to take his first sip before she continued. "So far, no one has found a way to kill me."

He opened his mouth to speak, but then closed it, and she took that as a sign to continue.

"When I was in Wonderland, there was a doctor who knew my real name. He knew that I was a healer. I'd never met him before. Or at least I have no recollection of meeting him. But he knew me in ways that, well, I guess in ways I wish he hadn't.

"He tortured me. Though I'm sure he didn't consider it torture. T-The drownings, the stabbings, those were just experiments to see how quickly I recovered. To analyze *how* I recovered. I won't go into details, but Josh stayed with me. He was there for me. He stayed by me, so to speak, during the worst of it. And then he risked his life to come for me."

There was a long moment of silence while she gave him time to process what she said.

"Is he connected with you now?"

Of all the questions he could have asked about what she had just shared, she was surprised that was the first thing to come to his mind, and she wasn't sure how she felt about that. But then again, this moment wasn't about her, she reasoned. It was about finally telling him the truth.

Rox shook her head. "I've learned to block him. After I left him I had to. But now, he's learned to respect my space."

"He still has feelings for you."

Rox smiled sadly. Josh made no effort to hide his true feelings from her. "He has a son. Sixteen, no seventeen now, and Jay and I were quite close. We *are* still quite close. He lost his mother when he was young, and when I woke up, all I had was this feeling that I belonged somewhere, but ... well ... to make a long story short, I filled a void for him and he filled one for me."

Michael swallowed the rest of his cognac in a single gulp and then nodded like he understood, but she knew better.

"Who's Meita?"

Rox laughed. "That's a great question I honestly don't know the answer to. All I know is that when I left Josh, he hired Meita to find me, but she had her own agenda and now we're all working for her – still not sure how that happened – but she, too, helped me escape from Wonderland."

"You don't have any idea what happened to you when you disappeared? I mean, you were on assignment in Peru. You were only meant to be gone for fourteen days, but then, there was an earthquake and you stopped communicating. All this time and we just thought you were one of the many who died."

Rox thought about what it must have meant for them to lose her that way. The fear and confusion. Mostly the not knowing until their minds were forced to make up a story so they were able to move forward. She understood that more than he knew. "There is a very good likelihood that I did die," she said softly. "Damn thing just won't stick."

"How many times have you, you know … "

"I lost count a long time ago," she said.

They both sat there, enjoying the burn of the cognac and the warm night air. She stared at the lights that flittered across the sky from the light show below. The kids had taken her to see it a few times, but she had never seen it from this height.

"I keep wanting you to be her," Michael said some time later, after the show ended.

"I know. I keep wanting to be her."

He rested his head on the back of his chair. "Tara was … she was kind. She liked to laugh. And she was so talented." He turned his head to gaze out into the night and got lost in his memories, and she let him.

When he lifted his head to look back at her, he gave her a sad smile. "She could capture an aspect of someone with her camera that the human eye just couldn't."

He leaned forward in his chair and studied her like a piece of art. He was looking for a flaw, something that could help him reconcile the fact that he had gotten his wife back, yet at the same time, lost her forever.

Michael got up and went over to the bucket with the champagne. "Shall we open this? Paid a ridiculous amount of money for it. Hate to see it wasted." He popped the cork and let it fly across the room while she got them new glasses.

"Tell me something about you," he said.

There wasn't really much to tell if she were honest. "I … ugh … "

"Anything. Just say something."

"… I spend an exorbitant amount of time afraid," she chuckled, then stopped. That wasn't a smart thing to say. "I mean—"

"To fear!" Michael held up his glass for a toast. "And conquering it."

He could have responded in any number of ways to her confession, and the fact that he didn't make fun of her brought tears to her eyes. "To conquering our fears." She smiled at him as they both drained their glasses. Then he poured them another.

They spent the next few hours getting to know each other. The champagne went down smoothly, and so they ordered more. For the first time since she returned, Rox relaxed. It was nice talking to him and not worrying about Tara. She wished she had talked to him sooner, let him get to know her instead of trying to live up to some memory she didn't even have.

Sam's pulses swept through her the entire time they talked, but the last one was so intense that she half expected him to be there behind her when she looked over her shoulder. For a moment, she forgot where she was. Maybe a few glasses of spirits and two bottles of champagne weren't such a good idea no matter how quickly she processed the alcohol.

"Tara?"

When she turned back to Michael, he was kneeling in front of her. He took the empty glass from her hand and placed it on the coffee table without breaking eye contact.

Rox's heart started to beat faster when his hand cupped the side of her face. His eyes slid closed, but hers remained open as their lips met. There was something different about his touch. Gone was the awkwardness, and in its place was a need she wasn't sure she fully understood.

When another of Sam's pulses swept over her, she sighed, and Michael mistook that as a response to their intimacy. His kiss deepened, and for a moment, it felt nice to know exactly what he was thinking. She sensed he had given up on wanting his old life back and was more interested in trying to find a path forward. She wanted to give him that, even if her heart was a few doors down on the left.

Rox could taste the champagne on Michael's tongue as another energy pulse slipped through her a little sooner than expected. Her mind shouted at her to stop, but then a part of her wanted to give Michael *something*. Her eyes slid closed as she opened to him. Their kiss was unfamiliar, neither forced nor urgent, more like a silent exploration.

His hand slipped up to remove the combs on either side of her head and her hair fell around her shoulders. He cupped her chin between his thumb and forefinger and gently pulled her to him.

She leaned in and decided to let go. She was so tired of being afraid of saying and doing the wrong things. She would figure everything out tomorrow.

Sam's energy slammed into her and she moaned in pleasure. She kept her eyes closed as Michael's lips explored her neck, and then her shoulder. He slipped down the strap to her dress, leaving her sitting there with the top half of her breast exposed. When his lips closed over her nipple through the fabric, she cried out, desperate to feel Sam pulsing through her.

The rhythm of his energy coupled with Michael's mouth left her breathless. Her head fell back as his tongue continued a path across her chest. She surrendered, allowing him to take control as he lowered her back on the sofa. He cupped her cheeks with both hands and she almost looked at him, but if she opened her eyes, she'd have to reconcile who was in front of her against who she wanted to be there.

It was selfish, the way she kept reaching for Sam, but she needed him if she were going to do this. He must have understood that because his pulses became more intense. They came to her in hard waves that took her back to the woods when they first met. To the time he cradled her in his arms while he pumped her full of tranquilizers. To the absolute peace she felt whenever their skin brushed. The kiss at Crossroads and his embrace when he finally pushed through the door at Wonderland.

The night breeze from the balcony excited her skin and she realized her dress was gone. Fingers that weren't the ones she was imagining entered her as she lifted her hips to meet them. Her hands gripped his shoulders while she sent her energy in search of the one's whose touch she craved. It collided with his, and if her eyes were opened, she would have seen the lights flicker.

She could have sworn she heard his voice in her head, but that wasn't his ability. In fact, she had no idea what his ability was, but they communicated in a way that went beyond words. She turned her head into the sofa to hide her face from the shame of the pleasure she was finally allowing herself to feel.

Lips touched her in places that hadn't been aroused since Josh. She cried out as she imagined Sam's hands on her thighs, moving them apart so that it was he who was entering her.

When their bodies joined, Rox let go. She stopped caring about the name Tara Alexandra Harding. She lowered all her defenses and let the waves of pleasure take over.

Michael moved with a gentleness that brought fresh tears. He kissed her lips, and she tasted herself as well as the hope he had for them.

Sam's pulses ceased and left in its stead a constant hum of his energy. It was as if he were all around her, teasing her with a release she didn't yet know how to achieve. Her breathing quickened as she sank deeper into the moment, her hips moving faster as she focused on how to direct his energy to that specific point inside that cried to be set free.

Michael lifted to his elbows, his rhythm set by hers. "Look at me."

Her heart stopped. She pretended not to hear him as she latched on to Sam. She wouldn't be able to hold on much longer, so she did what felt the most natural. She pulled. Normally, she only pulled when she felt threatened, but this time she let instinct guide her.

Sam's energy slid inside her with such force it lifted her up off the sofa. Wave after beautiful wave of pleasure rippled through her, and she cried out as strong hands gripped her thighs. She was floating, her eyes closed, and her mind blessedly empty as Michael achieved his own orgasm not long after.

She wasn't sure how long they lay there, him on top of her, both of them trying to slow their heartbeats.

Eventually, he slipped to the side and tucked her under his arm. When she made a move to get up, Michael asked her to stay. She hesitated, but then resettled with her back to his chest as silent tears slid down her face. He placed a kiss on the back of her neck, and then another one just under her ear.

Rox would analyze everything tomorrow. For now, she would lay there in the arms of the man she knew at one time she had loved and who had loved her in return.

As she laid there, she waited. Waited for the pulse she had tried to forget these past ten months, the same pulse that had destroyed any chance she had to rebuild the family she had died searching for.

CHAPTER THREE

~

Miles

4th August, 7:40am
East Coast Park, Singapore

Emotions, Miles had learned, were layered and complex. What a person felt at any given moment was a culmination of many different experiences and the memories associated with them. Most people understood their happiness; it was all the other emotions that left them with feelings of inadequacy and frustration.

For example, the woman to his left wore a smile, but if anyone cared to analyze it, they would see that it was forced. She didn't realize it herself, but she was unhappy and it emanated off her like a tidal wave of misery. Miles didn't know what made her that way. Perhaps it was the children who ran ahead of her and kept calling for her attention, or maybe it was the man – her husband, Miles assumed – who was buried in his mobile phone, ignoring all of them. He was a happy man.

There was a couple walking toward Miles, both of them living in a tangible fear hidden behind blank faces. Kids ran amok on the climbing frames of the nearby playground. The emotions that generated their screams and shouts were the most simple to identify. They were either happy or afraid.

Miles had decided that once you analyzed and brought every emotion back to its core, they were all based on two pillars: love and fear. He had read the scholarly papers, some saying there were five or eight different types of emotions, but he had learned that every other sentiment was simply built upon those two. Oh sure, there was a huge, long range of emotions that stemmed from them, but basically everyone was searching for ways, things, and people to help them feel love and mitigate fear.

He had learned that in his own house. When he first developed his ability, it took him over a year to work out that what he was feeling wasn't always manifested within himself. At first, it was confusing, but like most kids who discovered something out of the ordinary, it rapidly progressed to "cool". He could gauge how someone would react and even guess the likelihood of a response based on how they were feeling. He knew when to ask if he could go out with his friends or if he could have money for a video game.

It wasn't too long before Miles began to pick up on latent emotions, emotions that hung around long after the person feeling them had left. The first time he felt his mother's sadness, he locked himself in his room and cried for hours. It was ironic because her love was all over their house. It was in the bathrooms and the kitchen, the dining room and living room, everywhere except her bedroom. The more Miles analyzed it, the deeper into her feelings he sank. He realized just beneath her surface was a raging anger that confused him. When he spoke to her about it, he felt even more sorrow emanating from her, quickly followed by regret, and then a love so intense he felt he could never understand it.

That's when he tried blocking emotions out, but it was like he had opened a doorway into his abilities that wouldn't close. Everywhere he turned, there were people, and they were feeling things. Confusing things. Things that made them happy, but mostly things that left them feeling scared and angry. Anger was the most powerful latent emotion. It lingered in stores and on the clothes racks. It was in coffee shops and the library. Everyone felt angry and it seemed that they left their anger behind like fingerprints.

Over time, Miles learned they were more afraid than angry *per se*, but anger was respected while fear was seen as a weakness. So people hid behind anger when they couldn't pay their bills and thought they were going to lose their jobs. Or, like his mom, they hid behind anger when they realized they were in a loveless marriage and stuck with it because of the kids, because of the bills, and because there was nowhere else to go. She had taught him that on the other side wasn't a greener pasture; just more things to fear.

Teenagers were rife with unimaginable emotions. Lust. Apathy. Confusion. The cafeteria was so saturated with fear that he started missing school. It became too hard to concentrate. His grades slipped and he stopped hanging out with his friends.

Miles went to therapy where the doctors were all too eager to start talking about medication. But he didn't want to *stop* feeling, he just didn't want to feel everything from everyone else all the time: his father's fear of what the neighbors were saying, which led to a growing disdain at having a son too weak to cope with everyday life; his friends' pity, mixed with an odd sense of excitement at having known "the boy who suddenly went crazy"; and his mother's guilt. She blamed herself for everything, things that had nothing to do with her, yet she saw them as a result of her own failures. Miles felt like he was drowning in misery at home and being flayed alive whenever he ventured out.

So Miles ran to his brother, Tyson, in Seattle but he was too busy building his own life and had little interest in helping a teenager with emotional problems. So Miles ran farther. That's when Dr Tusk got him.

The place where Tusk held him captive was nothing shy of horrific. It was like an emotional cloud of noxious gas surrounded the compound and it only grew thicker the farther inside he went. The sheets, though freshly laundered, had the stench of paralytic terror. And the things they did to him – and to one another. Everyone who worked there was afraid – afraid of being the next one strapped to a bed, reduced to nothing more than a lab rat with no hope of escape beyond death.

But then Miles found Rox. Or she found him. She burst into his room like the hero he had long ago stopped dreaming about. He felt nothing from her. No fear. No anger. She was peace. But then the others came to help her escape and with them they brought more anger and fear. Confusion and love. The closer he stood to Rox, the easier it was to block out their emotions, but then Rox left. She left him with people who were so wrapped up in their own misery that they created latent emotions everywhere they went.

For a while, Miles trained with them and learned enough basic self-defense that he felt confident about taking care of himself. Then one evening, he overheard where Rox was staying, and he knew he would have to find her because remaining at Halo had begun to feel like nothing more than an extension of Wonderland.

His flight to Singapore was an exercise in self-restraint. The anger in economy class was palpable. Everybody was frustrated, even the flight attendants. The passenger seated next to him grew agitated with Miles' bouncy knee, but he needed some way to exercise all that pent-up frustration. When the flight landed, he couldn't wait to get off the plane, but the airport was a mix of anticipation and reluctance.

He checked himself into the Village Hotel at Katong V, a place that said it had authentic Peranakan designs – whatever that meant. He took the last of his brother's codeine pills with a small bottle of overpriced wine he picked up at the grocery store. He slept for eighteen hours. When he awoke, it was with a renewed sense of hope.

Miles looked out past the sand to the ocean. It would have been a beautiful view if not for the many shipping vessels lining the horizon.

Rox was here. He was certain of it. He wasn't sure how, but he was going to find her. How hard could it be to find a mixed-race American woman in Asia?

He just needed to know what it was she did that helped him shut out emotions. He needed her to show him how because it was getting harder to get through the days. The emotions were building up inside him and he was beginning to feel like he was going to burst. Miles didn't want to turn to drugs or alcohol to numb the pain, but what other options were there? A life locked away inside some asylum or a lifetime on pills that not only blocked out other people's emotions, but also prevented him from feeling anything?

Miles spun around in the middle of the path and realized he was beginning to spread his feelings onto those passing by. People were starting to slow down and stare. It was the expressions on their faces that signaled they were becoming afraid. A few of them clutched their chests at his feelings of hopelessness.

He had to get control of himself. He had made it this far. Surely that was the hard part. Besides, there was no way that Sam or anyone else at Halo would have noticed his disappearance. Even if they did, no one would think he was here.

He would find Rox. Then she would help him. Just like she did before.

He followed the signs off the footpath to the public toilets, focusing on the breathing exercises one of his therapists had taught him a few years back. The restrooms were housed in a small building with orchids and other colorful flowers around the perimeter.

Singapore was lovely, but the air was thick and damp. Butterflies as large as the palm of his hand flitted around him as he stopped to admire the care that went into keeping the park clean.

He was getting calmer now. Practicing his controlled breathing helped, but so did just looking at his surroundings. He would splash some water on his face and then head to one of the top expat destinations. His guidebook said Dempsey Hill was popular with the wealthy expatriates. He wasn't expecting it to be as easy as bumping into her, but he was certain someone would know her. In a city of six million on an island of about three-hundred square miles, how hard could it be?

He heard a few others enter the toilets behind him, but it was the angst they projected that gave him cause for concern. He stood up from the sink and used the mirror in front of him to look over his shoulder.

Three men stood in a semi-circle behind him. Two were Chinese with tattoos covering their left arms like they were wearing a shirt with just one sleeve. The other man was from a race that had given him a darker skin tone, but Miles couldn't identify it. He was the one who stuck Miles with a needle that injected liquid fire into his veins while the other two held him down.

Fear radiated from Miles with such intensity that the three men lost their focus for a moment and took a step back. But then everything went black and Miles fell to the stone floor, the others too petrified to catch him.

~

Eye spy

4th August, 8:30am
Marine Parade, Singapore

Sam climbed out of the taxi and the abrupt change in temperature caused his sunglasses to fog. He was in his teens the first time he had visited Singapore. He had expected to hate it. He was sure he would stick out amongst the many Chinese, but he quickly discovered that Singapore was an eclectic mix of everything, a little bit of everyone from everywhere. He understood Mika's draw to its cosmopolitan pace and easy lifestyle, but unlike his younger brother, Sam needed open space, the fresh air of the countryside, and the slow, steady march of seasons.

Rox had spent the last few years of her life trying to disappear on streets just like these, busy with people going through their daily routines. She had learned how to be invisible until she needed to be seen. Not many people understood the power of blending in without losing oneself. Had finding her family changed her? Did she fall in love with Singapore's hustle or did she crave the peace of nature like he did?

Sam cleared his throat when the image of her dying in front of him resurfaced. He wasn't sure if her ability was a blessing or a curse. Yet, there was something undeniably special about her. She affected too many people for her to just be another EO like the rest of them. She amplified Josh's ability to connect over greater distances, she helped Miles block out the emotions of others, and she allowed him to slip farther through time than he had ever been able to achieve on his own. It seemed like everyone was drawn to her.

"Buck up," Mika said, and pushed off the wall he had been leaning on to stay out of the heat. "He's here."

Guy Koh was an older Chinese man with a natural tan that said he wasn't afraid of the Singapore sun. He had an easy smile, but a handshake that proved he hadn't gotten to his position through delegation alone. As the head of the International Cooperation Department (ICD), he would assist them – unofficially – with their search for Miles.

"You must be the big brother he's always going on about," Guy said. "Pleasure to meet you."

Guy patted Mika on the back the way a father might do at seeing his son, and for a moment, Sam felt uneasy about their familiarity.

"Mika says you have a person of interest who checked into this hotel," Guy said as he led them up the stairs and into the lobby.

"Yeah, he's one of ours, actually, but we're a bit concerned about him because he's gone off reservation," Sam said.

"Alright, well, let's see how I can help," Guy said. "If he doesn't turn up within the next couple of hours, I'll authorize a team to track his whereabouts—"

"Uncle, I was hoping that Sam and I could be that team. Miles is, well, he's a bit like me and we don't want to spook him. He's not had it easy, and Sam recently rescued him from one of those facilities like we're investigating in Myanmar and Laos."

Sam was surprised at how easily Mika spoke about being an EO in front of Guy, not to mention the extra detail about Miles that Sam wasn't sure he was ready to share.

Mika's nostrils flared, which meant he must have picked up on Sam's concern. "Guy is second cousin to my mom. He's literally family. We can trust him."

Guy nodded. "I've been watching over your brother ever since he entered NS. I won't let anything happen to him."

Sam wanted to believe him. He had no reason not to, but Sam was feeling a bit more protective of his younger siblings since Val's disappearance. He knew that Mika could take care of himself. Hell, he was probably the only one who stood a chance at taking out their old man, but still, that didn't make him infallible.

"I thought you might ask that," Guy said, going back to Mika's earlier question. "But I can't let you two operate on your own without local oversight. I'll assign this case to one of my mentees over at OD."

Mika rolled his eyes. "Not—"

"Yes," Guy said, his tone of loving uncle gone. "She has jurisdictional oversight, so I suggest you find a way to make it work."

Sam raised an eyebrow in question, but Mika shook his head. "Long story."

The hotel lobby was decorated in Singapore's Peranakan heritage, which created a unique style that was popular among tourists who couldn't afford the Central

Business District hotel prices. Bright colors and intricately designed furniture, as well as antique *tingkats*, decorated the lobby.

Guy walked up to the counter with the confidence of a man in his position. He was dressed in dark blue jeans and a white business shirt that fitted well enough to show he was in charge of his aging. His cufflink made a heavy clank when he placed his arm on the counter and began to speak in a hushed voice to the manager, who nodded a few times and then began typing something into his computer. A few seconds later, the manager reached under the counter and pulled out a piece of paper.

"This your guy?" Guy asked as he showed them a photocopy of the passport the hotel had on file.

"Yeah," Sam said. This was the proof they needed even though it wasn't a photo of Miles, but his older brother, Tyson.

"Manager said he checked in two days ago," Guy said.

At least that was one question answered – Miles was definitely in Singapore. Now they just needed to locate him.

Sam ran his hand over his face. He had spent months trying to forget about her, to *not* think about what she was doing and with whom she was doing it, but after last night, he had accepted what he refused to acknowledge since the first moment her energy swept through him in the woods at Halo. He was in love. He didn't want to be. Aside from it complicating things, it made no sense. Who fell in love with a woman they didn't even know?

It took all his self-restraint not to burst through her room door last night and ... what? What would he have done? Ask her to abandon her husband and family so they could go on a first date?

"Sam," Mika whispered, breaking through his thoughts, and Sam realized he had missed part of the conversation. "Whatever's on your mind, I need you to concentrate on something else."

Sam spun away and pinched the space between his eyes.

Mika's ability reminded him of Shaira. Both of them could hear someone walking up to the front door long before anyone else in the house. Mika could see in the dark almost better than their father, and he could smell fear and other powerful emotions, which meant whatever Sam was thinking about was making him put out a scent that his little brother could detect.

"Take two, and then meet us on the fourth floor," Mika said, as he and his uncle followed behind the hotel manager.

Sam missed Shaira. She would brush against his leg or give a low and friendly bark whenever his thoughts drove him to distraction. He needed that a lot recently. He didn't like being here without her, but getting a wolf into Singapore required more time than they had, and they needed to find Miles before whoever killed his brother killed him.

He walked over to the elevators and pushed the button when a bell chimed behind him. Three men entered the hotel from the rear entrance at the back. The door was tucked away in the back corner and led to the shopping mall attached to the building. He waited to see if they were going up as well, but they continued over to the front counter. Only one of them spared Sam a glance, so he allowed the elevator doors to slide close.

The sound of a vacuum cleaner was the first thing he noticed as he stepped out. Two chairs sat either side of a small end table with an old-fashioned telephone on it. The chairs looked antique, but were more likely fabrications. Sam passed a housekeeping cart that filled most of the hallway and peered into the room to see a worker with headphones on placing empty bottles in her plastic trash bag.

"Find anything?" Sam asked when he walked into Miles' room.

Mika shook his head. "An empty bottle of pain pills and an empty bottle of wine."

Sam thought about that for a moment. He wanted to say that didn't sound like Miles, but then again, how would he know? It's not like they had spent any time together. Ever since they returned to Halo, Sam had been holed up in his office, and from what everyone else had said, Miles kept to himself. Sam wasn't even confident he would have been able to recognize the boy if it hadn't been for the picture he studied on the flight to Seattle.

"Safe's empty. Manager opened it," Mika said. "He must have his passport and wallet on him. Any thoughts on where this kid would go?

"No, not really." Sam pinched the space between his eyes again. "I'll phone Dad and see if he's found anything in his room at Halo."

Guy shook the manager's hand. "Call my number on the card if he returns. There's no need to let him know we're looking to speak with him," he said as he walked the manager back into the hallway and closed the door.

The three of them started in separate corners and searched for anything that might give them a clue to Miles' whereabouts or why he was in Singapore.

Sam went over to the safe and felt along its walls to make sure nothing was taped or attached with a magnet inside. Mika focused on the bathroom and unscrewed the top of the cistern, while Guy looked inside, behind, and underneath all the furniture that wasn't bolted or glued in place.

Three-quarters of an hour later, Guy leaned back against the desk. "I'm afraid there's nothing here."

Sam hated to agree with him, but even Miles' suitcase only turned up a few changes of clothes. "I'll phone Meita," he said. "Let her know there's nothing in the room itself, but we now have confirmation he's here."

"You think she's in danger?" Mika asked.

"Rox?" Sam asked. "From Miles? I doubt it."

But whoever was looking for Miles had proven they weren't above using violence to get what they wanted. But then perhaps all of this was unrelated. Perhaps Tyson had gotten himself into trouble. Maybe no one was actually looking for Miles. Miles could have shown up at his brother's house, found the place ransacked and decided to confiscate his brother's passport and head to Singapore to look for Rox on his own. Or maybe Tyson's murder happened after Miles' visit. Both were equally plausible. Josh was never able to uncover why they killed Tyson or what they were hoping to get from him. It was nothing more than conjecture that Tyson's death had anything to do with Miles.

"I'll head back to the office and authorize the use of CCTV to track this kid," Guy said. "And just to confirm, his name is Miles Li, not Tyson Li?"

"Yeah. We think he took his brother's passport."

Sam thanked Guy for his help and then phoned Meita to give her an update. He told her what they found, which was nothing, and she told him she had been able to track Miles to a park at East Coast. "But then I lost him. My software's still trying to decrypt the next bank of security cameras."

While Guy had just agreed to use CCTV, it wasn't like Sam could share with him the information Meita had found. If Guy knew that Meita had successfully gained access to even one of his cameras, let alone a bank of them, he would have no choice but to declare her (and the rest of them) a threat to national security. Their only choice was to wait for Meita's decryption to work or hope that Guy's intel would be more up-to-date.

"You find anything useful?" Sam asked.

"I see him head towards the vending machines and what I think are the public toilets. But then I lose him." Her voice held an edge of worry that made him think something was wrong.

"You think he's sick or something?" That was a possibility, given the pain pills and alcohol.

"No, it's not that. It's the three guys I see walking in the same direction a few seconds later that worries me. They just … they just don't look right, Sam. They look like trouble. And it's not just the tattoos all along their arms I didn't like. They kept looking over their shoulder, like they were checking to see if they were being followed. And one of them looked right up at the camera, like he knew it was there."

Three men? Tattoos?

"Shit!" Sam spun around and yanked open the room door. He raced down the hallway and punched the button for the elevator. Both were on the first floor, so he backtracked until he saw the exit sign and took the stairs three at a time. He pushed the door open, half expecting an alarm to sound, but it didn't. He stepped out into a narrow alley off the side of the hotel. He sprinted to the front just as a taxi pulled away, but it wasn't the three men from earlier. It was a family with a toddler in the back seat.

Sam entered the lobby just as Mika exited the elevator. "What did you find?"

"Follow me." Sam led them to the front desk and asked the manager if he remembered the three men with tattoos from earlier. The manager said yes and told them that they had needed directions.

"You remember where they were headed?" Mika asked.

"Katong Shopping Centre, they said."

"That's near here, right?" Sam asked.

"Yeah, just a block that way," Mika said.

But were they really heading there?

Mika must have thought the same thing because he asked the manager if they were local.

The manager looked surprised by the question, but nodded yes.

"You got a security camera?" Sam asked.

The manager nodded. "But as I explained to the other gentleman – the Director – it's not good quality. It's on a loop and erases every twenty-four hours."

"That's alright. I only need to see the last hour."

~

Neighborhood watch

4th August, 10:55am (-1 SGT)
Pak Tha, Laos

Leona felt the tingling sensation race up her arm when she ended the call. She ran her thumb over the tips of her fingers into a snap. Her contacts in Singapore had located the empath. Miles was in transit and would be with them in a day, or two at the max. And if that wasn't good enough, they had a confirmed sighting of Major Sam Watts. Her men were able to trace him back to his hotel. Leona had given them instructions to follow, but not to engage. With any luck, Major Watts would lead her team to the healer.

Despite her own research, Leona couldn't find any information on Sam's ability, or that of his father's. According to the records Harry had provided, the entire family could very well be duds – nothing more than EO activists fighting the good fight, but possessing no real abilities themselves. Tusk's research confirmed that with Sam's sister.

But Leona's instincts were telling her that Josh Mendez was in Singapore as well, and *he* had an ability. One that could potentially be worth more than the empath's, but there was no way of finding out what it was without actually interacting with him. She would have to think about that, right after she finished the next White Paper on genetics and human evolution Tusk had recommended.

According to it, no one could actually prove that EOs were actually "evolved" because it would require an entire historical genetic mapping of their family, whilst accounting for each member's specific social and environmental influences … from birth.

Leona rolled her eyes. Getting their hands on a single EO was one thing, but if entire families were to start disappearing, she doubted Tusk and his research would remain unnoticed for long.

She rubbed her thumb across her fingertips and waited for the tingling that ran down her arm. The world was standing at the precipice of a fundamental change in the way it defined humanity. Most people were happy to return to their everyday lives when they realized just how mundane EOs were, but if Tusk could identify a pattern, perhaps which specific gene sequence determined who evolved and what ability they would possess, well, that would create a new seat at the top of the food chain.

The door slammed opened with the force of broken hinges as Tusk walked in. This facility was probably a lot less glamorous than what he was accustomed to. It was one large warehouse with many smaller areas partitioned by heavy plastic that had yellowed with age and inactivity. Faded colored lines cut through the dust on the floor to explain each area's purpose. Tusk had said red and yellow meant restricted, while blue and green meant open to all workers. None of it mattered now.

The central area acted as their office space as its two desks had the only working computers. Most of their equipment was scheduled to arrive in a few days, but the locals had left them with enough to make do for now.

Leona and Tusk weren't too dissimilar. He had worked for over fifteen years to better understand EOs. He had come further than any of the scientists in his field in understanding how EOs gained their abilities, but he was still decades from evolving the un-evolved. What she liked most about him was that he wasn't in it for the money. No, if money motivated him, he would have stopped a long time ago. Tusk, like her, wanted to leave a mark on history; he wanted his name credited with a discovery that changed mankind. Simple wealth couldn't do that.

"I swear I'm surrounded by idiots," Tusk said as he dropped into a chair that threatened to collapse under his weight.

"You are," Leona said as she put down the paper she had been reading.

"One of the backup generators doesn't work and no one thought to tell me until – wait for it – until the main power went out."

"You don't pay them enough to own issues like that."

"I don't think it's a matter of pay," Tusk snorted.

"Sure it is. You pay peanuts, you get monkeys."

Tusk's problem was that he thought he couldn't find competent workers in Pak Tha, but the truth was, there were smart people everywhere. Most employers looked at potential employees in terms of qualifications, but qualifications meant paper trails. There were no more hardworking and loyal people than those who couldn't afford paper qualifications, but went ahead and learned how to do the work anyway. Those people were grateful for an opportunity and loyal because you gave them one. And the thing was, you only had to pay them a fraction more than you paid the monkeys, which was still a lot less than you had to pay for the paper trail.

"Their English is appalling," Tusk ranted.

"And how's your Lao? But if you prefer, I'm sure they're willing to speak with you in Thai."

Tusk gave her a look that said he wasn't in the mood for fair play, and Leona chuckled.

"Doc, it looks like you're in need of some good news."

"What? You found us an energy source that doesn't rely on the local power grid? I swear I don't remember this place being this bad the first time we opened here."

"I'm told some of the best music ever played was done on a piano that was out of tune."

Tusk fixed her with another hard stare.

"It is the rare woman who can see beyond her limitations to create new possibilities, to compensate for what she doesn't have by revaluing what she does. She is the true genius."

"Did you pick that up from some motivational app?"

It was obvious he considered her young and inexperienced, and like most of her previous partners, he too underestimated her capabilities. It was the same silly game she was forced to play each time she started a new venture. But he would learn. They always did.

"Do we have any empty rooms?" Leona asked.

"Yeah. The guy we picked up in Chiang Rai was just looking for a free ride. He wasn't evolved."

"I thought you said you could sense EOs," she said.

Tusk raised an eyebrow. "I can." Then he sighed. "I had a feeling something was off about him, but jet lag, wishing I had more to work with," he gestured to their surroundings. "I made a mistake."

She nodded. "Any of the others seem promising?"

"Just one. The girl. I'm told she can make you fall asleep." Tusk crossed his arms. "Well, supposedly. I had her try it out on a few of the workers, but of course she's a bit of a legend around these parts, and so they were all reluctant to do it, and the few I managed to convince to give it a try immediately fell to the floor from the merest of touches."

Leona ran her thumb over the pads of her fingers. Something was telling her this was more than psychosomatic. This could be an active ability, something they could use. "Run more tests. I have a feeling you might be on to something with her."

"I plan to. I'll test her on some live animals while I wait for more subjects."

"Why not use the ones we have?"

"There's only four of them, and I've already started their treatment," Tusk explained. "We'll certainly lose two of them by morning; they weren't in a good way to begin with. The others will probably go within the next thirty-six hours. I've never had such problems getting quality subjects—"

The door opened with such force it ricocheted off the concrete wall behind it. The tin roof shook and a small cloud of dust drifted its way over the four men dressed in army fatigues who entered with their automatic rifles raised. A fifth came in behind them, his weapon holstered on his hip and his hands loosely folded at his back.

"Can we help you?" Leona spoke first.

The men ignored her as they looked around.

"Are you the owners?" It was the one with the relaxed stance who spoke.

"Yes. I'm Leona and this is the doctor. Can we help you?"

"This not a good neighborhood."

Leona ran her thumb across her fingers and cocked her head to the side for a moment. "No, it is not." She got the feeling she wasn't due to die here today, and that gave her the confidence she needed to steer things in a less hostile direction. "We were just talking about hiring better security."

The leader gave a shout of laughter before crossing his arms over his chest as if to say *please continue.*

"Know anyone interested? Patrol the facility and maybe let us know if any … curiosities come to town that might impact the work we're doing here."

The leader stepped around his men and the two nearest him lowered their guns as he passed. This wasn't some neighborhood gang of locals with nothing better to do. All of these men had formal training. Their aim was steady and their eyes were fixed on the different quadrants of the room.

"Are you expecting trouble?" the leader asked.

"Nothing that a few of the right men can't handle."

The leader turned his attention to Tusk, and for a moment, Leona felt that tingly sensation in her hand begin to subside. "I'm told you have the Dream Weaver."

The leader didn't like the doctor, or hadn't made up his mind about him. Either way, the tide was changing, and a lot more now depended on how Tusk responded.

Tusk looked at Leona and then back at the tall Laotian man who had spoken. He wore an army fatigue shirt just like his men, but had on dark blue jeans tucked inside ankle boots. "If you're referring to who I think you are, then yes, she's here. But she came voluntarily. We didn't take her."

The man smiled at Tusk's comment like he already knew the punchline. Leona rubbed her fingers again and the tingle grew.

"I know you did not take her because she is not the type who can be taken." The leader turned around and looked at the warehouse she and Tusk had been establishing as their office. "You have not touched her." It wasn't said as a question.

He slowly made his way across the warehouse to where Tusk and Leona stood. He looked over the doctor like he was dismissing him as a threat, but then extended his hand.

Leona had never been able to get a read on Tusk. It was as if her ability couldn't locate him, but she didn't need her ability to know if Tusk refused to shake hands, her earlier feelings that all was well would be invalidated. She was about to say something, anything to fill the silence, but then Tusk reached out and clasped hands with their new head of security.

The leader threw back his head and shouted another laughter. He turned to his men who seemed to relax a little, but kept their weapons raised. "My name is Khamkong. I will be in charge of your security. My fee is seven hundred American dollars per month. My associates will take five each. We will collect the first month now."

A smile spread across Leona's face. She was happy to pay Khamkong whatever he asked, because she had a feeling Khamkong would not live long enough to enjoy it. She wasn't going to kill him. In fact, she sensed she would do all she could to save him.

"Come," Leona said. "Follow me."

CHAPTER FOUR

~

Same-Same

4th August, 11:55am
Beach Road, Singapore

"You know, some people have called you the anti-Christ," Josh said.

Michael looked up and their eyes locked. Josh didn't need his ability to know he was the last person Michael wanted watching over him.

"But the same's been said about every great visionary," Josh continued. "So I wouldn't take it personally."

"Is this really necessary?" Michael sat back in his office chair. "No one's going to attack me. This is Singapore, you know. This Miles kid couldn't just come up the elevator. He would need an access card to even enter the doors from the lift lobby. Not to mention someone would stop him before he made it down the hall to my office."

This was the last place Josh wanted to be, too. Katherine had arrived and gone with Meita to meet the President of Singapore at the Istana to discuss Article 31. Apparently, Rox was meant to join them, but she sent him a cryptic mental message about having drop-offs and errands to run. Sam was off with Mika trying to enlist the locals to help them locate Miles, which left Josh alone and available to babysit Michael. Neither of them were happy about it. Josh had volunteered to watch the kids, but Katherine said school was the safest place for them at the moment.

He would rather be with Rox, but she had shut him down each time he tried to connect with her. He had promised her he would never pry into her thoughts again without her consent, and while technically he hadn't, it was hard not to notice the link between her and Sam had left her unsettled.

"How is she?" Josh asked.

Michael looked confused. "What?"

"Rox. How is she?"

"You mean Tara."

Josh hated that name. He pushed his chair back from the small conference table and went over to the window. It was midday traffic below and if he concentrated, he could make out the sound of a horn blowing.

Michael's office was nice, but it had a minimalist feel more reminiscent of a start-up than one of Michael's actual accomplishments. There wasn't anything wrong with it *per se*, but he had thought Michael would have moved the headquarters to Mapletree Business City like all the other tech companies. Josh had been to Singapore a few times for work, but never here, in this building. But then again, he could see the charm in this view. It was the early afternoon sun and the way it bounced off the buildings around him. It felt distinctly Singapore in a way that a business park couldn't quite capture.

"Look, I don't have time to play these games. I've got actual work to do, so unless you know there's a real threat, just go. I'll be fine."

Josh turned around and the lines on his forehead deepened as he invaded Michael's thoughts.

Michael was angry. He thought Josh was after his wife, and that brought a smile to Josh's face because he was, but not in the way Michael suspected. Yes, he was still in love with Rox, but so much had happened between them that right now friendship was the best option if they were ever to have a future together. No one knew her like he did. He had been inside her mind and seen the goodness, the confusion, and the fear she had lived with – the fear she *still* lived with.

"Did you hear me?" Michael asked.

Josh inhaled deeply without dissolving the link. "Yes, but I'm afraid if anything happened to you, *Rox* will never forgive me."

Michael pushed to his feet, and Josh's smile widened. Michael was thinking about punching him. "Her name is Tara."

"So you've said."

"What is it with you? You want her back or something? 'Cause that's not happening."

Josh had pushed him too far. He could hear Michael's internal struggle to regain control, but the images of punching Josh in the face were simply too enticing. The only thing holding Michael back was that he didn't want to cause a scene in his office. He was the boss. Cool. Calm. Respected. A physical altercation could unravel all he had worked so hard to build.

"Whatever contract you made her sign, it was done so under duress. No court in any country will uphold it. She's not going back with you," Michael said.

Josh felt a little sorry for him. The man had lost his wife, spent six years as a single parent, only to have a complete stranger returned to him in the body of the woman he had loved. Michael was trying desperately to re-establish the life he had lost when Tara died, and he had mistakenly thought Rox's return would do that.

Josh probed a little further and followed Michael's trail of anger back to its source. Michael was insecure and scared that Tara would disappear on them again. He was trying desperately to fall in love with her, but she just wasn't who he remembered. Rox was quieter than Tara. She lacked opinions and was afraid of saying the wrong thing. Michael wanted the woman who had been bold enough to call him selfish. To shout in his face when he was out of line. He missed their passionate lovemaking. He missed reminiscing with someone. He missed her talent, a talent he had never really cared about when she was alive, yet he saw the beauty in her pictures only after her death. Michael missed wanting to leave her and yet realizing he could never live without her. He wanted his wife back, and Josh and Meita represented a real fear that he could lose the closest thing he had to Tara all over again.

Josh could see the truth that Michael was fighting to ignore: he had never really gotten Tara back. What was a person without their memories? Instinct had led her this far, but instinct wasn't enough to fill the space that Tara's death had created. And after Rox's confession last night, Michael was left feeling vulnerable and in desperate need to circle the wagons and protect his family, even if that family was broken and unrecognizable.

But what hurt Josh the most was seeing the fear that Rox lived with through Michael's eyes. She had been petrified of saying the wrong thing. Josh didn't want her trying to be someone she wasn't. He didn't want her caring about whether Michael loved her or not. She deserved happiness as the person she had become.

Josh was beginning to think her coming back here had been a mistake. There was no way she could live up to the expectations that everyone had created for her.

"She's not the woman you married, and trying to get her to be that person is only drowning who she really is," Josh said, his tone harder than he had intended.

Michael stepped back from the table separating them. His office wasn't big, but it was large enough that Josh would see an attack coming, and right now, Michael was short on reasons not to initiate physical contact.

"You think because you spent two years fucking her that you know who she is?"

Josh took a deep breath to reign in his own temper. He knew what Michael was trying to do, but he also knew if they fought, it would only make things harder for Rox.

"She's my wife. She sleeps in *my* bed."

Josh couldn't help follow the thoughts that came to Michael's mind as the implication of what that meant hung between them. Josh saw that Rox *didn't* sleep in his bed, but in an annex at the back of the house.

Josh thought she had been here rekindling her relationship with her family, but instead she had been living on the periphery.

Michael winced and grabbed his forehead as Josh increased the pressure on Michael's mind to see more.

Josh saw her once more through Michael's eyes: a beautiful woman, trying to fit in, but failing. Only one of their children took to her, and that was MJ, their boy. Emma was confused and afraid, Ruby was downright hostile towards her, and Michael was conflicted over his own feelings. He couldn't move past the wife and mother she had been to see the person she was now. Michael didn't know this Tara. She was so different. She smelled differently, she behaved differently, and he was afraid he would never be able to love her.

Last night at the hotel was the first time they had been intimate. Josh squeezed his eyes shut against the onslaught of emotions he hadn't been prepared for as he relived the moments when Michael made love to Rox. Michael knew she had sex with him as a way to build a connection between them, a way of saying sorry for not being who he wanted, and that tore at Josh on a whole new level.

When Josh opened his eyes, Michael was staring at him.

"Are you trying to do to me what you did to Tara?"

"Don't flatter yourself," Josh said.

"She doesn't want you," Michael said.

Josh took a step forward then stopped. There was a time when he would have had Michael kicking his own ass by now. But Rox, she changed him. She helped him become a better father to his son. She showed him that not everyone was out to get him, and she did that by loving him with an innocence that only existed once.

"Sit down," Josh said.

He didn't wait for Michael to comply, and instead forced him to his seat. Then he took the one across. Josh opened his mind so that there could be no doubt about his ability.

I found your wife in a facility, unconscious and who knows how long away from being a guinea pig.

What the? Are you in my—

And yeah, my initial actions weren't exactly noble. Josh paused to allow Michael's mind to come to terms with what was happening before he continued. *If she chooses you, so be it. But you will love her as* Rox *because the woman you married? She's dead. ¿Entiendes?*

The door swung open and a woman slightly taller than average walked in. She was dressed in a black skirt and a white camisole that was too risqué for Corporate America, but made sense in Singapore's heat. The sounds from her red stilettos were subdued by the carpet in the room, but it was her stride that announced she had something she wouldn't be deterred from discussing.

Josh relinquished his hold, and Michael shot to his feet.

"We need to talk," she said before Michael gathered himself.

Josh latched onto her thoughts and discovered she was upset about next year's anniversary launch. This was going to be nothing more than a work conversation.

"I thought we discussed the patent absurdity of making the platform free for twenty-four hours," she said. "Almost all of our revenue is from ads and avatar-related purchases." Her breathing was accentuated, which made her neck and face match the color of her shoes.

"I'm in the middle of something at the moment," Michael said, and Josh had to cough to hide his laughter when he heard Michael wishing that Josh would interrupt them.

The woman turned to Josh. "Excuse me. I'm sorry to interrupt, but this won't take long." She turned back to Michael. "You're walking away from an untold amount of revenue!"

Something switched inside of Michael, and Josh noticed that their earlier encounter was forgotten as Michael focused on the woman. "No, I'm showing gratitude to everyone who helped me get here."

"Put out a message. Record a video where you give your heartfelt thanks, but anniversaries are usually the time when there's a huge spike in revenue. Wanna know why? Because more people log on. They get curious to see what we're going to do differently. Some even get nostalgic. They remember when they first joined and created their first avatar. And that makes them spend more money! Advertisers know this and that's why we can charge a premium to advertise on that one day."

Josh looked at Michael. The man was calm on the outside, but seething inwardly. He hadn't liked her tone or the presumption that she needed to explain to him the sales and marketing side of *his* business. In fact, Josh realized that Michael had never really liked her.

Josh wanted to tell the woman to stop while she was ahead, but she continued on before he could place the suggestion in her thoughts.

"If the marketing team starts down this path, we're walking away from potentially hundreds of millions—"

"If the marketing team wants a job tomorrow, they'll do exactly what I tell them and not question me about it," Michael said. "And that also applies to you."

Josh leaned back in his chair and covered his smile with his hand. He didn't want to like Michael. The man had slept with Rox, but Josh understood the change that took over when he was talking about his company. Michael had a vision, an ideal of what he wanted V-R to be. And another money-grubbing, insincere social media platform designed to hook its users without a single consideration for their lives as actual people wasn't it. Michael wanted to show his users and all the companies that advertised their products through his system that he was grateful, and the only way to do that, the only way to *meaningfully* do that was to put some money back in their pockets.

The woman gave Josh an angry look as she spun around and marched out of the office.

Josh whistled. "You know she's going to quit."

"She's already accepted another offer at a competitor."

"She's going to tell them everything she can about your platform," Josh said.

"I know. But all I can do is make her take her garden leave."

"You can enforce the NDA."

Michael shrugged. "Proving that it was her who leaked

intellectual property isn't as easy as it sounds. Her problem is she's smart and she knows it, but she's not willing to put in the time. She's looking for an easy way to the top."

Josh had come across a few of those in his time. They were either later humbled by a mistake and then went on to rise to greatness or they became bitter, toxic employees who placed blame on others for their lack of success.

"How did you know she was quitting?" Michael asked.

"Body language," Josh said as he reached into his pocket and pulled out his phone. It was Meita calling him.

"Any luck?" he asked her.

Josh turned his back on Michael as he listened to Meita explain to him they had confirmation that Miles was in Singapore.

~

Sacrifice

4th August, 7:53pm
Siglap, Singapore

The ground floor of Michael's home was an open design with two separate steps separating the three areas. It was modern with clean edges, or maybe this was considered post-modern? Whatever label best described its design, the difference between this and Halo could not be more apparent.

Halo was functional. It had a kitchen large enough to feed at least ten all together and a dining room that could seat a few more. Each room had walls as its divider and the furniture was chosen for comfort and maximum durability. Perhaps Michael's home was what comfort and maximum durability looked like at a much higher price bracket.

A hand touched Sam's leg under the table, and he realized he had been bouncing his knee. He looked at Meita, but she kept her attention on the conversation between Josh and Michael.

Sam had only been working with Meita for ten months, but there was something unique about her. It wasn't just that she made him look like an old-school LAN administrator with her network systems and cloud architecture navigational skills, it was also the way she brought everyone's strengths to the forefront. While she was their official team lead, she didn't hesitate to pass the reins to him when they were in the field. She managed to somehow patch things up with Josh, which was no simple feat after the stunt she pulled when Josh hired her to find Rox. She also convinced Katherine to send Sheppard to university.

Kamal Sheppard was a young man who had gotten in over his head masquerading as a geneticist at Watership Down, when in fact he was nothing more than a paramedic. Meita saw potential in him and argued that they would one day need a geneticist they could trust, so she made the case to invest in Sheppard. Sam had agreed. Sheppard had a lot of potential and had more than proven he could keep his head under pressure.

Meita's hand slipped off his knee, and Sam felt a bit of the tension release. If he didn't know better, he would have sworn that Meita was an empath, but she didn't have abilities like the rest of them. She could sense other EOs, but was immune to them. Josh couldn't hear her thoughts and Rox couldn't heal her or siphon her energy.

Sam closed his eyes and tried to feel Rox, but again nothing happened. Everyone at the table was worried about her, and Josh said she wasn't letting him inside her thoughts.

Sam looked at Michael and had to give him credit. He had been through a lot these past six years and yet he sat at the table confident and seemingly unphased. It made Sam feel even more guilty for his feelings. How could he sit here knowing that if Rox would have him, he would happily take her away from all of this. That wasn't the man he wanted to be.

"Yo, Bro?" Mika said.

The conversation stopped and everyone turned to his younger brother. He had been wandering around, ostensibly looking at photos, but in actuality committing the family's scent to his memory.

"Let's go for a walk," Mika said.

Sam hesitated and looked over at Meita.

"Go," she said. "I'll let you know if I hear anything."

Sam eased his chair back, careful not to scratch the marble floors, and followed his little brother onto the front porch.

"You're doing it again," Mika said when the front door closed.

Sam lifted his arm and sniffed. He didn't smell like he had stepped out of the shower, but neither did he feel like he was giving off a bad odor.

"You know you can't smell it," Mika said. "Talk to me."

Where should he begin? He was struggling to make sense out of all of it himself. Was this how Josh felt?

Then an energy slipped through him with such precision he stopped to wonder if it was only his imagination. He looked down the road, but the rain had just started.

He stepped off the porch, his feet moving on their own. His breath held as he waited.

"Sam?" Mika called from behind him, but Sam held up his hand and signaled for his brother to be silent.

He wasn't sure how he opened the gate without looking, but the next thing he knew he was on the sidewalk, the rain pelting down on him as he peered through the narrow cones of visibility the streetlights offered.

"She's here," Sam whispered.

His walk turned into a jog and then into a full-out sprint. Something was wrong. Lightning lit the sky and he could make out figures at the bottom of the street. Her energy slammed into him again, and this time he felt her pull. Rox only ever took energy when she needed it.

Josh!

Sam used his ability and the raindrops slowed as if frozen. He inhaled a deep breath and slipped into that place where time seemed to open up to him and spit him out a few seconds into the future. His lungs burned as he fought against his muscles' need for fresh oxygen. It was an odd sensation, running while holding his breath. When his abilities first manifested, it felt like an impossibility, but now, it was a habit he had taught himself through years of practice.

Before he met Rox, the farthest he had passed through time had been three seconds. A lot could happen in just three seconds. He had used those precious moments to save lives, and to end a few.

Reality yanked him back and the raindrops fell in a deafening crash around him. He took another breath and used his ability once more. He glanced to the right and stumbled. Tree trunks as wide as his body appeared on either side of him. He looked up for the cones of light, but there were no street lamps. No rain. Shock caused him to suck in a mouthful of air, and a sweetness like he had never inhaled before filled his lungs. He grabbed hold of his chest in wonder and tripped over a tree root that wasn't there just moments ago on the asphalt. Reality reasserted its hold and yanked him back.

Rain slapped against him as loose gravel cut through the skin on the palms of his hands. He looked over where the trees had been, but gated houses once again lined the streets. Rox's energy collided with his as he struggled to his feet and continued towards her.

She was facing three people, two directly in front of her and one making his way into her blind spot. Sam shouted her name as one of her attackers threw a quick jab, but she blocked it and then countered with a right, right, left. She was a lot quicker than he remembered, but the one who had remained on the fringe of the fight managed to flank her. His heart soared as she spun around, her guard lifted to block the attack from above. But the strike came in low.

Sam arrived a second after her legs gave out and her

head hit the sideview mirror of a parked car as she crumbled to the ground.

The guy who struck her only had time to look up as Sam's fist broke his nose, and then his cheekbone and finally his jaw. Someone moved in behind Sam, but he had trained for multiple assailants in close quarters so he led with his elbow over his shoulder. He spun around and grabbed hold of the man's shirt before he fell back out of range and brought the man's face down into his knee. A sharp pain radiated through Sam's shinbone, but he blocked it out as he turned to face the last attacker. But instead of joining the fight, the man spun around and ran for a van that was blocking the entrance to the street a few meters away. Sam took one step after him and was tackled to the ground from behind. He flipped over and was about to launch into another attack when he realized it was his brother.

"Get off of me," Sam roared, but Mika kept him pinned.

"This isn't the States. You gotta stop," Mika shouted, but Sam still struggled to break free.

"Rox. Think of Rox," Mika said.

Sam stilled. He looked past his brother and saw her curled on her side, unmoving, but waves of healing energy were pulsating off of her.

Mika relaxed his hold allowing Sam to push free and crawl to her. Sam rolled her onto her back, and she took a blind swing he easily caught.

"Rox, it's me. It's Sam." Tears slipped down his face and onto hers to mix with the blood running across her forehead.

He watched as awareness focused her vision.

"Sam?"

"Yeah. You OK?"

What a stupid question. But then she lowered her fist and sat up. A smile so beautiful spread across her face that he forgot where they were. He watched in disbelief as she tilted her head to the side and leaned forward to kiss him.

Rain slid inside the back of his shirt, but he ignored it because she was in his arms. He couldn't explain their connection any more than he could explain what he had just witnessed while using his ability, but he knew whatever existed between them was real. And her kiss was proof she felt it too.

She mumbled something between their lips, but he kept his mouth locked on hers because he didn't want their moment to end. He had forgotten about the two men lying on the ground or Mika who was standing behind them on the phone to Guy, and Josh who was sprinting down the street because he had heard Sam's call.

He cupped her head with his hands and held her still as he deepened their kiss. Thunder rumbled, but he took no notice. It wasn't until he realized she was crying did he pull back.

"Hey, it's OK," he said.

"I'm sorry. I, I—" She lowered her head and wept in his arms.

Mika would handle the men who had attacked her. Sam wasn't sure if the third one got away, but he didn't care anymore. The way she curled into him made him want to take her away from all of this. He would find a small island nearby for a few days – or a year – where they could get away. Meita and Josh would handle GFO, Mika could take over field operations if Singapore ever signed the petition for Article 31, and his father would take care of Halo.

Sam was tired of fighting. It seemed like death was all he had ever known since his mother had died, then his daughter two hours and eleven minutes after her birth, followed by his wife. He had even prepped for the death of his baby sister, Val, but then Rox saved her, and just like that Sam realized for the first time in such a very long time, he wanted to live. Not just to spare someone else the pain of his death, but because he wanted to live as there was something in his life *he* wanted. And she was finally in his arms.

Val would help their father with Halo as soon she got back on her feet. Her thoughts were still a bit scattered and she retreated into herself too often to call it normal, but she was getting better each day. His stepmom said so.

All that mattered to Sam now was safe within his grasp. He would never try to keep her from her family. She could visit them as often as she wanted. Hell, he would move here if she preferred to live close by. But he needed her, on his sofa, in his bed … in his arms.

Sam heard Mika and Josh talking, but he couldn't make out what they were saying. With their abilities, they would make an unstoppable team. All would be fine.

He slid her off his lap and then scooped her up into his arms as he stood. She laid her head against his chest as he started back towards the house. The memory of him carrying her onto the plane played in his mind. They had been through a lot together, but he struggled to remember a time when they actually just sat and talked. Maybe the plane ride to Crossroads? Or was it before they got the call Josh's son had been taken? There were those few moments in the SUV after Wonderland when she told him her real name.

There never seemed to be enough time. From the moment she arrived on their doorstep back at Halo asking for help until now, so much was happening around them that he wished they could get away, for a little while, so they could see what they had the potential to be. To hell with saving all the EOs. He had saved enough lives for the both of them. He wanted to be selfish. No, he had earned the right to be selfish. Sam finally had something worth living for in his arms, and he would sacrifice everything to keep her there.

~

Till death

4th August, 8:43pm
Siglap, Singapore

"I could've taken them you know," Rox said softly as she slid out of his arms onto the porch of Michael's house.

Sam's eyebrows met in confusion, then a slow smile spread across his face. "But then I couldn't be your hero."

She had been training for ten months and had come a long way since he had last seen her fight. Mika may have driven her to her knees and turned her stomach inside out, but one thing was certain, she knew how to get back up. Third rule of training with Mika, get up swinging. "It'll keep 'em back until you regain your footing."

Fourth rule, never fall down.

"They've found me, haven't they?" she asked.

He cupped the side of her face, and she leaned into his touch. She should be thinking about securing their position or figuring out how she was discovered, but instead she was distracted by Sam. His energy was more potent than before. She felt it across a wider distance, much farther than she had when they first met. And now when he touched her, the pulses stopped like usual, but in its place was the constant hum of their energy.

She sucked in a sharp breath as an unexpected jolt of pain ran below her rib cage. Sam put his hand over hers where she cradled her side.

"Breathe through it," he said.

"I have to sit down." She lowered back into one of the chairs on the porch, and that shifted the pain but did little to alleviate it. Whatever internal damage she had was healing itself, and nothing hurt worse than recovery. "Sorry I kissed you."

He knelt in front of her. "I'm not."

It was too humid for her to feel cold from the rain, but she shivered anyway. There was so much to think about that her mind was having problems focusing. She had finally figured out what she wanted, but the guilt from choosing the man she loved over the man she married was suffocating.

"We don't have to figure it all out now," he said. "We can go as slow as you need."

"I love my children," she said through silent tears. "If I had to choose between you or them—"

"You'll never have to." His finger traced her bottom lip. "I'll never ask that of you."

Rox wasn't sure if the physical pain was heightened because of the emotional one, but she turned to her side and groaned.

Sam went to pick her up, but she shook her head. "It'll pass. I just need to get through the worst of it." She curled up in the chair as best she could and focused on healing. She pulled from the storm and let its energy replace her fatigue and repair her injuries.

She had spent the day trying to find an easy way forward given her feelings for Sam. She had forgotten about Miles and Tusk, and anyone else who wanted to understand her abilities, so when the van pulled to a stop beside her, she checked that she was on the sidewalk, but didn't pay the vehicle or its occupants any further attention until one of them grabbed her. It was instinct to wrench her arm free and strike out with her other. She didn't have time to think, just defend. Evade. Fight back.

She laid her head back and tried to make sense of the last twenty-four hours. She finally had a real conversation with her husband. It had taken ten months and a lot of false starts, but they got there. Despite the awkwardness of Josh and Meita's sudden appearance, they found a way to speak openly and honestly about their past. Sure, making love to Michael complicated things, but she didn't regret it because she needed to see if there was some small part of Tara inside her that remembered his touch. But then she felt Sam and knew all she would ever be able to give Michael was that one moment.

"Better?"

The concern in his voice brought her out of her trance, and she sat up a bit straighter. "Was that Mika down there?"

"Yeah, about that," he said, but the gate to their front yard scratched open and Mika and Josh walked up the pathway, their shoulders hunched against the rain.

"You alright?" Mika asked her as they came up the steps.

Rox forced a smile on her face. "Yeah. Never been particularly grateful for our sessions until tonight."

"You did well." Mika crossed his arms over his chest in a way that reminded her of Sam. "Held your own against three bigger and much stronger opponents until helped arrived."

Mika had thrown her, flipped her, punched her, kicked her, pinned her, and made her cry; he had caused her food to come back up more times than she would ever admit, and despite the fact that she continued to get back on her feet (albeit sometimes slower than others), not once had he ever told her she did well. Not even a "you're getting better" when she was able to run ten kilometers without stopping or slowing her pace.

"The two that I took down?" Sam asked as he stood up.

"They're with two officers. I've had them watching this place since earlier today when we got confirmation about Miles."

"Well, they've done a shit job, wouldn't you say?" Josh said.

"They did as they were instructed. They watched the house, not anyone in particular." Mika turned away from them and inhaled, like he had caught a whiff of something through the rain.

Rox was about to ask him why he did that, but Sam spoke first. "What'd you pick up?"

Mika closed his eyes and tilted his head to the side for a moment before he shrugged. "I don't know. C'mon, help me question those guys before they're taken in."

Sam nodded, but turned back to Rox. "You going to be alright?"

"Yeah, I'm fine. I'm through the worst of it."

She watched Sam and Mika walk out into the rain and disappear back down the street.

"Where were you?" Josh asked. *I tried connecting with you repeatedly today, and you blanked me. Ever think I could have been trying to warn you? Give you some kind of vital information that could – oh, I don't know – help you avoid a showdown against three opponents "much bigger and stronger" than you?*

Rox needed some time away from everyone today. Everything had become so convoluted since last night. She was supposed to have two more months to figure things out, to find a way to have a normal life.

Oh for fuck's sake, Rox. Grow up. You were never going to have a normal life. Never. The question is do you wanna wind up back in a box with water rushing in at your feet?

"What did you just say to me?" She pushed to standing.

I think you heard me the first time. We've got confirmation that Miles is here, in Singapore, and you run off because you can't work out your feelings?

Fuck you.

Yeah? Fuck me, Rox? Well, I hope it's nothing like the mercy fuck you gave Michael last night because I gotta tell you—

The sound of her hand connecting with the side of his face echoed through the rain. He hadn't seen that coming because she didn't know she was going to do it. It was pure instinct.

The look he gave her teetered between disgust and surprise. She had never struck him, not even when she confronted him about how he had manipulated her feelings.

It's not just you and me, anymore. Your life just got a whole lot more complicated, and we don't have time for you to play the confused schoolgirl.

Why are you being like this? How was I supposed to know that Miles would come here? Or that I'd be attacked on my way home?

Because I taught you better than this!

You mean you manipulated me.

He smirked. *Fine. You need me to be the bad guy, I'll play that role. But the woman I found, the woman I trained would've never had sex with a man out of obligation.*

He caught her hand before it made contact again. *If you were to get captured today, did you ever think about what it would do to those kids in there? What it would do to Jay?*

Rox yanked her hand free.

Yeah, I get it, they haven't taken to you yet, but that's because you're trying to be someone you're not.

It's not that simple!

But it is, mi amor. You think I like what this family has done to you? The last time you felt trapped or like someone was asking you to be someone you weren't, you left. In fact, you ran and I spent over a year and a ton of money looking for you. Why are you letting them define who you are?

He looked away from her as if he couldn't bear her face, and she was surprised at how much his opinion mattered. That's when it hit her. Josh and his son were the closest thing to a real family she had. Maybe it would never be textbook, but Jay loved her despite the fact she left, and Josh had come for her time and time again.

She lowered her head. *They're my children, Josh. Don't you think I've hurt them enough?*

He tilted her chin up. *You didn't hurt them. You died, and I'm guessing you didn't do that on purpose. Yes, they got hurt. Their worlds got rocked. I get it. Jay's mother died too, remember. But he loves you for who you are. So should they.*

She's everywhere in this house. Her mind screamed. *Everyone expects me to say what she would've said or do what she would've done. But I don't know her, and now I have these children. I don't know how to be a mother.*

He stepped closer and lowered his forehead until it touched hers. "No one knows how to be a parent. We kinda just wing it."

A small burst of laughter broke free, and he wrapped his arms around her and pulled her close.

His lips touched her cheek. *I can't lose you again.*

For a moment she stood there, acknowledging all the emotions she had been bottling up since she returned as the lost mother and wife with no memories. *I don't know what to do. It's like everyone wants something from me, and I'm so afraid of making the wrong decision.*

Josh stepped back, but kept his hands on her arms as he looked down at her. *Start with what you know.*

I know that I don't want to lose my kids. I don't want to lose Jay. You. And Sam ... Her thoughts went on a tangent as she stared off into the rain.

Yeah, I get it. You chose Sam. You gotta find a girlfriend to talk to about him. That's where I draw the line—

The front door opened and Meita stuck her head out. "Either of you seen Ruby or the little boy?"

Rox wiped the last of her tears away and shook her head. "No. Why?"

Michael came out of the house and looked around into the darkness. His energy flowed around him in fitful waves that were hard to ignore.

"What's wrong?" Rox asked.

"I can't find them," he said. "They're not here!"

Rox closed her eyes and reached out with her energy. It was the first time she had tried using her ability to make contact with her kids. She hadn't done so before because she was trying to fit in, but she was finally learning the difference between fitting in and belonging.

The first to answer her call were the kinetic forces

from the storm. Clouds gathered above her and the lightning altered its direction, creating a loud crash of thunder that shook the ground. She blocked out the elements and focused on what was right in front of her. The electricity created from Josh's heartbeat, then Meita's and Michael's. She pushed further and felt the helper just on the inside of the door, Katherine on the ground floor, but a little further in. There was someone upstairs, but it was just the one, and she knew that had to be Emma.

Rox opened her eyes. *Can you go upstairs and find out what you can from Emma?*

I'll talk with her, bring up their names, and see where that leads.

Rox nodded. She hated the thought of someone invading her daughter's thoughts, but if Ruby and MJ were missing, then time was of the essence.

"Everything alright?" Sam asked as he and Mika walked up the pathway.

"We can't find Ruby or MJ," Rox said, and with those words a fear like nothing she had experienced took root. If Tusk took them, he would want to experiment on them, but they weren't evolved. Or at least they weren't *yet.* Neither of them showed signs of having any ability, but then again, she had purposefully strayed away from talking about anything evolved with them. She had been too busy trying to be Tara to think about who she truly was, and perhaps the importance of them knowing about it.

Warm arms encircled her and she laid her head on Sam's chest.

"We don't know that he has them. They're kids. They could've just run off," Sam said.

"In the middle of a thunderstorm?" Rox said softly.

"Who has them?" Michael said. "What do you mean you don't know if 'he has them'? Who's he? This kid named Miles?"

Everyone looked to Rox for an explanation.

"Answer me!"

Rox stepped back from Sam. "Michael, we don't want to jump to conclusions, but the people who held me captive *might* be here in Singapore and—"

Michael stepped back and grabbed the railing to stop himself from falling. "You think that doctor, the one who tortured you might have them?"

"Let's not jump to conclusions," Sam cautioned. "It's more likely they ran off."

"Don't you speak to me about my children."

Rox was surprised by the vitriol in his voice. "Michael, he's just—"

"You come back to me broken, confused, and with no memories of the life we had. You lie to me for months, and now, two of our kids, no, *my* kids are missing because of you. I swear if anything happens to them, I'll find a way to make sure you stay dead!"

Sam launched himself at Michael too fast for Rox to stop, but Mika must have anticipated it because he caught Sam's fist on the backswing.

"Not like this," Mika said with a calmness that belied the situation.

Rox stood still, afraid of making any sudden movements

that would influence Sam's obvious struggle to regain control. She watched as Mika led Sam down the walkway and back out into the rain.

For the first time since she could remember, she didn't wonder about who she had been, but instead asked herself who she wanted to be.

CHAPTER FIVE

~

Like mother

4th August, 9:17pm
Siglap, Singapore

It struck Rox as odd how little she had been in her children's bedrooms, and that only highlighted how much of an outsider she had been during these last ten months. Each room was reflective of their age as well as their personalities. MJ's was situated between Ruby's and Emma's, its walls covered with superheroes. He had two bookshelves, one filled with a mix of children's classics and comics, and another for his action figures. In so many ways he was the average ten-year-old boy, full of energy and smiles and questions and conversations that ran from one stream of consciousness to another. He loved with an innocence that made her feel special. She wished he and Jay could meet. They would like one another.

Ruby's room was at the far end of the hall, and was, Rox had learned, typical of someone who had a live-in helper. Clothes were left on the back of her chair and on the tops of every available surface until Marie entered to collect the day's laundry. At sixteen, Ruby should have known how to clean her own room, but then again, Marie knew her children better than she did. Who was she to say anything?

Rox had only been in Ruby's room while she was at school. It was filled with medals, certificates, and a few trophies. Ruby practiced judo and had placed in a few tournaments, but never won any. She was a good kid who struggled with anger management issues, Michael explained.

Rox and Ruby began their relationship at a stalemate, and no matter what Rox tried, she couldn't get Ruby to open up. In fact, Ruby would often leave the room whenever Rox entered.

Yes, it hurt, but how do you break through to a teenager who had so much pain bottled up inside?

Rox ran her fingers across the faces in the family photos arranged to form a collage in the hallway. She studied Tara's smile. It was bright and joyful and filled with memories. She had been happy.

She had also been a different person, and that version of herself was never coming back. It was time to accept that.

The guilt she had been carrying around for the past ten months began to lift. Josh was right. She wasn't to blame for the loss of her memories. It was nothing more than an unfortunate circumstance of life.

She thought back to the moment when Walter had given her the choice to help him find his daughter, Val, or return to a life on the run. He told her that life was rarely fair and sometimes bad things happened without explanation, and spending too much time trying to figure out why or who was to blame was a dangerous distraction that robbed you of healing.

Rox was done trying to be Tara. She glanced back at Ruby's room but didn't go in. She would never give up on her eldest daughter, but she was done feeling guilty.

She entered Emma's room where Josh was seated across from her engaged in a jovial conversation that allowed him to read her thoughts with ease.

Emma's room was perfect. It had all the right colors and accoutrements for a happy, well-adjusted teenager, but it lacked depth. The bookshelf, desk, and beanbag were tidy, no clothing out of place. She had a white bedside table with a pink lampshade that matched the throw over the footboard. A soft teddy, presumably from her childhood, rested on top of her pillows.

Rox studied her youngest daughter for a moment. Emma always said the right thing and knew the right questions to ask to appear perfect, just like her room. But right now, she was hiding something.

It was there in the bags under her eyes that teenagers don't get from studying all hours of the night. It was in the perpetual slouch of her shoulders and her lack of eye contact.

How on earth had Rox not seen that before?

She shook her head. There was no point in beating herself up about it. As soon as they found Ruby and MJ, she would have a talk with Emma – whether Emma wanted it or not.

"Find anything?" Rox asked Josh.

"You're wet, too!" Emma said.

Rox had forgotten about how she looked. Her wounds had healed and the rain had washed off any blood, but nothing but a shower and fresh clothes would change the waterlogged look she sported.

"Went running in the rain," Rox said to Emma. "On hindsight, not such a good idea."

Emma nodded like she understood, but then her head tilted to the side like she was studying something. "Are you leaving us?"

Josh stood. *We need to talk.*

Rox sucked in a breath. She had to tell them at some point she wasn't staying forever, and the more she thought about it, the sillier it seemed to have waited so long. But she couldn't change the past. She had made her choice to remain silent, now it was time to start communicating.

"Emma," Rox began. "I, ugh, I was given a year with you guys before I have to work for an organization that helps people."

"So you *are* leaving." It was the sound of her voice more than the tears filling her eyes that hurt Rox the worst.

Rox opened her mouth to say something, but then quickly decided against it. What could she say? Yes. She was leaving.

Emma's evolved.

Rox opened her arms, and Emma walked into them as a sob escaped. She had wasted so much time all because she was afraid of being rejected. It seemed so trivial now. Maybe if she had just been herself, they could have come together as a family much sooner. Maybe she would have patched up her relationship with Michael so that when

Sam came looking for Miles, she would have already fallen back in love with her husband.

Rox placed her cheek on her daughter's head. "I'm so sorry."

They stood there, each holding on to one another until both their tears subsided.

"Emma," Rox slowly pulled back. "What's your ability?"

Emma's shoulders stiffened, and she looked over at Josh. "I don't ... " She stared up at her mother. "Do you have an ability too?"

Rox nodded. "No more secrets."

Emma placed a shaky hand on her mother's chest. "I can feel what's in here." Her voice was small, almost as if she could somehow make it less true if she whispered.

Empath. Like Miles, maybe, Josh said.

"Can you feel the same thing?" Emma asked.

"No, I'm a healer." Rox didn't know any empaths, well, except Miles. "You can feel what other people are feeling?"

Emma nodded. "Sometimes, but not always. It lessens when you're around, but I can normally tell when someone is speaking a truth they believe in because they give off stronger emotions."

"What do you mean it lessens when Rox is around?" Josh said.

Emma shrugged. "Like when you came up here, I could feel that you were upset, but mostly you were worried. But then there was something else underneath all of that, but it's hard to explain. Like I know the questions you were asking me weren't what you really wanted to know."

This day has been far too long.

"What can you do?" Emma asked her mom.

"I can heal people. Sometimes."

Emma looked impressed. "Like physically or spiritually?"

"More like physically."

"Wow." Emma considered that for a moment. "Is that how you lost your memories?"

"I don't know how or why I lost my memories, Em."

Her daughter smiled. "That's what you used to call me."

I hate to cut it short, but she knows where Ruby and MJ are.

Where?

~

Alchemy

4th August, 8:25pm (-1 SGT)
Pak Tha, Laos

Mockingbird had been his favorite facility. It was the first one he had done right: the most modern surveillance equipment, the best scientists and doctors in their fields, and he had learned the importance of investing in medical engineers who could build the types of tools he needed to extract, analyze, and one day reconstruct a wide variety of EO abilities.

Research laboratories for evolved humans were still very much in their infancy. Tusk remembered back to Su Kim, the EO with extraordinary hearing who Tara helped escape from Watership Down. Just about any medical lab in the world could have analyzed her auditory abilities because an otacoustic emissions probe already existed and was in large supply. It wasn't identifying or even isolating her ability that had become too expensive to continue researching; it was the *measuring* of that ability that had become cost prohibitive. Tusk suspected she could hear sounds that no other human could, and he wasn't talking about the sound of a mosquito from twenty meters away. He was referring to sound waves that humans were biologically incapable of hearing because those sound waves operated on a frequency that the human eardrum couldn't detect – perhaps even on a frequency all known devices were incapable (or unaware) of detecting. To test his hypothesis, he would have to build equipment that could not only identify, but also isolate sounds that even when amplified, the human ear remained unable to process. Then he would have to test if Su Kim heard those sounds. Very few investors were interested in abilities as banal as advanced hearing; therefore, his funding for her ran out and he had no other recourse but to sell her.

Yet the ability to stop aging, that was something every human wanted. Young ones like Leona wouldn't find it as interesting because they were still too fresh from the womb, incapable of comprehending the implications of time. She was most interested in the empath because she was still in the phase where *feelings* mattered and uncovering their impetus was somehow enlightening.

The door swung open and hot, humid air filled the room. The air-conditioning unit gurgled and then slowly switched on. "You told our men to engage?"

It was her tone that gave him the most offense,

followed swiftly by her sudden appearance in his lab. The fact she was asking the question meant she already knew the answer. What she probably wanted to know was *why* he had told their men to engage when she had given orders to the contrary.

"They should always engage when the healer is present. Regardless of the circumstance." He didn't bother to look up from the results on his screen. He had spent much of the last six hours trying to make sense of how such a negligible amount of body oil transfer could render an eighty-kilo man unconscious.

"Yeah, well, two of the men got caught. One barely managed to escape."

That was hardly noteworthy. For all her money and her ability, she was still so young. "Ever played chess?"

She was silent for a moment, then her eyes rolled with understanding. "Don't give me that shit. Only a fool sacrifices her pawns needlessly."

"The healer is worth an untold number of pawns." He gave her a reassuring smile like he might have given to one of his children, and for a moment he realized she was young enough to be his child. If he had started early. "What about the secondary team?"

Leona lost her look of frustration and in its place confusion set in. "Secondary team? You sent another team?"

He had to admit, he missed Nancy. She would have considered this new facility a derelict warehouse in desperate need of a demolition crew. For the first time, he held conflicting feelings about Tara. If it weren't for her, Nancy would still be alive and he would be discussing the results of this new EO they found instead of defending the wisdom of deploying more than one team.

Alchemy. That's what he was going to name this facility.

"You gonna fill me in about this second team or what?" Leona asked.

"There was a second team in place following the first one."

"And you told them to engage, too?"

"No, their job was to simply observe and report."

Leona crossed her hands over her chest. "You don't think that's a waste of resources?"

"Not in the slightest," Tusk said as he leaned back in his chair and almost fell over. He stood up and was tempted to laugh at the absurdity of their situation, but decided to look at it as a return to his humble beginnings. There were other facilities he could have gone to, but with Harry no longer running GFO, he couldn't risk inadvertently leading anyone to his other locations.

"Look," he continued. "The three men you hired are good at scaring people into paying a debt they owe, but they are not cut out for surveillance. They have sleeve tattoos! People tend to notice that, Leona."

"I've worked with them before," she added.

"Yes, and I'm sure they did a commendable job scaring off whoever it was you needed gone, but what we need is a bit of finesse."

Her mouth thinned and she did that thing with her fingers. She was smart not to trust easily, but he was beginning to think that some of her bravado had been an act. She was old enough to have some experience, but not enough.

"The people who have Tara not only have money, Leona, they have the law on their side. Make no mistake about it, I aim to get that healer back in my lab regardless of the cost. Now, the secondary team noticed that Josh and Major Watts were at a house. So while I instructed your guys to try to apprehend Tara, I had the other team watching on the periphery to see what happens."

"And did something happen?"

"Yes. The house they were staying at is owned by a Michael Leon Harding. You might've heard of him. Inventor of V-R, that virtual reality social media thing targeted at your age group. He's worth over $130 million, not including the house, and is the father to three children, and a widower no more."

Leona leaned against the desk. "Go on."

"His *deceased* wife, Tara Alexandra Harding, recently returned from the dead." He paused to let that sink in. "So while your men were attempting to capture Michael's not-so-dead wife, aka *my* healer, two children were seen climbing out the back window of said house."

Leona nodded slowly. "So, you *assumed* my guys were going to mess up?"

"No, not at all. In fact, I was hoping they would have been successful. It was three against one; they should have been able to take her with relative ease."

"My guy who got away said she had backup."

Tusk thought about that for a moment. "She knows I'm coming for her."

"Well, she knows now, that's for certain," Leona said. "Anyway, what about the kids?"

"I'm waiting to hear back from the second team shortly with an update."

"They're at Fort Canning Park."

There was a moment of pause while Tusk tried to figure out if he had heard her correctly.

A smile spread across her face as she stood to her full height and placed her hand on her hip with the swagger of a woman who knew she had been underestimated and was moments away from proving why that was always a bad idea.

"The three guys who you so aptly described as obvious are meant to be obvious. They're meant to be noticed because while everyone is looking out for them, they *don't* notice the team who comes in and actually completes the objective."

Impressive. Maybe she wasn't as inexperienced as he thought. "And what is your team 'who comes in and actually completes the objective' going to do now?"

She shrugged. "Whatever we tell them to, but they've followed the kids to the Fort Gate. Looks like sneaking out of the house is what kids do these days."

Tusk chuckled. Regardless of the time or culture, kids remained the same. "Do you have a recommended course of action?"

She crossed her arms over her chest and gave it serious thought before she answered. "It'd be easy enough to take them, but as you say, we also want the healer. We could offer an exchange."

Tusk shook his head. He'd tried that before. He still hadn't worked out exactly how they had found

Wonderland, but he wasn't going to risk exposure again. Besides, he wanted the children too. "A family of evolved ones," he whispered to himself.

"Think the kids are evolved as well?"

Tusk sat back down in his chair. "Fifty-fifty. There're just as many evolved ones who are one-offs as there are families of them."

"Makes sense. Evolution takes time, and I'm sure even Mother Nature has a few test runs before she gets it right."

"That she does." But the evolved have been around forever. They've just finally reached a population density to not only be noticed, but large enough to provide a statistically relevant sample size. Well, he was stretching the definition of "statistically relevant", but if he waited for that, he would be dead. Luckily, most of the world had lost interest in them, which suited Tusk just fine. The longer they stayed under the radar, the easier it was for him to conduct his research. Once the government stepped in, there would be regulations and protocols that would render any scientific study too difficult and too costly to conduct.

"I guess we have Miles to thank," Leona said. "Any idea why he was looking for the healer in the first place?"

Tusk had none. "Where is he?"

"In the air," Leona said. "Your healer risked her life for him once, think she'll do it again?"

The question was, would she risk her life to save her children?

~

No misunderstandings

4th August, 9:41pm
Siglap, Singapore

Sam hated entering Michael's house for many reasons, and none of them was the rainwater he was dripping on the marble floor.

"We've got a problem," Katherine said as she met him at the door. "Someone's breached the Singapore ICA firewall earlier this afternoon. Their tech people were able to catch the hack and boot him out within minutes of the breach – the authorities will make an arrest within the hour – but it looks like yours and Josh's details have been compromised."

"And Meita's?"

Katherine smiled. "What do you think?"

They both looked over at Meita where she sat at the table having a quiet discussion with Michael. Her hand was on his arm and she was nodding at something he was saying. Meita's strength was not that EO abilities didn't work on her, but it lay in the way she guided people through their crisis and made them feel like someone was on their side.

The first time Sam met Meita, she was pretending to be Josh's secretary. She was dressed in a designer outfit completely ill-fitted for the weather and the circumstances, but one thing he learned about her was she knew how to maintain a level head. He had only seen her worried once, and that was when she had to tell Josh his son, Jay, had been kidnapped. As much as Sam didn't want to, his mind catalogued that moment because it was the first time he saw her calm professionalism waver.

Children. Maybe she had one.

"I need Michael on our team," Katherine said.

Sam covered his mouth as he exhaled a deep, heavy breath.

"Look, I get that you have feelings for her, and they're obviously reciprocated. But Sam?" Katherine waited until he was looking at her before she continued. "If you want her kids to be able to live a life without being swept off the street and thrown into some Mockingbird-type facility like the one Josh found her in, or in some building like the one you rescued your sister from, then I think you need to reprioritize the mission."

Sam rolled his shoulders back to release the knot of tension that was forming along the base of his neck. He crossed his arms over his chest in a manner that not only gained him an inch in height, but one in girth.

Katherine placed her hand on his wrist and gave it a squeeze that showed she too had strength, and some of it had just weakened his resolve.

"That man is father to her three children and was trying to patch things up with her. She's the most valuable evolved one that we know of. I believe that one of her kids, Emma, the middle child, is also evolved."

Sam's arms dropped to his side. "What makes you think that?"

"Ever since we discovered Rox's identity, I've been keeping an eye on them. No, nothing intrusive," she added when he raised an eyebrow. "Look, if I'm going to be spending *that* kind of money protecting this family, I better damn well know what I'm investing in. And something about the kid is off."

Rox, Josh, and Emma came down the stairs and into the living room. His eyes locked instantly with Rox's, but then he looked at her daughter. The girl was fourteen, but barely looked twelve. Her shoulders were rounded forward and her head tucked down like if she had a choice, she would rather be invisible.

"She's either going to blow something up," Katherine whispered, "or she's evolved. My money's on evolved."

"Ruby snuck out to see her boyfriend," Rox announced.

Sam released a sigh of relief.

"Wait, she snuck out with MJ?" Michael said.

Emma nodded like she were afraid to speak. "MJ followed her when he caught her sneaking out the window."

"And you didn't think to come tell me?" Michael shouted.

His anger was justified. Ruby could not have picked a worse time for a late-night rendezvous, but kids were like that. They struggled to see the bigger picture. Many of their emotions were so new to them that they struggled to put them in perspective. Sam remembered the first time Val had said she was in love. Sam had his abilities for a number of years by then, and a small smile spread across his lips as he recalled paying the boy a visit.

His smile slipped when he realized his choices weren't too dissimilar from Val's first love. Was he going to run like the young boy he warned away from Val and give up on his relationship with Rox before it even got started?

I'm surrounded by drama queens. Everywhere I turn someone is having some existential crisis. You like her, she likes you, Bob's your uncle. Will you two please stop already! Now listen. Emma's evolved. That important enough to take your mind off your one *and only true love* for a minute? *Can we not focus on finding the hormonal big sister, the little junior, and then Miles, so that we can get out of here? I mean, Rox was just assaulted and we're all standing around like we've got all the time in the world. And if you don't tell your brother to get from behind me, I'm gonna make him eat his own hand!*

Sam liked Josh. He didn't want to, but he did. The man was fiercely loyal and smart as a whip. He made mistakes, but instead of beating himself up, he simply analyzed them so he didn't repeat them. In the past ten months, Sam had come to trust Josh. He didn't always like his tactics or his intrusiveness, but they didn't need to be friends to develop a mutual respect. Sam knew Josh would come if he called. No questions asked. But Sam had watched Mika grow inside his stepmother. He was there when Mika and Val were born. He had been woken up by their cries in the middle of the night, and on occasion, he had gotten up to help. So that made Mika more than just the little brother he grew up with, but one he had responsibility *for*. And that was Sam's line in the sand.

You touch my brother, and I'll kill you.

Josh nodded like his life hadn't just been threatened. *You hurt her, and I'll kill you.*

They stared at one another, both lines drawn and both declarations irrevocable.

"Alright!" Meita jumped to her feet, her eyes locked squarely on Josh's. She didn't need to hear their conversation to know that it hadn't been going well. "Do we know where she is?" Meita continued.

"Fort Canning," Rox answered.

"Where in Fort Canning?" Michael snapped. "It's a big place."

Emma shook her head. "I don't know. Sorry, Dad, but she really is in love with him, and MJ was going to tell on her if she didn't take him. And you guys seemed to be discussing something really important, so I thought how bad could it be? She always comes back before anyone notices anyway."

"What!" Michael jumped to his feet. "What do you mean 'always comes back'?"

Katherine stepped to the center of the room. "Rox, you, Sam, and Mika head to Fort Canning. Get the girl and her brother. Meita, you and Josh take Michael and Emma. We'll meet back at the hotel. We booked a few extra rooms just in case; use one of those."

"I'm going to Fort Canning; I don't care what the rest of you do," Michael said as he walked around the table and held out his hand. "Emma, you're coming with me."

Emma hesitated, and in that split second, Sam watched a mix of emotions run across Rox's face, but they all fell away as joy took root.

But then the girl started to cry, and everyone stilled.

"Dad, I'm so sorry, but I think I'm evolved and I didn't know how to tell you and I don't think I should go to Fort Canning because, well, because honestly right now everyone is wigging out and when people do that, it's hard to be around them when they have such strong feelings." Her hands were shaking and it reminded Sam of his sister after she had finished polishing her nails. "I just need some quiet time for a little while. I'm so sorry, but I think we should go to the hotel with Josh."

No one spoke.

Then Rox cleared her throat. "Michael, I don't think Ruby or MJ are in danger, especially if she just ran out to be with her boyfriend. But if I'm wrong and they are, things can get … dangerous, and as their father, they need you."

In some ways, Michael made the decision a lot easier for Sam. The look he gave Rox spoke volumes about his feelings for her. Sam doubted Michael would ever trust her again, or if he did, it wouldn't be with the same trust he had for Tara. He already looked at Rox like she were a stranger, like he had finally accepted his wife was dead and she wasn't coming back.

"Marie?" Michael said, without breaking eye contact with Rox.

"Yes, sir?" The helper's voice was soft and uncertain.

"Take Emma with Meita back to their hotel, but do *not* go anywhere else with them until you've heard from me."

Emma ran to Marie, who pulled her in for an embrace and kissed her head much like a mother would.

"We can use our family safe word to communicate," Michael said. "Don't tell them."

"Dad—"

Michael looked back at Emma, and she stopped talking. Then he turned to Katherine. "I'm coming with you to get my daughter and my son. Then afterwards, I want you and everyone that's come with you out of my house. You are not to make contact with me or my children ever again."

He turned to Rox. "And that includes you." Then to Katherine. "Do I make myself clear?"

Katherine placed her hands behind her back and spread her legs in a manner that drew attention to the fact she was wearing a skirt.

"Mr Harding, I can only imagine just how … uncomfortable this has been for you, but it was only a matter of time before this life you have so admirably constructed came to an end anyway."

"What are you talking about?" Michael said.

She took a step toward him. "You see, the evolved ones of today don't get to live in such comfort. Someone would've discovered Emma's abilities eventually, which would've put a target on her back. And you can just ask anyone here," Katherine pointed to Sam, "his sister," then she pointed to Josh, "his son," before turning back to Michael. "No one with an ability goes unscathed. Yet, what's remarkable, perhaps even a bit ironic, is that in each case, it was your wife who got their loved ones back home. She died so that their families could be whole again."

Michael was about to speak, but Katherine held up her hand, and surprisingly he stopped. "Just so we understand one another, you threaten to take my agent's kids from her again, and I'll bury you. I'll bury you so fucking deep down in the ground you'll think you're dead. And who knows," she shrugged, "maybe you will be. Now, I get the need to make sure your children are safe. Therefore, I will *allow* you to accompany my team in case your daughter decides not to cooperate. We'll rendezvous at the hotel. Sam, you have one hour. I suggest you don't dawdle."

Sam stepped out of Katherine's way as she turned around and walked out the door into the rain. He wondered where she was going, but Katherine always had an exit strategy. Always.

CHAPTER SIX

~

Fort Canning

4th August, 10:02pm
Fort Canning, Singapore

Michael hadn't felt this level of fear since he returned home to tell his family that their mother was missing. Tara had been on assignment in Peru when an earthquake hit. He hadn't even known about the earthquake until his secretary told him the next day. Then it took him a couple of hours to find the emergency contact details Tara had sent him in a text message a few days before she left. Looking back, he could have located those numbers in just a few seconds, but it had been a busy day at the office. He was in the middle of launching his second major update and there was a barrage of phone calls and endless email queries. There hadn't been the headspace to find those numbers. Besides, she always came back home.

His secretary booked him on the first flight out of Singapore to Lima. There was nothing direct, so he had a five-hour layover in Amsterdam. He spent the entire time in the executive lounge taking phone calls, not once thinking about Tara unless he gave in to his annoyance at the huge inconvenience her disappearance was causing. But he had expected her to turn up. If he had known she was actually missing, dead, then he would have handled it differently. But she always came back home. Always.

His flight from Lima to Yurimaguas landed in the center of town. Even then, he remained oblivious to the severity of the situation. It wasn't until he stepped onto the runway, the air clouded with a snow-like dust that dampened sound, did he finally stop thinking about work and allow his thoughts to contemplate something else.

Destruction rode on the tails of the breeze like smoke. Aid workers hurried passed him with a purpose that alerted him to the fact he was approaching ground zero. A few of his fellow passengers paused beside him, also in a horrible state of wonder.

He had told the kids he was going to "get" mommy because she had "gotten herself" lost. Even though she was a professional photographer who had spent years in jungles, traveling to remote locations, living with cultures that had chosen to remain indigenous, and surviving on cuisines that most homeless people in Singapore would decline, he still only saw her as the mother to his children, and that meant she had no other option but to return.

Tara had thrust single parenthood upon Michael like an unwanted child. Looking back, he couldn't recall much of that trip. He ignored the many calls he got from Ruby. It wasn't until one of Tara's surviving colleagues told him his secretary was calling that he actually spoke to someone back in Singapore.

The long connecting flights back home went by quickly. When he landed at Changi, he was filled with an anger and a hatred that clouded his judgment. Ruby knew from the look on his face that her mother wasn't coming back, and it didn't take her long to completely shut down. He watched as if through someone else's perspective as she developed a shell around her heart. Anger became her go-to emotion, and he did nothing to stop it.

Emma, his most talented yet immensely shy daughter, collapsed inward. She stopped talking. She went through the motions of each day completely detached from the things that made life worth living. He kept telling himself that she would come out of it, but she didn't.

MJ regressed to toddlerhood, and Michael dove headfirst into work. He had commitments to his users, not to mention his employees. Everyone was counting on him. So he left the kids to Marie, an Indonesian who had left her own son to become a domestic worker in Singapore where she could earn just enough money to lift her family up a rung on the economic ladder of poverty.

It took Michael over a year before he accepted they all needed help. By then, the kids had morphed into people he no longer knew. They had lost their friends because without Tara, there was no one to take them to playdates or buy birthday presents or organize holiday parties.

Then six years later, *she* shows up.

He looked over at her where she sat beside him in the back of the car. She alternated between bouncing her knee and tapping her foot on the floor mat. He looked down at her lap where her thumbs were tucked against the palm of her hands just like Tara used to do when she was nervous.

Outside, the bright lights countered the heavy rain. He had to stop thinking of her as the woman he married. She might have the same birthmark, but that was where the similarities ended. He had hoped that if he took things slowly they would rekindle what they had, but now, that felt like a child's dream.

He prayed that Ruby and MJ were okay. He wasn't sure whether to beat the hell out of them when he found them or pull them in for a hug and then lock them in their rooms for all of eternity.

Michael Leon Harding grew up close enough to the tracks to see how people lived on the other side. He went to an Ivy League university on a combination of academic scholarships, work-study programs, and loans. He wasn't sure what he wanted to be, but he understood the importance of an opportunity. So when the company he was working for a few years after he graduated offered him an overseas assignment, Michael didn't hesitate.

Singapore was Michael's first trip outside the US, and at first it was hard living in another country; he missed *his* people and the parts of his culture that brought him comfort. As a dark-skinned man in a sea of Asians, he felt like an outsider and that no one understood his perspective. But it wasn't long before he realized his perspective was shifting. He began to see the diversity in Singapore and noticed that a fair number of the faces wore his same complexion. People looked upon him with curiosity and interest rather than fear and mistrust. Slowly, all the baggage he carried around because of his race and gender began to dissipate. When he let his guard down, he found a freedom he knew would never exist for him back home. Here, he was an individual, not an amalgamation, and in finding himself, he found his passion and became an entrepreneur.

It wasn't long after that he met Tara, and they clicked in a way that was refreshing and effortless. Her mother had been a single parent who had discovered the joys of international school teaching, which meant Tara had lived in a few different countries during her childhood. She had never met her father, and her mother explained that he was a fellow teacher she had a brief relationship with, but who wasn't interested in starting a family.

Michael wanted *that* Tara back.

When he received the phone call informing him she had been found, he went through a range of emotions, but it wasn't until he saw the birthmark on the back of her neck did he allow himself to feel the first tremors of hope that his family could be whole again. Everything was going to return to normal. Ruby would soften, Emma would re-emerge, MJ would stop being so needy, and he could finally let go of the crushing guilt and feelings of inadequacy that strangled each moment of joy before it had a chance to take root.

But looking at the woman beside him now …

Memories were built upon life experiences, and all those moments they had shared, the cement that held them together through different approaches to parenting, sleepless nights, personal failures, and a hell of a lot of lovemaking ... she had none of them. She might as well be a stranger they were living with.

The one and only time Michael had cried was when Ruby was born. He had never known a vulnerability like that before. He knew he would do anything to protect her. He would work harder – no – smarter because everyone worked hard, but only the smart worked smarter. He wanted her to have all the opportunities she deserved. He wanted to see her in pink ballet tights on a stage, he wanted her in a jersey one size too big and a basketball gliding off the tips of her fingers during her teenage years, and he wanted her to be poised and sophisticated when she graduated from college. Tara had wanted the same thing, too. But the woman who returned to them didn't know them well enough to want anything for them. She was so afraid of saying the wrong thing she never let her guard down.

Michael looked down when he felt something brush against his hand. She was attempting to comfort him, and in truth, he didn't know how to react. He was torn between blaming her and seeing her as an innocent victim in all of this. He knew if Tara had known she wasn't going to make it back from Peru, she would not have gone. Family had meant everything to her. But this woman wasn't Tara and he needed someone to blame right now because without a bad guy, none of this made sense.

"I'm so sorry I didn't tell you everything sooner." It was a whisper, but he knew both Sam and Mika heard. Those two were brothers, something about different mothers, but Michael wasn't interested in their family history. He just wanted his children back and these people gone from their lives.

Katherine had threatened him if he took the kids away from Rox, but truthfully, Michael knew a bluff when he heard one. He grew up on the outskirts of the inner city where the ability to read a situation – to know when a threat was real or nothing more than a simple act of posturing – was a necessary life skill. She wouldn't kill him, but he did believe her when she said she would ruin him. While he wasn't afraid of starting over, he didn't want to have to drag his kids from their exclusive lifestyle to the streets he grew up on. It would be like releasing a bird into the wild after it had spent its entire life in a cage. They wouldn't make it.

The car stopped at a traffic light on the corner of Hill Street and Coleman Street. Time seemed to stand still until Sam turned around.

"Here, put this in," Sam said to him.

"What is it?"

"It's an earpiece," Sam explained. "It'll allow us to keep in touch when we split up at the park."

Sam passed Tara a small backpack and a handheld radio transceiver.

"She doesn't need one of these?" Michael asked Sam, pointing to the earpiece.

"Me and technology aren't exactly on the best of terms," she said lightly.

"What does that mean?" Michael wasn't in the mood for game playing. They were here to find his daughter and son. If she wanted to be with Josh or Sam afterwards, he couldn't care less. Right now, everyone and everything represented a means to an end.

"The energy from electrical equipment doesn't sync well with my energy. It's like we cancel one another out, and it usually breaks."

Michael hadn't realized he was leaning forward until he sat back. "Hmph." Now, that he thought about it, had he ever seen her on her laptop? "Is that why you don't use the phone I gave you?"

Tara nodded.

The arrow turned green and Mika followed the procession of cars queuing to turn.

"We're getting out at the Registry of Marriages." Sam handed them a color copy of the map he printed for them before they left. "I've divided the park into four quadrants. You're to search the area that's highlighted on your map."

"And if you see anything that doesn't feel right," Mika said as he maneuvered around a taxi picking up a passenger, "don't engage." He turned to give Michael a brief glance.

"I'm not just gonna let someone take my kids, man."

Sam nodded. "We're hoping that Ruby and MJ are just being kids – sneaking out of the house when they're not supposed to."

"And if the same people who attacked Tara followed them?" Michael asked.

"We will not let anyone take them," Tara said. She had taken his hand into hers.

Michael wanted to pull away, but something kept him still. He looked at the street lights that cut through the darkness and the rain. At a time like this, husbands and wives were supposed to band together. They were supposed to share thoughts, finish one another's sentences, and cry on each other's shoulders. He realized after six years as a single dad, he just wanted someone to share the load with.

He intended to yank his hand away, but instead he squeezed hers back. God, help him, he thought as he sent up a silent prayer that Ruby and MJ were dancing and laughing in the rain, that they were high off the adrenaline and excitement from being on an adventure they weren't supposed to be on. He prayed that Ruby was smiling. His baby girl hadn't smiled in so long his heart hurt and he caught himself as the first hiccup of despair hit. MJ just needed attention. He wasn't so needy when someone actually listened to him. Why was it so hard to play with his son? Why did he find it so difficult to simply stop working and go home to be with his family?

Mika pulled into the nearest parking space at the Registry of Marriages, and they all climbed out into the rain. Keeping their map dry was going to be a challenge, but Michael knew the park well enough. He had been given the section with the lighthouse which, now that he thought about it, seemed like a good place for teenagers to hook up. He thought he had a few years yet before Ruby would be interested in boys, but then again, she was sixteen. Where had the last six years gone?

"Wait." Michael just remembered something. "If she's hesitant to come with you, tell her that I said no hoverboard until she's saved up half the money."

"Or I'll just give her the earpiece," said Mika. "She can talk to you through it."

"Right!" He had forgotten about that.

He glanced at Tara, but she was looking at Sam who had just asked her if she were alright.

She nodded. "A bit sore, but nothing that I'm not used to."

Michael wasn't sure if Sam's move was instinctual or he simply didn't care anymore that her husband was standing beside them, but he pulled Tara in for a brief hug and then leaned forward so their foreheads were touching. "No heroics. You see something wrong, you call me."

"Same goes for you," she told him.

Michael couldn't deny the intense feelings of jealousy that leapt to the surface. No matter where their relationship stood, Tara was his wife and the rules for that were simple: no one touched her. But the way she seemed to relax in Sam's arms and the look they shared allowed him to see, perhaps for the first time, that she wasn't Tara. She was Rox, and he was once again a widower.

~

The Fort Gate

4th August, 10:23pm
Fort Canning, Singapore

Rox used her ability to reach out, but only the storm responded. It was hard to see in the rain and her map had long since disintegrated. Mika had taken her running here a number of times, so she knew the layout of the park fairly well, but she would have liked to reference her map just for reassurance. The flashlight Sam gave her provided good light, but only in the areas she aimed. Outside of that was complete darkness. She was expecting solar-powered lights to illuminate the footpath like many of Singapore's parks, but if Fort Canning had them, they weren't on.

She paused at the next turn. Was that music? Kids liked music. MJ had told her a few stories about Fort Canning Hill being haunted, but she didn't believe in ghosts.

Rox couldn't imagine Jay sneaking out to meet his friends in Central Park. No, Jay would know better. But it wasn't fair to compare Ruby with Jay. They were two different children raised under very different circumstances.

Jay knew his father was evolved. He grew up around evolved people and had been taught to protect himself from the moment he could stand. He had also been kidnapped, so he understood life's dangers and the bad people often waiting in the shadows. But Ruby had led a very different life. She had grown up in a metaphoric utopia. Beautiful blue skies. Warm weather. Wealth that allowed her to travel and to participate in activities that some kids had long ago stopped wishing for. But both children had experienced the loss of their mothers. Jay, before he could form a lasting memory of her, and Ruby, well, Tara died at that critical point when Ruby was just coming into her own identity. Sure it would change, many times in fact, but this was the first one where it would be independent of her parents.

Rox picked up her pace and came upon the Fort Gate. A row of stone pillars just over waist height marked its entrance – or exit, depending on the side you approached from. It looked like it was built in the time of castles. Dark, heavy wooden doors with ingot studs and a curved top to match the archway were pushed wide open. Light from two camping lanterns were just inside the tunnel, and it cast a shadow against the walls that made the teenagers look misshaped.

The sounds of laughter and drum and bass drowned out the rain for a few seconds. These were children having fun, completely unconcerned about the storm raging around them.

A large cooler box sat open just inside the tunnel, and a kid much too short to be the same age as the others wound his way through those dancing to grab a drink. He sat in one of the empty camping chairs, his shoulders slumping like he might be bored.

This was not their first time partying here. They had been here before and knew to bring gear to make the moment more enjoyable. For some odd reason, Rox appreciated their cleverness, even if she doubted that most of their parents knew their children were using Fort Canning Park as an after-hours hangout spot.

Each of Rox's steps squelched as she called out with her energy. Even though she had never used her ability on her children, she felt something familiar return as she drew closer. She was grateful she hadn't changed out of her running gear because even though she smelled of sweat, her clothes were fitted and didn't weigh on her.

The kid heard her approach before she called out his name. He shot to his feet and dropped the drink he had in his hand. He lifted his arms to protect his eyes from the flashlight.

It took him but a second to recognize her. "Ruby," MJ shouted without turning around. "Mom's here."

Lightning cracked as Rox pulled her son into her arms and held on until she was certain he wasn't some sort of apparition. His clothes were damp and his curls had turned to frizz, but he was safe. She purposefully inhaled his scent of rain and sweat with the hopes to sear it into her mind. She didn't need memories of his birth or his first step to be his mom. He was hers, and she knew that with absolute certainty. Some moms gave birth while others took over afterwards – neither of them offering love of a lesser degree, and she was a bit of both.

Rox was tempted to laugh at the mixture of excitement and fear on his face when she heard his name being called. She stood up and positioned herself between her eldest daughter and her son.

The look of disgust on Ruby's face was apparent if not by the set of her jaw then the forward slash of her brows.

An echo of shouts for the music to be turned off bounced around the Gate, and when the speaker quieted, a wave of curiosity swept over the teenagers.

"What are you doing here?" Ruby snapped.

There were a number of ways Rox could have responded, and none of them seemed adequate against the amount of hostility emanating off one so young. Rox had a right to be there for a plethora of reasons, but the most important one was she was their mother, and Ruby's displeasure with that was simply a waste of energy.

"Are we in trouble?" MJ asked from behind Rox.

The Gate had taken on a new level of commotion as the other kids wisely began packing up.

"MJ, come here." Ruby held out her hand.

Perhaps Ruby had become the closest thing to a mother that Emma and MJ had since Tara disappeared six years ago, but none of that mattered at this point. Rox reached out and grabbed her son's arm to keep him at her side. She kept her eyes on Ruby as she unclipped her transceiver and told Sam she had found them and gave him her location.

"Do you have any idea how worried we were?" Rox said.

"As you can clearly see, both MJ and I are fine. You can run along now."

Rox was unsure of the kind of mother she used to be. Was she a tough disciplinarian or maybe she led with a gentle, guiding hand? But at that moment, she wanted nothing more than to throttle her eldest.

"Get your things; we're leaving," Rox said between clenched teeth.

The Gate was empty now and the only light came from her flashlight, the lanterns gone with their teenage owners. But Ruby made no move to gather her stuff. Instead, she widened her stance and crossed her arms over her chest.

"Ruby, I get that you have no idea what's going on, but we need to leave. Now."

Her daughter snorted, and her arms uncurled and slipped down to her waist where she pushed one hip forward. Rox took a step closer without thought. She had no idea what she was going to do when she reached her child, but this level of disrespect was too much to ignore.

Then MJ screamed.

The blow to her head happened too fast for Rox to bring her arms up to block it. Everything went black for a moment, and the only sound was the thunder fighting its way across the sky.

Something took hold of her wrist and yanked her to her feet, but she had no recollection of falling. She toppled over onto someone's shoulder and would have succumbed to unconsciousness if it weren't for MJ's second scream.

"Ruby!" he shouted, and Rox lifted her head.

The flashlight had fallen and now lay on the ground by her attackers' feet.

Rox swallowed the nausea and landed a sharp elbow jab to the back of whoever was carrying her. The grip on her loosened just enough for gravity to take hold.

She dropped to the floor of the tunnel and rolled out of her attacker's reach. She had gone farther than intended because rain pelted her face and neck. Mud threatened to swallow her hands as she pushed to her knees. She sucked in a breath to call for MJ when a boot slammed into the center of her chest, stealing the little breath she had just regained and seizing her muscles.

She inhaled a wet blade of grass and choked as a second kick knocked her onto her back. Large hands grabbed the front of her running shirt and pulled her upright much too quickly for her to process. The night teetered on a complete blackout, and if it weren't for the countless hours she spent training with Mika, she would have succumbed to it.

Instead, she used her attackers leverage to help support her weight and brought her knee up with a solid kick to the groin. There was a moment of perfect stillness before the grip on her gave way and her attacker fell back to the ground.

"Mommy!" His voice was barely audible above the thunderstorm, but then the sky flashed with light and she saw him being hauled back into the Gate.

Rox stumbled forward and lost her balance. She fell hard to the pavement as the pain in her forehead built until it burst, causing fresh blood to run down her nose and into her mouth. Her stomach rose like she were heading downhill much too fast. The protein bar Sam had given her just before they left forced its way up and out.

Lightning lanced across the sky and the hair on her arms rose. Her skin broke out in goosepimples like it had back at Watership when she was climbing up the side of the cliff. Energy from the storm rushed into her like an injection of adrenaline. She pushed to her feet and saw Ruby disappear after her brother.

The sky rumbled into blackness as Rox shouted after her children. She managed a single stride before sweet agony consumed her. All other thoughts were eliminated when her heart refused to take its next beat. Her body temperature spiked and the familiar scent of skin burning filled her nostrils. The joints connecting her bones expanded as she slowly began to be pulled apart. The only sound she could comprehend was the snap of lightning winding its way through her body.

Rox wanted to scream as thin lines of scarred tissue erupted down her chest and back and along her arms and legs. Her head thrust back as an arc of lightning jumped from one eye to the next, stealing her sight.

Her brain attempted to sever the link between her nervous system and her consciousness, but instead she convulsed, feeling all 200,000 amperes of electrical current travel from her right shoulder down to her left heel.

The first millisecond felt like she was stuck in a loop of never-ending torment. If she were capable of thought, she would have compared this to the pain of Wonderland and realized that drowning to death was nothing against being struck by lightning. Lightning was exacting. Every drop of rain felt like a drop of acid that had bypassed her dermis and was setting fire to her insides. Her bones felt stretched, like they were trying to contain something that desperately wanted to burst free, and her heart still refused to take its next beat.

Then an energy pulse slipped beneath the pain and blood started to flow through her veins again. Sam was here. She tried to turn around, but the lightning rooted her. Her mouth opened as if to speak, but sparks flew forward, cracking her teeth in its escape, and for the first time she was grateful for the death that followed.

~

Lightning strikes

4th August, 10:38pm
For Canning, Singapore

Michael skidded to a halt and slipped on the wet grass. He had never seen anything like it. People have been known to get struck by lightning. It happened. It wasn't as much of a phenomenon as one would think, but to witness it was … breathtaking.

The bolt of lightning glowed bright enough that he had to cover his eyes and squint through his fingers to make her out. He half expected to hear her scream, to watch as she collapsed to the ground, but instead she stood frozen, the lightning still feeding her too much energy for a single human to accept.

Michael had always thought of lightning as a flash, a viper's strike or a fraction of time that was as simple as an eye blink … then poof, the event was over. But this lasted longer. A small part of his brain reminded him he was here looking for his children, but instinct kept him still and his legs rooted to the spot.

He glanced over his shoulder to see Mika join him a second later. He, too, had to lift his arms to give his eyes time to adjust to the intensity of the brightness.

"Rox!"

The voice came from behind them and was muffled and hard to hear, like someone shouting underwater.

Michael watched as if in a trance as Mika tackled his brother. The two rolled on the ground, and for a moment, Michael wanted to warn them of getting too close because he could have sworn he had read something about lightning having the ability to jump. But instinct, fear, or simple curiosity kept his gaze returning to Tara – to Rox.

Electricity had sound. Michael thought of a lightbulb and of walking under the street lights late at night in the neighborhood he grew up. Once, he had put his ear near the power socket on the wall and listened. He couldn't have been more than seven, but he remembered hearing something, and the hairs on his ears rising, and the uncontrollable urge to scratch an itch he couldn't possibly reach.

But lightning, he had just learned, operated on a different decibel, and right now it appeared to be amplifying.

Instinct told him they needed to run. Whatever was happening wasn't natural, and while he didn't like the idea of leaving Rox, he knew there was nothing any of them could do for her.

Michael kept his eyes on her as he sidestepped his way over to the two men still wrestling on the ground. He reached down and grabbed the person nearest to him, only to realize it was the wrong brother when Sam jumped to his feet and continued toward certain death.

A lot can happen in three seconds. First, Michael wondered about the beauty and the insanity of love. It seemed to defy the natural order of things that Sam would want to reach Rox when he must have known that doing so would result in his own electrocution, and that made Michael curious about the depth of Sam's feelings for his wife. But then Sam disappeared. Michael looked left, right, and then spun around in a circle. When he turned back to Rox, the lightning bolt flashed out as if it had never been there, and in that same instant Sam reappeared, about a hair's breadth from Rox, who should have fallen forward, but her chest bowed out as her arms lifted at her sides. Then something he could not describe and wasn't sure he even comprehended pushed her to her knees. She fell to the path with such force the concrete and stone cracked under her weight. A tidal wave of energy pulsed from her as if she were a pebble released in placid waters. Sam was lifted off his feet and thrown back in the direction he had come like a leaf caught in a backdraft. His horizontal, airborne flight was silent, like he was passing through an invisible portal – first his head, then his shoulders and torso, followed by his waist and hips, and finally his legs disappeared as if he were being erased from time and space in swift, apathetic strokes.

Michael looked down at Mika, whose look flashed from disbelief to resignation as he curled into the fetal position, protecting his head like he knew what was coming. Michael squeezed his eyes shut and braced himself as the wave of energy consumed him.

~

In or out

4th August, 10:39pm
Fort Canning, Singapore

It was the constant drops of rain that woke Michael, and a hardy slap to the face. Mika was standing over him asking him a question, but Michael's ears were ringing. He shook his head and tried to communicate that he couldn't hear, but his body was having trouble following instructions.

He was hoisted to his feet and motioned to stay. Or he hoped he was told to stay because he wasn't sure he was capable of walking just yet. He swayed from side to side as Mika ran over to Rox and rolled her onto her back. He lurched away, and that's what set Michael's legs into motion.

His breath caught in his chest as a horrible moan escaped. Her clothes were melted into her skin and parts of her body were black, like logs left in a fireplace. He hadn't wanted this for her. Tears flooded his eyes and he turned away from the burnt corpse.

Michael choked on his vomit as it came out, grateful for the rain that would wash it away. How on earth was he going to explain this to his children?

His head lifted. "Ruby!"

He raced passed Mika towards the Gate. Chunks of stone were missing from the facade about shoulder height. It ran along the inside of the tunnel in a straight line.

Michael came out on the other side and called for MJ. He waited and listened, but the only sounds were of the rain and the distant wail of a siren.

Someone came up behind him, and Michael spun around.

It was Mika. "We need to get out of here."

"Not without my kids. She said she saw them. She said she had them. Where are they?" Panic was rising, and he knew that a calm head was best, but he was struggling to process everything. He shouted their names again, but still no answer.

"Listen to me," Mika said. "We've got satellite footage. Drones. Surveillance. We can see what happened and track it. But we *don't* want to be here when the authorities arrive."

Michael heard the words, and the words made sense,

but he wasn't sure he *could* leave. Fear like nothing he had experienced gripped him. What if Ruby and MJ were struck by the wave of lightning like he had been? Then he remembered Sam. "Where's Sam?" Did his children disappear like he had?

Mika's jaw tightened as he turned his head to the side. Michael saw one of the man's nostrils grow to about double its normal size. Michael backed away, his head shaking in disbelief. This was all too much. He needed to find his children. Then they needed to get as far away from these people as possible. They could mourn Rox later. Maybe he wouldn't tell them what he saw. Perhaps he could just say that she left with the others.

For the first time, he was grateful for the life they had without Tara. It was normal. Sure everyone had issues – he could see that quite clearly in hindsight – but they were *safe*. No one went missing and no one showed up with nostrils that looked like they belonged on some science fiction creature. In fact, people couldn't read thoughts and the woman posing as his dead wife wasn't a healer. This was some kind of scam.

"What do you people want from me?" Michael asked.

Mika tapped his ear and swore, like he wasn't paying him any attention.

Michael remembered the earpiece. He pulled it free and dropped it.

"Don't!" Mika said, and picked it up. "We don't want anything tracing back to us. We've got to go."

"Stay away from me. I need to find my children and then I want you people gone." He didn't care if he had to start over and his children were forced into a life less privileged. He had survived. So could they. Survival was in his DNA, which meant it was in theirs.

Mika grabbed him, and Michael tried to yank free, but stilled.

"Josh?"

Michael, listen to me!

Michael froze.

I know things seem a little crazy right now, but you need to do what Mika tells you.

"Get out of my head!" Michael shouted.

You don't want the police to find you there. It'll slow things down, and if you want to find your kids, you gotta trust us.

"I'm not trusting any of you!" His family was fine before Tara – Rox – returned.

I know it seems that way, but you were always going to be in danger. There was a moment of silence. *Where's Rox?*

Michael's breath caught again. He wasn't sure how to describe what he had seen. Being struck by lightning, the burnt flesh, the lifelessness of death. He had never seen it before. Not like this.

He felt Josh push aside the pain from the images and refocused his thoughts. *I need you to help Mika. Help him bring her back to me.*

Michael was shaking his head before Josh had finished. *"I'm not moving a dead body, and I'm definitely not moving my wife's."* Or whoever she was!

Remember the night we met? Josh's thoughts were flowing faster with a sense of urgency that Michael couldn't ignore.

Remember how I cut my hand and she healed it? Look, I can't go in detail now, but Michael, I know she seems dead – she is dead, but—

"No! You didn't see what I saw. She's dead. I mean … I saw it … I saw her. It was like it wouldn't stop. It just kept, I don't know … "

"We don't have a lot of time," Mika said. "Maybe five minutes before they arrive. Less probably. I'm going to have to leave him." He was talking to someone else, but he didn't have a phone and his earpiece wasn't working either. Then Michael realized it had to be Josh.

It all became too much. Michael started to hyperventilate. He needed to find Ruby and MJ. He needed to make sure they were safe because things like this weren't normal.

I know. And I promise you we won't stop until we have Ruby and MJ back. I promise you. Listen to my thoughts, hear the truth in them. But you've got about five seconds to decide because Mika will need to leave if he's got to carry Rox back to the car without you.

Michael knew networking. Systems design. He knew programming and algorithms. He knew single parenting, and he knew he was failing at it.

I have a son, about Ruby's age, and there is nothing I wouldn't do to ensure his safety, but Michael, I know the type of people we're up against. They took my son, and Rox sacrificed herself to get him back.

I know. She told me.

Yeah, but she didn't tell you everything. Then all of a sudden memories that weren't his flitted through Michael's mind. He saw – no, he felt Rox's pain. The needles and the drowning. Cuts that were so small yet no less painful stole his breath. *Help Mika bring her back to me, Michael.*

"Is he in or out?" Mika asked.

Please.

CHAPTER SEVEN

~

Bender

4th August, 11:03pm
Bayfront, Singapore

"I don't think this is going to work," Michael said as they pulled into the underground parking garage of the hotel. He looked back at Rox, whose seat belt was buckled, but jostled around with each corner Mika took and each speed bump driven over.

Bile rose to the back of his throat. He was transporting a dead body. Michael hadn't familiarized himself with Singapore law despite having lived the overwhelming majority of his adult life on this tiny island nation, but he was sure there had to be some statute against what they had done.

Just follow our lead, and everything'll be OK.

Mika pulled into one of the handicapped parking spaces near the elevator. Josh told him that Meita and a security guard would be waiting for them, and there they were. Or he thought that was them. The woman that was supposed to be Meita was dressed in a charcoal-colored skirt and matching suit jacket with heels so high, Michael wondered how she walked in them. Her face was made-up with bright-colored cosmetics that made her look like she was about to go onstage, which made him doubt if she was Meita after all. It would have been better if Katherine met them because, in all honesty, the only one he truly remembered was Katherine, and that was because she had issued a threat.

"Sir." The security guard nodded at him as if seeing a man step out of a car completely drenched from the rain was an everyday occurrence at Singapore's most expensive hotel.

"Oh, très bien, you found her," Meita said with a heavy French accent. She was clutching a clipboard to her chest and waving her mobile like it were a conductor's baton. "We were so worried."

Mika nodded at the security guard and grabbed the wheelchair off him. "Meita, there's a blanket in the boot. She's drenched and … "

Say covered in mud!

"Mud!" Michael quickly supplied. "She's covered in mud."

"Can you hold this please?" Meita passed her clipboard and phone to the security guard and retrieved the blanket from the boot.

"Michael, come help me get her into the chair," Mika instructed.

Meita held up the blanket, effectively blocking the security guard's view as they lifted a dead Rox out of the car and placed her into the wheelchair. Her head rolled to the side, and Michael almost let go. There was no way anyone who saw her neck would think she had been rolling around in mud. There were fissures running down her charred skin that looked desiccated and cracked, like the simplest of touches would cause her to fall apart.

"Ho, ma chérie." Meita did well to hide her surprise as she turned back to the security guard. "Thank you so much for your discretion. If any of her fans were to get hold of a photo of her in this state, well, I'm afraid her career would be ruined."

"What—" Michael started.

Go with it!

Michael slammed his lips shut and helped Meita arrange the blanket so that it covered her body and most of her head, leaving just a small window so she could breath. Not that it was necessary.

"You're welcome, ma'am. But I still have to confirm she's breathing," he said. "It's hotel policy whenever someone is brought in unconscious."

"Bien sûr, bien sûr," Meita said as she took her clipboard back and turned to the lift lobby, hoping the guard would follow her. "We would just like to confirm once we're closer to the suite. There are so many cameras here that I simply cannot permit—"

"I'm afraid not," he said and reached out a muscled arm to prevent them from going through the sliding doors into the elevator lobby. "Before I grant you access, I need to check a pulse."

Josh, what do we do? Michael squeezed his eyes shut and sent the thought. He had never initiated a connection before, but this seemed like the most likely way to do it.

Touch the security guard.

What?

Touch the security guard! I'm going to try to establish a link. No matter what you hear or feel, don't let go.

Michael grabbed the security guard's arm.

The guard snatched his arm back. "Sir, please don't touch me."

Not like that! I need you to touch skin.

How am I supposed to touch skin? He's wearing a jacket.

The guard looked at the three of them and went for his receiver.

Michael reached out and grabbed his hand.

For a split moment, the car park was awash in tones of gray. He felt the guard's earlier confidence waver into concern. He was having doubts about the story Meita had told him – Rox, a famous model and spokeswoman for an all-natural, honey-based skincare product line had gone off her meds since arriving in Singapore and had gone on a bender. He wanted to radio in and ask for backup, but that idea ended abruptly as Michael was swept away into the many thoughts running through the guard's head. The most pressing one was that a dead woman overdosed on illegal drugs would be found in one of their suites. He would be immediately dismissed, which upset him greatly because this was a good job. The pay wasn't the best, but he liked the perks of meeting famous people, and sometimes he would earn extra if they hired him as a personal guard when they gambled at the casino or went shopping in the mall. His wife worked at reception and was pregnant with their first child. They needed the money because he wanted their baby coming home from the hospital to go into their own home, not that of his mother's. He didn't want his wife, Sumaiyaa, to go through the stress of being the sole earner while he looked for other employment. Besides, she had just started showing and the slight bump in her belly made his chest swell with pride. He would press his cheek against Sumaiyaa's stomach—

Let go!

Michael jumped back, breaking the link between him and the security guard. Michael shook his hand like he was trying to dislodge something wet and sticky from it. He looked up, but the guard was wearing a smile of compliance.

The guard led them to the elevator and pushed a button, then entered an access code that stopped them on one of the basement floors none of the guests had access to.

They followed him out of the elevator and into a busy hallway of workers before he entered a code on another door that led them down a much quieter hallway. It was narrower and had thick, red carpet running along the floor. The walls were painted a shade of off-white and wall sconces were intermittently spaced to provide maximum lighting without being too bright.

Sumaiyaa's husband stopped in front of another elevator and pushed a button. A minute later, the doors opened with a loud clunk and they got in. They went up to the floor for penthouse apartments, one level higher than where Michael had stayed last night, and exited into a short hallway. The guard opened the door leading out into the main hall.

Michael looked down as Mika wheeled his dead wife up to a door at the end of the hall.

A thin line ran across Josh's forehead when he opened the door. There was a glazed look in his eyes that said his attention was divided as Mika wheeled Rox in and locked the wheels. Meita turned to the security guard, said thank you, and closed the door

Michael couldn't believe what had just happened. Did they really sneak a dead body into one of the most infamous hotels in the world?

The doorbell rang, and Michael jumped. Josh held up his hand to silence them, but Meita smacked the back of her head with the palm of her hand.

"I got this," she said and opened the door. "S'il vous plaît! I must sign to acknowledge that all is well, no?"

The guard nodded. "Yes, ma'am." He handed her a cell phone from his pocket and flipped it horizontal to allow for her signature. "You can read it if you'd like, but a copy will also be included in your checkout paperwork."

"Bien sûr, bien sûr," Meita said as she slipped her finger across the screen.

She closed the door, and Michael breathed his first sigh of relief.

~

Luck

Date/Time & Location: Unknown

Sam slipped into consciousness with reluctance. He was lying on his back, and training had taught him that was a bad position to be in – too many vital organs exposed. His mind readied to turn him over, but his body quickly sent the message that everything hurt and he shouldn't try to move just yet. It requested approval for a nap.

But a body not in motion was an easy target, his mind countered.

His body conceded to an opening of the eyes, and a sky much too verdant for immediate recognition greeted him. Pain lanced across his chest and he coughed. His mind and body were under agreement for the urgent need to clear his lungs, so he sat up as blood spewed from his mouth to decorate the ground between his legs.

Luck was on Major Sam Watt's side because gravity took control once he lost consciousness again. It tilted his torso forward instead of back. Sam was seated in a dead man's position: legs spread out, his torso upright but leaning forward and just a smidge to the side, his chin resting on his chest. It was the way his arms lay across his lap that kept him from falling backwards, which was the only thing that kept him from drowning in his own blood.

~

In retrospect

4th August, 11:18pm
Bayfront, Singapore

There were three moments in Josh's life when he had to claw his way out of the maze of his own thoughts. The first was when he discovered he had a son, and that son was already nine months old. The image of Jay's emaciated body and the look of detachment in his eyes still haunted him. The second was when he received the call that Rox was missing. It felt like his day of reckoning had finally arrived, and the accompanying shame threatened to crack the foundation of how he defined himself. And the last was when Tusk took his son while he had been out trying to atone for his misdeeds.

This was his fourth.

Five years ago, Josh found Rox unconscious – presumably dead – strapped to a gurney inside a facility he had infiltrated and was beginning to fear he would never make it out of. In truth, he had entered her room because it was the first door on the right. He was in search of evidence about the type of work done at these places so he could finally show the world the atrocities his kind were forced to endure. He had only gotten as far as he had that night out of pure luck, and of course, his ability. But using his ability didn't come without side effects, mental fatigue being the prime one. He had stretched himself well past his limits and was beginning to struggle to maintain the barrier that separated his thoughts from those he controlled.

His hands were shaking and he was limping down a hallway so redolent with the smell of antiseptic that he could almost taste it. He needed a quiet place to gather himself, so he slipped into Rox's room with a plan to crouch behind one of the counters to rest his mind for a few minutes. And then he felt this energy – this heat – encase his ankle. It itched at first. Then his tendons felt as if they were being stretched and twisted. He clenched his jaw against the growing pain until something snapped. His eyes flew open, and when he got to his feet, he discovered his ankle was able to bear his weight again.

He wasn't sure how much time he had wasted arguing with himself about the (im)possibility of a dead woman healing him, but by the time he decided to test his theory, he was already quite far behind schedule. He ran the palm of his hand along the jagged edge of a peeling counter top and broke his skin on the second try.

It took him ages to find a wheelchair, but when he did, he wheeled her out the front door and into another kind of prison he hadn't realized he was building until it was too late.

Josh remembered the moment he decided to manipulate Rox. It was shortly after he discovered she had no memories. At first, he started small, just planting seeds that she was safer with them, which wasn't difficult for her to believe since she couldn't remember anything about her life.

He started training her as soon as she showed signs of coordination. When he discovered she could also heal *herself,* he took her training in a new direction. He didn't know what her life was like before he found her, but at the time, he reasoned he was just trying to help her fulfill her true potential. Besides, it wasn't like he was killing her – that would come later – he was just testing her capabilities and helping her to gloss over the parts that would have stopped her from wanting to participate further.

It wasn't like he started out with stabbing. The first time he intentionally harmed Rox was when he broke her finger. It was the pinkie one, so it was the least valued amongst them, but nevertheless, his memory of her bone snapping back in place was only rivaled by his memory of her screams when it happened. That day, he learned she was able to heal herself, but she was defenseless against pain. But a tolerance to pain could be learned, he reasoned, and God knows he made sure she developed one.

The funniest part of it all was that he couldn't remember the exact moment he fell in love with her. He had her in his bed long before he developed any lasting emotions for her, and that part shamed him. All of it shamed him, but there was no going back and making it right. He couldn't erase the memories even if he wanted to. His ability didn't remove memories, it altered and shaped them, and helped to form new ones that were as real as the mind made them.

Josh loved Rox the way a man loves a woman. Completely. Unforgivingly. Selfishly. But he had been working on that last part ever since she left him, and the proof of that was when he hadn't hurt Sam. It was tempting, especially when they were at Crossroads, but he knew he would have to prove himself different if he were ever to win her back, and so he sat himself down and did just that. He accepted that she would be with Sam for a while, and it was his just punishment that he would have to watch her with another man. He had hoped that witnessing her with someone else would make his feelings for her fade. He had never been one to chase a woman, but as he watched her give herself for his son, then break their connection in her time of need so he wouldn't have to share in her suffering, Josh fell in love with her all over again.

He groaned as he lifted the blanket from her face. Her running shirt was seared into her neck and shoulder. The left side of her head lacked hair, like it had been held over an open flame until the fire reached the roots. The skin along her jawline was not quite melted, more charred until it flaked. The rest of her body was a patchwork of burn wounds and scar tissue that left her unrecognizable.

"Can you fix her?" Mika asked.

Could he fix her? Josh had never been able to fix her. At one point, he had tried accessing her memories, the ones she had forgotten, but there was nothing there. Nothing to retrieve, alter, or restore.

Josh laughed. Could he fix her? "No." She was dead, not broken. Besides, Rox fixed herself. That's what she did. She improvised, she jerry-rigged, she held on until she either figured it out or until—

"Wait!"

Josh tore the rest of the blanket away.

Rox held on!

Josh wasn't exactly sure if she could come back from a lightning strike like he had witnessed through Michael's memories, but she held on.

Josh pushed Mika back a step without lifting a finger. "I need to cut those clothes off her. Out of her."

The door opened and Katherine walked in. "Meita's getting Michael, Emma, and the helper situated in one of the spare rooms on another floor. I trust you guys have this situation under control or do you need me to make a few phone calls?"

"I need something sharp enough to cut those clothes off her," Josh said.

Katherine covered her mouth when she looked at Rox lying on the bed. She turned away and cleared her throat before she spoke. "You, uh, you're going to need a scalpel. And a surgeon's hand. Why don't we wait and just let her heal herself. You think she can ... I don't know ... heal the clothes off?"

Josh started to pace. Rox was coming back, well, he hoped she was coming back. He gave her a sixty percent chance, but that was all she had ever needed. Someone to believe in her. He had failed her once and he would be damned before he would do it again.

"Then get me a scalpel. And a surgeon."

"Won't her skin just heal itself?" Katherine reiterated. "I mean, that's what it did when the surgeons operated to get the bullet out after you guys rescued her from Wonderland."

"Yes, and need I remind you how smoothly that went." Josh's voice was filled with sarcasm. Working on Rox while she was alive was a pain in the ass. Firstly, the amount of anesthesia it took to put her under was astounding. Secondly, regardless of how much you gave her, it never lasted long enough. Her body would begin healing any incisions made faster than the surgeons could operate.

No, their best bet was to help Rox now, while she was dead. Or at least that was the theory he was going with.

"We need to make it easier for her to heal herself when she wakes up. From something like this … " His shoulders slumped and he sighed as he gestured to her body, "I've never seen anything this bad before, so my best guess is maybe one, two hours before she wakes up?"

"I think I know someone," Mika said. "Well, maybe."

"Do it," Katherine said. "I'll make some calls, but it's going to take me at least thirty minutes before I can even have the right person on the phone, let alone en route."

Mika pulled out his phone from the front pocket of his jeans. "Dammit!" It was dead.

Katherine typed in a passcode and slid her finger across the screen before tossing him hers.

"In the meantime, help me take off whatever we can," Josh said.

Katherine came around, and they worked together in silence. At first she was gentle with her movements, but he told her to hurry. They had already lost an hour with transport and getting her up to the room. "Besides, she can't feel anything." She was, after all, dead.

They peeled off what they could and then cut away the

material that wasn't melted into her skin with a pair of scissors they had to wait for room service to deliver. Josh's hands were shaking when he put the last of her clothes into one of the laundry bags they got from the closet.

"How will you know when she wakes up?" Katherine said. "I mean, other than the fact that she'll be awake."

Rox awoke in many different ways, but he hadn't witnessed her rebirth since she left him. In the past, a few times she had screamed when her consciousness slammed back into her. In the early days, it would take hours for her confusion to end and her cognitive thinking to resume. But with practice, she got better, and faster.

This time? He wasn't sure what to expect. She would be incredibly itchy, more so than she had ever felt if the amount of flesh she had to regenerate was anything to go by.

When there was nothing more they could do for her, he and Katherine joined Mika in the living room to wait for his contact to arrive.

~

Can't trust 'em

5th August, 12:02am
Bayfront, Singapore

A small woman no taller than five-two was escorted up to their apartment, followed by a man a good six inches taller. She was dressed like she was the entertainment at a kid's party: bright, candy-apple red shirt and a pair of bright red, yellow, orange, and white striped trousers that stopped just above her ankles. Her shoes were orange flats with little fox ears and whiskers on the front of them. She was clutching a bag on one shoulder and a smile that didn't quite fit their situation or the late hour. She was about to introduce herself when she caught sight of Mika. Her smile fell.

She spun around like she was going to leave, but the man accompanying her grabbed her shoulders and stopped her. "Hear him out. Director Koh wouldn't have sent us if it weren't important." He placed a kiss on her forehead and spun her back around. He was dressed in the opposite fashion, black jeans and a long-sleeved black T-shirt that was pulled across a chest that did a lot of weightlifting.

Josh had read about Zen masters, people who could live in the present, their thoughts only focused on the task at hand. The man dressed in black had a mind as clear and clean as a newly opened hardware store. It was a maze of thoughts and ideas, but everything was organized into a practical and relevant space. Nothing was pressing to get to the top or bleed into the moment. His goal was singular: to protect his wife while she uncovered how she could help a woman in need.

"You know I wouldn't call if it weren't important," Mika said.

The man dressed in black nodded and they shook hands.

Mika turned around and introduced them. "This is Dr Dotz and her husband, Mal. They work on retainer with my uncle at ICD."

How much do they know about our kind? Josh asked Mika.

"They're evolved, too," Mika said.

Well, that explained the man's ability to focus. "This way," Josh said, as he led them to the bedroom.

Dr Dotz stopped, causing her husband to bump into her. The look on her face was one of disbelief. "What—" She took a step forward and sniffed.

Josh invaded her thoughts and was surprised that the Doc was more curious than repulsed. She glanced over at Mika twice, and each time her intention was to say something, but she stopped herself.

Rox intrigued her. She represented a challenge, a shift out of her comfort zone, which was a refreshing change from how she normally dealt with her patients.

"Wait!" Josh said. "You're a fucking psychologist?"

Dr Dotz nodded like he was only half correct. "Technically, I'm a psychological anthropologist—"

Josh turned to Mika. "Are you shitting me? We need someone to surgically remove burned clothing out of her skin and you think this woman is going to … what? Counsel it off?"

Mika held up his hands, but it was the way Mal moved in front of his wife that stopped Josh from continuing.

"Is there something I need to know?" Mal asked Mika without taking his eyes off Josh, who he was quickly categorizing as a threat.

Josh studied Dr Dotz's husband. There was something about the way the man's shoulders squared that said all patience and amenable introductions were over. He was now focused on a new task, and Josh hated to admit he wouldn't find it as easy to control him as he did others.

"Look," Josh said more calmly. "I was under the impression that we were getting a surgeon." Josh pointed back to Rox who was partially naked, but he doubted anyone took notice. "We don't need a—"

Dr Dotz walked around her husband and squeezed between Mika and Josh. She placed her bag on the floor, leaning it against the bed. She rubbed her hands together and closed her eyes before she held them over Rox's body like she was about to actually perform some sort of magic. The Doc's shoulders slumped and her head fell forward like all the muscles in the upper part of her body had diverted its efforts to keeping her arms up.

Josh moved closer, but Mal's hand on his arm – gentle, but insistent – brought him back a step.

Were those tears slipping down the woman's face? Oh for … ! This was the last thing they needed. Josh needed someone to work on Rox in the physical sense.

"Look, I'm sorry to have wasted your time—"

"Tsst." Her tone was sharp, but her eyes remained shut and her hands had begun drawing figure eights over the space above Rox's body. "This woman has endured great suffering."

No shit! She's dead. *I'm going to kill you!* he said to Mika.

Be patient. Mika responded. *She knows what she's doing.*

Yeah, really? Or is this the part where she tells us that Rox has crossed over into the spirit world and it's going to cost us a thousand dollars to make contact?

"Honey, can you look in my bag and pass me a scalpel."
She was now standing up straight, her eyes opened. She
relaxed her arms and rolled her shoulders back like she
was trying to stretch out a kink. She leaned forward and
poked the burnt flesh at Rox's neck. "Let's start with the
twenty-four."

Mal took out a black cloth and unrolled it, exposing
about ten different kinds of scalpels. He ran his fingers
across several handles before he pulled out the one Josh
assumed was numbered twenty-four.

Josh had to admit, he was intrigued now. He reached
into the Doc's mind and followed her train of thoughts:
*This is so interesting. I've never dealt with a dead body
before. Especially one that's coming back. Oh, I can feel it.
The energy she's emitting is growing stronger. We don't have
much time. Wait …* Dr Dotz looked up from Rox's body
and then slowly turned her head as if following an invisible
line leading to Josh. "Is this your wife?"

"Uh …" Of all the moments for his mind to stop
processing thought, this would not have been the one he
would have chosen. "I think I messed that opportunity
up."

She looked surprised and squinted at him behind
glasses that were too large, but matched her trousers. "Oh.
OK, never mind. It's none of my business. Just that right
now she's searching for you. Or, wait. Not really 'you'
per se. It's kinda complicated because she's searching for
you while at the same time her energy is searching for
someone else."

Josh decided it would be infinitely easier to read her

thoughts, but they were just as jumbled and tangential as her speech and provided no more of a clue to her actual meaning.

"Anyway, help me get something disposable under her because she will bleed. I mean, I'm good, but I'm not an actual surgeon so sometimes I go deeper than I should. But I'm learning." She smiled.

"You do know what you're doing, right?" Josh asked, as he and Mika helped to lift Rox off the bed while Mal spread the extra blanket from the closet beneath her.

"We shall find out!" Dr Dotz shrugged and then returned her attention to Rox.

Mal placed his forefinger over his lip, signing to remain quiet, and Josh rolled his eyes. If they weren't so desperate, he would have told the good Doc and her husband to get out, but they *were* desperate and he agreed when she said they didn't have much time left.

Very little blood flowed at the beginning, but then Dr Dotz made her next few incisions and a pool formed on the blanket. Everyone stopped.

Dr Dotz looked up at Josh. "Ugh … " Josh read her thoughts. Rox might wake up any moment. The doctor started to move quicker, her cuts less precise and in some cases she cut much deeper than he thought was necessary, but he too felt the sense of urgency.

"Run me a tepid bath," she instructed without looking up.

Mika ran into the bathroom's en suite.

"But make sure the tub is sterile!"

"We aren't getting a sterile bath in a hotel room," Josh said, fighting the temptation to throttle her. "And I don't think we want to call room service at the moment to come clean it out."

She nodded like she understood, but continued to work. "Can you get me a woman?"

"What?" There was a woman lying right in front of her.

Mal left the room and returned quickly with Katherine following him.

"Oh, good," Dr Dotz said. "I need you to use the shower gel and give the tub a cleaning like you would an operating table."

"Excuse me?" Katherine said.

"Oh, and make sure to wipe out the spout as well ... you know, where the water comes out?"

Katherine looked at Josh. "She's joking, right?"

"Sorry, I don't trust men to clean properly." Dr Dotz glanced at her husband and blew him a kiss. "No offense, honey."

He smiled. "None taken."

Katherine looked at Josh, and then at Mika who had stuck his head out of the bathroom. "Neither do I," she mumbled and went to give the tub a medical-grade clean.

CHAPTER EIGHT

~

Pain

5th August, 1:07am
Bayshore, Singapore

Death was a fast-acting depressant: one minute you were conscious, the next … nothing. Time ceased. Or more accurately, it flowed; you simply stopped being part of it. The return journey, however, was slower. It demanded reverence and patience.

Rox floated on a sea of energy, unaware of her unawareness. There was no pain or joy, no conflict; therefore, no peace. She was nothing more than a probability, an idea on its way. She remained in that state – on the precipice of being – as waves of energy washed over her in search of that tiny opening that would be the catalyst for life.

The water in the tub swirled slowly at first, responding to an unknown yet undeniable call. Then its pace increased, and Rox was pulled under. Seconds turned into moments, causing minutes to feel like hours. Energy circled beneath her until it had gained enough momentum to slam into the base of her skull where it ignited the first synapse. An electrochemical message raced across her neural network, alerting all the muscles in her body to relax. Blood flowed into her heart, causing it to contract and send more hurtling through the rest of her veins.

Rox resurfaced, but was still unaware of her existence as she passed through the different stages of conscious evolution. There was a slight tingling in her extremities as the new blood flow tickled her nerve endings. The itch rose fast and it tore through her body, leaving a trail of goosepimples that aggravated her skin as they rose.

"Rox?" The voice was a noise that only added to her confusion. "Just relax."

The words felt familiar, like a language she had studied a long while ago, but which her ears had fallen out of tune with. She ignored it as the itch grew, and she drew her nails against skin still too thin to withstand such an assault.

"No!" The voice had become louder. Harder. "Don't scratch."

Something grabbed her and a new kind of fear took root. She slipped beneath the surface in an attempt to yank free, but whatever she was sitting in leaked into her eyes and up her nose and down into her stomach. She shot back up, coughing and confused as new pain settled in.

"Look at me, Rox." *It's me, Josh.*

Instinct kept her muscles taut, but her eyes opened to a soft shade of gray, void of color.

You're OK. Just relax.

Rox stared at the lines and curves that shaped his face. For a moment, she forgot to breathe and instead focused on the intimacy of his voice and how it touched her in places she didn't know it was possible to reach.

Did she know him?

The corners of his mouth rose, and she copied his movements, but then something moved behind him.

"Keep her in the water." It was another voice. A softer one, but foreign. "She's still got a lot more skin to grow."

Rox wasn't sure what those words meant, but she sensed something was wrong. She tried to get up again, but the one with the intimate touch held her down.

"No, don't, mi amor."

But her right arm hurt like it had been held against a hot surface far too long. She opened her mouth, but her jaw locked in a bittersweet agony, trapping the sound in her throat.

The face in front of hers frowned into a familiar sorrow that released the lock on her memories. *This is the hard part.*

Total awareness flooded her as she remembered who she was. She moved her mouth to say his name, but a pain so precise stole all other thoughts and kept her focused on self.

Just breathe with me.

Rox wished she hadn't looked down.

"No, no, está bien. Just look at me, mi amor."

But she couldn't. Her breathing became too erratic. Her muscles started twitching.

"I have a sedative," the woman behind Josh said, but it wouldn't do anything.

"Josh …" Her voice was weak. Broken. Scarred.

"See, it's starting to grow back."

Straight lines ran across her forearm creating deep canyons where her flesh should have been. Her right hand was curled, like she was holding an invisible ball she was incapable of releasing. She couldn't see in color, but they were dark like soot, and the edges of her skin were lifted as if ready to be peeled.

Who … Who did this to her?

"Keep her in the water," that same foreign voice said again, and Rox tried to sit up so she could get a better look at who was speaking, but then the itch overloaded her pain.

Whatever happened was far worse than anything Tusk had done to her.

For a moment, she thought Josh was going to lift her out, but instead he climbed in beside her. "Take my energy." She wasn't sure she heard him, but then he repeated it.

Images of Ruby and MJ surfaced. Lightning and Sam's pulse.

The water sloshed up into her mouth as she tried to call for Sam, but arms much stronger than hers held her down. His touch on her half-healed skin was like being struck all over again. On instinct she drew, and energy from every source responded to her call, bombarding her nerve endings.

Her grip on consciousness slipped.

Those same strong arms lifted as more water rained down from above. As it touched her jaw and trickled down her neck, a crackle started in her ear that made her think she might die all over again.

It hurts, she told him.

Yo se, mi amor.

Rox synchronized her breathing with his like she had done so many times in the past. The crackling grew louder as it traveled up her jaw and branched off into the roof of her mouth. She thought she was growing new teeth the way her gums ached. Then her eyes started to itch, and if it were not for Josh's strong hold on her, she would have scratched them out. Miniature bubbles of balloons floated behind her eyelids, each one bursting to release an array of colors.

Rox curled into Josh and grabbed the front of his shirt with fingers that were rapidly regaining their dexterity, as well as their natural color. She ground her newly formed teeth and moaned with the ache marching across her chest like thousands of ants establishing a colony.

She reached out once more for Sam, but again everything but his soothing pulse returned.

"Sleep," Josh said.

She wanted to ask him about Sam, about Ruby and her son, but instead she allowed the pain of healing to swallow her whole.

~

Samaritan

5th August, 12:15am (-1 SGT)
Pak Tha, Laos

Leona walked into the lab with an exuberance that belied their environment.

Tusk sighed at the interruption and was about to slump

back in his chair, but remembered what had happened the last time.

"Let's have it," Tusk said.

Her smile was bright with pluck, and it made her look even younger. "My guys just called. They cleared Singapore waters and are on their way to Indo to switch vessels. We got 'em."

Tusk had been awaiting an update from his team, but he had misplaced his phone and then got distracted with the samples from the only subject he had who was showing any progress. He missed Nancy. She usually took care of planning and appropriating subjects for him to study. He had been forced to become a jack of all trades, and multitasking – he had quickly learned – wasn't a scientist's strength. "And the healer?"

"We got the kids," Leona said.

Tusk tore off his gloves and threw them on the small surgical trolley. The kids were good, yes, but they were not as valuable as the healer. He spun around the lab and stubbed his shoe on the leg of his chair.

Space! He missed space. And air-conditioning units that worked, and fans that didn't rattle, and Nancy. Goddammit, he missed Nancy. She would have sorted this place out. They would have had reliable electricity by now, she would have handled the local "security" they were forced to pay by either reaching a better agreement or having them removed altogether – the latter, more likely. She would have also been able to capture not only the children, but the healer as well, because she would have understood the importance of a woman who could heal herself.

Tara's ability meant a fundamental redefining of what it meant to be alive, which would impact the definition of humanity in a way that being able to *feel* another's emotions simply couldn't achieve. Life was death. Without one, what was the other?

"Aw, c'mon, don't be like that, doc. She'll come for her kids."

"Yes, I know, but I've dealt with two situations like this before, Leona, and neither of them ended well for me or my research facilities." He gestured around the small room they were in. The only thing state-of-the-art about Alchemy was that it had electricity … sometimes. "Either of the children have an ability?"

She shrugged. "The boy's too young, and we had to sedate the girl. She's a fighter. My guy said she had some kind of training and it was a good thing he was there or else your team wouldn't have been able to take her."

That piqued his interest. What sort of ability enhanced fighting capability? "What's the age of the girl again?"

"Sixteen."

It was the right age for an ability to manifest, if not a few years late. But regardless, what evolutionary benefit could there be to physical dexterity? In fact, physical dexterity, he sadly hypothesized, had reached its evolutionary peak. With more humans performing cognitive labor coupled with more sedentary lifestyles, the need for skills like agility and fortitude were becoming superfluous. "Do we know anything else?"

Leona cocked her head to the side and looked at him with sympathy. "I know you wanted the healer, but I've got a bit of bad news about that."

"What?"

"She, uh, well, she got hit by lightning."

Tusk blinked like he wasn't sure he understood. "You mean actual lightning?" He raised his hands above his head in an attempt to mime lightning.

"Not sure what the *figurative* kind would be, so I'm going to go with, yes, 'actual lightning'," she said, mimicking his movements.

Tusk began to pace. He wasn't able to get three proper strides before he had to spin around, but it was enough to allow his thoughts to flow. The steady clicking of the fan acted as a metronome and helped him to focus.

"Doc—"

He held up his hand, and she stopped.

He had measured Tara's thermal energy, and even when she was in a state of rest, it was high. He wanted to say it was correlated to her ability, but truthfully, she could just as easily be one of those people with a naturally higher body temperature. It wasn't unheard of.

He had never thought about using her as a lightning rod, though. There were certain tests that were simply too risky to perform. He knew, for example, that decapitation was a definite way to kill her, but there would be very little to gain from such an experiment. In fact, finding ways to kill her wasn't his goal. Tusk wanted to understand *how* her cells replicated with such precision and speed. What made her skin knit itself back together moments after being sliced apart? How had her lungs managed to expel water after being filled for over ten minutes? OK, so she expels water ten minutes after being drowned – a medical miracle, yes, but again, not necessarily unheard of. The more cogent question was why no brain damage?

"How long till the boy gets here?"

"The empath? Miles? Tomorrow, late evening. Provided the weather cooperates. Why?"

"Have the kids come straight to us. No need to route them through the warehouse like the empath."

Leona looked confused. "But you said never break protocol. Mistakes are made when short cuts are introduced."

He knew exactly what he had said because he said it. "Yes, dear, but we are halving their capabilities by sending them in two different directions. GFO has deep pockets, but they lack manpower."

"You really think they'll still come after Miles now that we have the kids?" Leona asked, and then rubbed her thumb over her fingertips.

"What do you think?"

She didn't respond right away, but then she nodded. "I can't figure out the connection between the healer and the empath."

Tusk stopped pacing and circled his chin with his forefinger. He was going to need a shave soon. "Well, we know there's no family connection." Was their connection even germane? What he couldn't understand was how Tara's ability of perfect cell regeneration impacted emotions. Nothing about his research showed she could do anything more than heal herself. The surveillance video at Wonderland showed she could absorb – there was no other name for it – other people's consciousness, their awake-ness. What Nancy described happening to her, what the security guard in the room with Dr Philippe had said happened to him, and by Philippe's own accounts, Tara's ability was not limited to healing. But none of them had mentioned an emotional aspect. But neither had Tusk asked. He needed to look over the surveillance footage again. Maybe he could spot something that would explain Miles' reaction to her or her impact on Miles.

"What're you thinking?" Leona asked.

Tusk lifted his glasses and rubbed his eyes. "Just trying to figure out the Tara-Miles connection. It doesn't make sense."

Leona ran her thumb over her fingers again. "Maybe there is no connection."

Tusk shook his head. "Why else risk her escape?"

"Maybe she's altruistic. A good Samaritan."

Tusk snorted. "No one in their right mind—"

"Maybe she wasn't in her right mind."

Tusk sat down heavily in his chair, grateful when it stayed intact. Leona was on to something. They had pumped Tara full of sedatives. She had been through rigorous testing.

Tusk sighed and jumped to his feet. He pulled out a pair of surgical gloves from the box and began to put them on. "Either way, the boy will confirm it. And I don't think her getting struck by lightning was coincidental." In fact, he was sure it wasn't. He'd been looking at her ability completely wrong. "And one of your guys saw it?"

Leona nodded.

"How soon can your guys get the kids here?" Tusk

pressed the button on top of the pipette and a small drop of the oil he extracted from the only viable patient he had fell onto a small white lab mouse.

"Well, if you want them coming through LP, then theoretically soon, but—"

"Great."

Tusk expected her to leave, but when she just stood there, running her hand over the back of his chair, he turned around. "What?"

"Look, I don't know anyone who's been hit by lightning, but I think you should manage your expectations about the healer. I don't think it's something one walks away from."

"You'd be surprised."

~

Delicate

5th August, 2:07am
Bayshore, Singapore

Her eyes opened and she was greeted to color for the first time since re-awakening. She felt herself sinking and instinct made her reach out. Her hands were a milky brown; the earlier flakes, dissolved.

Rox ran her hands along her body to check that all her skin had reformed. Goosepimples sprouted as she released the breath she had been holding when everything felt as it should. There wasn't a new scratch or scar on her.

Intellectually, she understood that her ability was a gift, but emotionally … physically … It was hard to focus on anything other than the pain and the suffering at the moment.

On the other side of the door were Josh and Katherine, Meita, Michael and Emma, and a lot of questions she couldn't answer, problems she couldn't solve, and pain her ability couldn't heal.

Tears slipped down her face as she reached for the bottle of shower gel, but it was empty. The next bottle was labeled shampoo, and she decided that was good enough. There wasn't enough water to wash with, so she turned the tap to the side with the red semi-circle. Hot water rushed out and she paddled it around the tub to distribute the heat.

She fought with herself to keep her mind focused on the present and the nice lather she was building in her hands. Her tears turned to hiccups when she realized her hair was gone. Fuzz was all that remained, and she wasn't sure if that was a result of the lightning or if someone had been kind enough to try and even it out while she … healed.

A flash of light tore through her mind, but she pushed it away and continued to massage the suds down her neck and over her chest. The walls that were holding back the specific sequence of events that led to her death were fragile, but she wanted everything to remain compartmentalized, just for a little while longer.

Rox reached up to wipe at her tears and got soap in her eye, but she didn't try to alleviate the sting. Instead, she let it remind her of what it meant to be alive. Life without pain was a long ago fabricated memory that seemed like manipulation at the time, but now, with the benefit of hindsight, a gift.

With her one good eye, she washed the spaces between her toes and the soles of her feet. She lowered herself beneath the surface of the water to wash away the shampoo and thought about inhaling. It's not like she could do any lasting harm. Besides, she'd drowned before. She didn't remember any pain, just fear. Lots of fear.

Rox resurfaced and wiped her eyes dry. She stepped out of the bath and reached for the hotel robe. It was infinitely better than anything else she could think to put against her new skin at the moment. She looked at the assortment of creams that lined the little glass shelf just above the sink and decided on the one with moisturizing in its name. It smelled expensive, and that reminded her of a time when there wasn't money for such luxuries, when food was eaten out of industrial-sized trash bins with padlocks that needed breaking, and nights were spent with shoes on because it took a skill that few possessed to steal them without waking the wearer.

She caught a glimpse of herself in the mirror and looked away. She wasn't sure if it was fear or a bit of self-hatred, but she wasn't in the mood to face that specific reality. She would have her post-death pep talk later. Right now, she just focused on the cool feeling of the cream sliding up her thighs.

Her stomach let out a rumble, and that reminded her of the urgent need for nourishment. She wrapped herself in the robe and took a deep breath.

When Rox stepped into the living room, the first person

her eyes sought was Josh. He straightened from leaning over Meita's shoulder, and his look of surprise said it all.

Rox slipped her hand up the sleeve to massage her arm where her tendons and muscles had been exposed not long ago. Her lips pulled up into a smile that looked as awkward as it felt, but she was steady. Calm. "I'm alright," she said softly.

His lips did that thing when he wanted to say something, but was having to fight to remain quiet. *You had me scared.*

Thank you. She didn't need to say it, but that's why she did.

"Mom?" It was a soft voice coming from the sofa. Emma sat up with a look of confusion, or perhaps wonder; Rox couldn't distinguish and it didn't matter. Emma ran over to her, and Rox lifted her into her arms like she were much younger than fourteen. She pulled her in tight against her chest and inhaled her scent. Flashes of Ruby and MJ threatened to steal the moment, but she pushed them back and simply basked in the joy that she now had a memory of her daughter calling her mom.

"I love you," Rox said, but it hardly seemed like enough. Surely there were words more powerful, more apropos than *love*.

"I know," Emma said. "I can feel it."

Her daughter was an EO, and thankfully, her abilities weren't healing. Rox stepped back, but didn't break their embrace. Emma had dark circles under her eyes that said she hadn't gotten much sleep. She was also frail, which made Rox wonder how she hadn't noticed it earlier. Emma needed to eat more.

Meita just hung up with room service.

Rox nodded at Josh without looking up. She wanted this moment to last, perhaps forever, but she knew she had two other children who needed her. Tusk had taken them and the fact that she wasn't able to save them tore at her in ways she hadn't known were possible. Guilt at failing them a second time made her question if she even deserved them.

Don't do that. We fail them repeatedly, but we never stop trying. That's what makes us good parents.

She sucked in a deep breath and turned to Michael. He had been standing patiently behind Emma with his own looks of confusion and awe. "I couldn't stop them," she explained to him. "I got hit from behind, and by the time I was able to get the best of one of them, I was … "

Struck by lightning. She curled her fingers into a ball and then stretched them wide at the memory of the pain in her joints. Her back muscles threatened to seize up as she turned towards the television mounted on the wall. Artificial energy had always grated at the base of her skull like a chisel looking to leave its mark. Smaller electrical appliances were more of a nuisance than painful, but she always knew where they were located and could tell the minute the refrigerator's compressor turned on to kickstart the cooling process. But now …

What's wrong?

She shook her head. *I don't know. It's like … I can't feel* … Wait … there, if she concentrated, she caught the silent pulse of electricity exiting the power socket at the base of the wall, but it didn't hurt like it used to. "Do you think I can still heal?" she asked Josh. She didn't feel different, but she sensed something *was* different about her. What if the lightning had taken her abilities? What if when she needed them most, she no longer had them?

Josh chuckled. *Mi amor. You just got hit by lightning and died, yet now you're here. I think your ability to heal is still intact.*

Now was probably not the time, not with Michael and Emma, Meita and Mika, and two other people's energy she sensed coming from the corner of the room present, but later wasn't promised. No moment beyond the now ever was.

She walked into Josh's embrace and let him hold her. They both needed it. Her life was messy and complicated. She was in love with a man who wasn't her husband, while another man who had become her best friend, her family, was in love with her. She wondered if anyone got the textbook definition of happiness.

Only the boring.

She laughed, and he laughed, too.

"Welcome back," Meita said.

Rox stepped free from Josh's embrace and put her arms around her daughter again. God, it felt good to say that with confidence. Her daughter.

The lock disengaged on the suite's door, and Katherine walked in with a bag in each hand. "There's nothing like shopping to cure what ails you." She dropped the bags on the step leading down into the living room like the act of shopping had been more gratifying than the actual purchase.

"Update," Katherine said to Meita.

"With ICD's help, we've got acccss to the surveillance drones. I can see when the kids were picked up, and then I've been able to track their movements to here, the start – or end – of East Coast Park."

"How long ago was this?"

"A little over two hours."

Michael cupped his hands over his mouth and nose as if he were praying, but Rox knew he was trying not to lose it. He reached for Emma, and she walked over to him and started to cry quietly.

"I've got an image of their boat," Meita said. "But … "

"Stealth?" Katherine asked.

Meita confirmed.

"Won't do us much good then." Katherine placed one hand on her tiny hip and the other on the bar top that separated the living room from the dining area.

"Why?" Michael asked. "Can't we notify nearby ports and tell them what's happened and to contact us when the boat docks?"

Rox understood his need for simple answers, but people like Tusk never did things simply. She understood that now.

Katherine was the one who answered. "No. You don't dock stealth boats at ports."

"Can we not use the surveillance drones? Just follow them until we can get to them?" Rox asked, pulling the belt of her robe tighter.

"We are," Meita said. "But ICD surveillance drones aren't meant for long range recognizance missions like we need. The batteries will simply run out before they reach their final destination."

"Not to mention they weren't designed to cross large bodies of salt water," Mika added. "A bad storm like the one we have now, choppy waters, salt-water spray—"

"The added strength of the wind during a storm will affect their navigation and their flight path," Meita said.

"It's a miracle the one following them hasn't fallen out of the sky yet," Mika said.

"Do we know where they are now?" Rox asked.

"The Riau Archipelago," Meita said.

"I know that place!" Michael said. "Nikoi is there. The kids and I holidayed there. Could that be where they're going?"

"Possibly. But not like you're thinking," Katherine said. "Besides, by the time we get there, they'll be gone."

"So, what? We do nothing?" Michael shouted.

Katherine snorted and stretched her arms out towards everyone in the room. "I hardly consider this nothing. Look, ICD's got a team in pursuit, but we have to play smart. *We* know who we're up against, and chasing after them without a plan is a surefire way to lose them. Permanently."

Rox's stomach dropped at the thought of never seeing them again. She had forgotten all about her need for food as they explained to her what she had missed. She had trouble concentrating, her mind jumping from the details of what they were saying to what she knew Tusk could do to them. It was more than the physical torture or the unwanted experiments. He would rob them of their innocence. He would steal the sparkle out of MJ's eyes, and that scared her more than anything. Ruby was prepared for this. Looking back, Rox saw a toughness in Ruby that would keep her thinking. Losing her mom had already taken that spark, which meant Ruby would fight Tusk, but the question was, could she win?

"They're not evolved. MJ is too young and Ruby would have shown signs by now," Rox said, interrupting Katherine.

"Unless she's like you," Meita reminded her.

Either way, they still had value to Tusk even if they weren't evolved. Rox remembered Val, Sam's sister, and knew there were a lot of bad things that could be done to the unevolved, too.

Rox reached out with her energy in search of Sam, but nothing returned. She wanted to ask what could keep him away when he would have known she had just died, but now didn't feel like the right time.

"My uncle's approved the decommissioning of the drones that are tracking them."

"What does that mean?" Michael asked.

"Means that we can follow them until the drone's battery dies," Mika explained.

"How many do we have following them?" Michael asked.

"Only one left."

"Any idea how much longer until that one drops?" Katherine asked.

"An hour," Mika shrugged. "A little more if we're lucky. But battery life isn't the main concern. It's the wind."

"Meita, thoughts?" Katherine said.

Meita took a deep breath as she sat back from her laptop. "Well, I think it's safe to say Tusk followed Miles here. We checked him for any tracking devices after his rescue, and he was clean, which means they've been waiting for him to resurface. Perhaps for you, too, Rox."

Katherine waved her hand for Meita to speed up.

"They tracked him here by watching Miles' family – same as us," Meita said, then paused for a moment before looking at Rox. "They grabbed him, but I don't think he found you. I think they scooped him up first. He hadn't been here that long and nothing leads us to believe he even knew where to begin looking for you."

"So how did they find her?" Katherine pointed at Rox.

"Had to be the men at the hotel," Mika answered. "Sam said that the men you saw snatching Miles from the East Coast were the same as the ones from the hotel." He snapped his fingers. "I bet that's how they found Michael's place."

"Any thoughts on their destination? Doubt they're taking the kids on an all-inclusive on Nikoi," Katherine said.

"You've got Thailand to the north," Meita said.

"Too busy. Too touristy," Josh countered. "Indonesia? They've got so much to choose from there."

"Wait!" Meita sat up, and her fingers flew across the keyboard. "Mockingbird was the first one to get shut down – that's where we found out about Josh." Meita was mumbling to herself as she typed. "Phone."

Katherine reached for her bag and tossed her phone to Meita who caught it with two hands. Rox wasn't sure what to do with herself while Meita spoke with the person on the other end. She didn't have any spare clothes, and she didn't want to know what happened to the running outfit she had been wearing when she got struck by lightning.

Meita hung up. "OK, I'll have more in a few minutes, but right now, all we can do is speculate. If not Thailand, then perhaps we're looking at Indonesia."

Michael spun around the room and swore, but then looked at Emma and reined in his temper. "You people have any idea how big Indonesia is? How many islands there are?"

"If I may?" It was the short woman standing in the corner. She was dressed in bright colors and wore a smile that said she had no idea the severity of the situation, or she was an eternal optimist. "I don't think it's Indonesia."

"Why do you say that?" Michael asked. "You know something?"

"Oh God." Josh shook his head in frustration. "Don't say—"

"I hear voices," the woman said.

The room fell silent.

"She's telling the truth," Emma said, quietly. "I can't tell when a person is lying, but I can tell when they're speaking their truth."

Rox wasn't sure she understood the difference.

"They tell me things sometimes. It's kinda hard to explain, but they'll feel better if you look more to the north." The woman stepped back like that's all she had to say, and the man she was with put his arm around her. "Oh, I'm Dotz. I helped to cut your clothes out, and this is my husband, Mal."

Do we trust her? Rox asked as the woman walked around the coffee table to come shake hands with her.

Yeah, Josh sighed. *Her thoughts are out there, but she's only trying to help. Plus she was the one who suggested we put you in the bath.*

"Thank you," Rox said.

"Oh, it was my pleasure. I've never seen someone return from death before." Dotz's smile was infectious, and Rox couldn't help but return it. When their hands touched, a surge of energy raced up Rox's arm.

"Wow!" Dotz said, yanking her arm back.

What happened?

I don't know. I just wanted to get a read on her energy, but it was like instead of opening the gates a little, they flew open and … I don't know, but she's got more energy than anyone I've ever come into contact with.

Josh grunted. *Maybe she does hear voices.*

Katherine's phone rang. Meita answered. "Sec," she said, and unlocked her laptop. "Kay." And then her fingers started to type. The conversation lasted no more than two minutes, but when she hung up, she exhaled. "Northern Thailand. Chiang Rai."

Michael breathed an audible sigh of relief, and everyone followed. Emma squeezed Rox's hand and then leaned into her father's embrace.

Dotz had been right. They could have spent days looking for MJ and Ruby in Indonesia and would never have found them because they were never there. How long had Rox looked for her family in the US, only to discover they were living in Singapore?

Don't do that. The important thing is we now have a location.

"What's there?" Katherine asked. She was the only one who hadn't visibly relaxed.

Meita hesitated, and Rox felt something tighten in her gut.

"A facility?" Katherine asked.

"I doubt it," Meita answered. "It didn't have its own separate file encryption like the other locations, but its coordinates were referenced in the Mockingbird documents."

"Supposition?"

"Supply route for the region. Maybe."

Katherine nodded like she understood, but Rox was far from understanding. So they hadn't found a facility, but had found a supplier to one of Tusk's facilities instead? Josh had told her that Mockingbird was the first facility GFO had uncovered and shut down, then there was Watership Down, followed swiftly by Wonderland. "How many facilities are there?"

"We have thirteen heavily encrypted files on thirteen separate servers located around the world." Katherine spoke like she was giving an update to a boardroom and not to the mother of two missing children.

"We suspect there are thirteen," Meita elaborated. "But we have no way of knowing until we can decrypt each server and read each file."

"And that's provided Harry didn't have private, non-GFO servers set up somewhere," Katherine added.

Her comments weren't helping. If they were wrong and went chasing the wrong lead, it would be harder to find MJ and Ruby. Ruby was a fighter, but facilities like the ones

Rox had seen were designed to quickly take the fight out of a seasoned soldier. What chance did a sixteen-year-old girl and a ten-year-old boy have?

"Look," Meita said to Rox and Michael. "It's a lead. And if we think about it, it makes sense. They had to get out of Singapore, and they couldn't exactly fly on a commercial carrier with two stolen children. The best way to do that undetected is on a boat. A stealth boat. But that kind of boat requires a lot of money and one highly sophisticated network."

Katherine nodded her agreement. "Time is also of the essence because they know we're on the ground here in Singapore, which means Tusk's only choice is to rely on his current contacts. Maybe there isn't a facility in Thailand, but there's something there that can lead us to one."

But how long was that going to take? The longer a person stayed missing, the less likely they were to be found.

You can't think like that.

It's exactly how you thought when they took Jay!

Yes. And we got him back. You got him back!

But you trained Jay. Her breathing had escalated too quickly and each inhalation sounded like she was hyperventilating. *MJ is just ten.* Her thoughts were merging together into a ball of panic. *Michael said that Ruby has been in judo since she was six. That's ten years of practice. But it's not the same.* She looked up with fear in her eyes. "Has she ever taken a hit, Josh? A real hit—"

"Stop." Josh started towards her, but she backed away.

Rox had tried to keep all her emotions neatly compartmentalized. The fact that she had just died, again;

the fact that she was now alive, again; plus Miles had been recaptured by Tusk, and she didn't want to think about the fear and pain he would be living through. Now, MJ and Ruby were missing, and more than likely, it was her fault.

"You can't think like that." Josh grabbed her arm, but she yanked free. He reached for her once more but she wasn't sure what to do. Where to go. How to save them.

"I can't heal what I can't see." She couldn't hold it back anymore. The walls she had put up were too delicate to hold back the tide of fear and uncertainty that washed over her. Her children were en route to a very sick and evil man, and there was nothing she could do about it. He was going to hurt them, and their best defense was the fact that they were innocent. But Tusk had shown he preyed on the innocent. He had taken Jay and traded him to gain her. She would never forget the feeling of the fire as Tusk slid the torch down her arm. "They're just babies, Josh."

She stopped fighting him and simply fell into his support. Her mind jumped back to Wonderland, and if it were not for her metabolic rate adjusting so quickly to the increased dosages of sedatives, she doubted she would have ever made it out. Then there was Watership Down. If she hadn't gone back for Sam and his father, who knows what would have happened to them. She remembered Val slamming her head into the wall to quiet the voices only she heard. Had Val recovered? Would she ever be her old self again? Was Sam racked with guilt over how long it took for them to rescue her?

Rox now understood the underhanded deal that Walter had made with her. She would do the same if given the opportunity. There wasn't a person she wouldn't sell out to keep her children safe.

She needed to tell Sam that she forgave him for what happened. She understood his desperation. Hell, she gave herself up to save Jay, and she would do it all again for MJ and Ruby.

Stop thinking like this, mi amor.

But how do you control your thoughts when all you have been left with was to wonder?

"Look at me." Josh cupped her face with his hands.

"Where's Sam?"

~

Lost

Date/Time & Location: Unknown

It was the soft, rhythmic drops of rain that ignited his second slide back into consciousness. A shiver raced down his spine as goosepimples exploded over his skin, and his eyes opened like the pages of an old book being turned, slowly and with care.

He inhaled thick, rich air that was so sweet he was tempted to stick out his tongue for a taste. His body instructed his mind to do a full scan to assess his injuries, and his mind unenthusiastically complied. His muscles felt as if weights had been attached to them and the simple act of stretching required more energy than he had. At least one of his ribs was broken, probably two. They would need taping, but from the little landscape he could see with his head still cocked to the side, he doubted he would find any lying around.

After a few more deep breaths, he slowly went about straightening his neck, moving through the pain until his head was upright. He tried to get his bearings, but the fading light made it difficult to see the environment he was in. Perhaps he was in a forest. The soft, steady fall of rain made him think a rainforest, but the air held a chill reminiscent of autumn.

He reached out with his other sense, that sense all humans have to help them identify place and time. What greeted him raised the hairs on his body and incited panic. A growl just behind him stilled every thought. A heated breeze tickled the goosepimples at the base of his neck, and he knew from its dampness that it was breath. His muscles froze. Fear made his heart slam against his chest as he struggled to figure out what was behind him.

Sam squinted through eyes that felt dry despite the rain running into them. He was unsure of what his next move should be. He couldn't see, so he couldn't attack. Then something pushed against his head, leaving a thick line of something else to trail down into his shirt. If he were in full form, he would have rolled with the movement and come up ready to strike. Or at least defend. But his muscles weren't cooperating from being in the same posture for too long.

How long had he been unconscious? How long had he been here?

His father's voice echoed in his head, and for a moment he wasn't sure if it were real or his imagination. It instructed him to be still until he could formulate a plan. If whatever was behind him actually attacked, then Sam would have no choice but to defend himself, no matter the odds. But right now, his father's voice was telling him that whatever lurked just outside of his peripheral vision was also weighing up the odds.

Another push just between his shoulder blades, and Sam tilted forward, but remained upright. He could hear breathing that wasn't his own and the slow rattle of a growl. His senses were telling him that it was an animal and more than likely four-legged. Most two-legged creatures had hands, and they used those for touch, but that knowledge brought him little comfort.

Circulation began to return to his extremities, but it would still be a while before they actually cooperated enough to form a meaningful defense. He was going to start shaking soon, the body's way of asserting itself into animation. He could feel it coming, and he just hoped that whatever was prodding him from behind wouldn't mistake his sudden, uncoordinated movements as a threat.

It started with a twitch in his leg, and he heard the animal step back. There was nothing left to do but hurry through the pain to get to the other side. He placed his left hand onto the ground, and it disappeared into grass that was so thick and soft it reminded him of moss. The tips of the blades tickled his palms, but he focused on the muscles in his left arm, tensing them so they could support most of his weight as he curled his legs to the side and pushed up.

It was like moving through water, there was so much resistance. Pain lanced its way up to his shoulder and his arm almost gave out, but starting over would be twice as difficult, so he kept going until he was standing.

The landscape tilted, and he realized the verdant canopy overhead was the thick branches of trees all around him. Night was approaching and the little light left from the day was quickly disappearing into the darkness of the forest.

For a moment, he thought he was going to pass out again, but then whatever prodded him stepped into his line of vision.

Sam froze.

This wasn't the first time his ribs were broken. He knew the burn of a bullet wound and the throbbing, disorientating ache of a dislocated shoulder. He had been bitten by Shaira just once, but that was all he needed to learn that animal bites were precise in their pain. But what stood before Sam caused a different kind of fear to take root. This was primal. No amount of intellect or quick wit would save him from an animal like this. Never before had he felt the need to submit to another being, to offer up the alpha status and take on a lesser position. He had spent a lifetime comfortable in the knowledge that he was not only at the top of the food chain, but he was also at the top of the social one.

Puffs of breath vapor formed in quick succession in front of his mouth, and if it weren't for his experience with Shaira, he would have succumbed to the fear he knew he must reek of and turn to flee. But that path led to certain death – predators chased, and so he focused on slowing his breathing. He wasn't sure why the animal didn't attack; its size and solid frame would ensure an easy victory, especially with Sam injured, but it remained staid, muscles taut and primed, but motionless.

Sam wasn't sure how long it took for him to get his breathing under control, but he knew when he succeeded because the animal before him took another long, deep sniff like it had noticed the change.

If there were more distance between them, Sam might have chanced breaking eye contact to search around for a heavy branch to wield as a weapon, but an animal of this size would have reflexes much faster than his own.

The creature suddenly exhaled, like it had breathed in something unpleasant, and the way it shook its head reminded him of Shaira. But whatever he was staring at was no wolf – of that he was certain. He would hazard a guess that it didn't belong to the canine family at all. Its long, curved fangs reminded him of saber teeth, and it had short, brown fur decorated with lighter spots. Its ears were long and triangular with thin tuffs of hair hanging from the tips. Its paws were wide and its nails out, ready to rip through skin if necessary. It was a tiger. Or some kind of rainforest cat-like creature with shorter, more stocky hind legs and fangs that looked prehistoric.

If it attacked, then death would be quick, and for some reason that gave Sam a small bit of comfort. One swipe from its paws or a bite from those curved teeth would definitely lead to rapid blood loss. Adrenaline would help numb the pain, but he would still have to live through about twenty seconds of fight.

They both stood frozen in indecision, and for the first time, Sam wondered if it were just as afraid as he was.

An animal on the hunt or protecting its territory would have attacked by now. Instead, this one behaved as if it were curious.

Sam took a few seconds to further slow his breathing. He carefully shifted his weight until he could widen his stance, which would give him a better defensive, as well as attacking, position.

It let out another soft growl and Sam stilled. They stood as if paralyzed, both afraid to move for fear of how the other might interpret it. The steady rain continued to fall, drenching them as the light from the sky faded into darkness. Sam found himself mesmerized as its eyes began to sparkle when night finally arrived.

Sometime later its head lowered, just a centimeter, but that was enough to signal that its muscles had relaxed and the standoff was over. Sam's breath escaped in an audible sigh, and the animal yawned as if it, too, were relieved the tension had ended.

Sam chanced his first look around since waking. The rain drowned out most sounds, but a few insects let their presence be known. Trees much larger and wider than anything he had ever seen surrounded him. He felt small, like perhaps wherever he was wasn't meant for his kind, or perhaps, wasn't meant for just *one* of his kind. Here, he suspected he would need a tribe to survive. There was no way a single man could take on beasts like the one in front of him alone.

Sam thought back to the last thing he remembered, and it was of his brother, Mika. They were fighting, and he couldn't figure out what would ever make him come to blows with his little brother. They had a few arguments, but never had it ever turned physical. Walter would have never tolerated that from either of them, especially given how much older Sam was.

He glanced back at the animal, which now sat perched on the root of a tree the size of a boulder sticking out of the ground. Thunder rumbled across the sky, followed by a flash of lightning.

Rox!

Pain slipped up his side as he looked over his shoulder for any sign that she might be there with him, but it was too dark for him to see anything.

The animal abruptly leapt down from the root and arched its back as if stretching before it turned around and walked off in the opposite direction. It quickly disappeared into the darkness, and for a moment, Sam almost called for it to stop. But then he saw its sparkling eyes looking back at him. A low groan pierced the rain, followed by another.

Sam wasn't sure what to do at first, but then a small laugh escaped. He had no idea where he was or how he had gotten there, but one thing he knew with certainty, and that was his newfound "friend" had just successfully communicated the time-tested sign for follow. Major Sam Watts shuddered against the growing cold as he clutched his ribs and hobbled after a creature he had no name for and too few words to describe.

CHAPTER NINE

~

Woman up

5th August, 2:32am
Bayshore, Singapore

Rox felt numb after watching the surveillance video of
Sam's disappearance. She had never really understood his
ability, but Josh explained that Sam was most likely wherever
he went when he passed through time. Rox remembered
the cracks in the stones. Sam had been so close to her he
could have very well touched her when she exploded. He
would be lucky to be alive. *She* was lucky to be alive. Most
people got struck by lightning and in the blink of an eye, it
was over. She got struck by lightning and there was enough
footage to analyze, pause, fast forward, and rewind.

Rox secured the Velcro straps on the compression vest
to her torso. It was designed to stop rounds fired from a
standard handgun as well as hollow point ammunitions.
On top of that, she wore a long-sleeved microfiber
performance T-shirt with the ability to keep her cool in
humid conditions. She tucked the elastic cuffs of the
cargo pants Meita had given her into the black boots

Katherine had pulled from one of the shopping bags. Rox asked where she had purchased them given the hour, but Katherine just pointed to the logo on the bag as if that were explanation enough.

Rox looked at her reflection in the bathroom mirror and counted her blessings to be alive. She stepped into the bedroom and was surprised to see Katherine waiting for her.

"Be foolish to ask if you're alright," Katherine said as she crossed her arms over her chest and leaned back in the chair.

Rox wasn't sure what to say. The last time the two of them had a private conversation like this, Katherine had threatened to withhold her true identify, causing Rox to retaliate by siphoning her energy. They had a few calls since then, but most of her communications had been through Meita. In truth, Rox wasn't sure what to make of the head of GFO.

"We'll get your kids back," Katherine said with a confidence Rox wanted to believe. "Tusk won't want them dead. Man's too clever for that."

"There're worse things than death."

"Says the woman who can't die." Katherine chuckled as she stood and slipped her hands into her trouser pockets. She leaned back against the work desk and crossed her feet at the ankles. "They found you here. Now, I'll take responsibility for that. I let Miles stay at Halo, and it was clear the boy had issues. I should have paid more attention."

Her words might have sounded like an apology, but they didn't feel like one.

"If I thought they could have tracked you all the way to Singapore, I would have never let you leave."

A flash of anger gripped Rox at the thought of anyone attempting to stop her from reuniting with her family, but Katherine took no notice.

"Feel any different after the lightning?"

Rox wasn't exactly sure how to explain how she felt. When she concentrated, she was able to feel the artificial energy running between the walls of the room, but without the pain or discomfort that usually accompanied it.

"Not many people can say they've been struck by lightning for seven seconds," Katherine said. "*And* still be alive to talk about it."

Rox wasn't sure *she* wanted to be able to say that.

"When this is over, there's a doctor I want you to see. He—"

"No doctors!" Rox was sure that whatever her future held, it wasn't going to include time as a test subject.

Katherine pushed off the desk and held her hands out in front of her. "I get it. But hear me out. When you were … well, dead, Meita did some research. Lightning strikes last for about thirty *micro*-seconds. That's like a nanosecond or something. Yours lasted for seven *full* seconds. When they brought you back here you were fried chicken, sweetheart. And if it weren't for Little Miss Rainbow Bright out there, I have to admit I don't even want to think about the state you would have been in when you woke."

Josh had told her that it was Dr Dotz's idea to put her in water, and Rox was beyond grateful. Each time she came back, there was suffering and confusion, and a gnawing itch and hunger that overrode reason. This time, however, all those things were present, but she felt more in control. Calmer.

"This is a very personal mission for you, which means I should keep you sidelined." Katherine held up her hands again when Rox was about to protest. "Children convolute things. They make you hold on to hope when common sense tells you it's time to move on. That makes you the weak link on this one."

Rox wanted to deny it, but she would sacrifice everyone accompanying her to get her children back.

"Mika's running point. With Sam gone, he's our best option. Josh is showing a lot of potential, but he lacks experience, and right now that's what we need most. Not to mention Mika speaks about three languages, two of which are relevant, to Josh's Spanish, which isn't worth shit on this side of the world, I'm afraid."

"What about Meita?" If experience was the deciding factor, surely she had the most.

Katherine nodded like she approved the question. "Meita's at her best when her attention is divided. Besides, she's more of a big picture kinda woman."

"What's more big picture than finding my children?"

"Apprehending a mad man. Shutting down a facility and all facilities like it so no more children go missing." Katherine's tone took on a harder edge, like she had been trying to play nicely, but now the gloves were off. "Creating a team of evolved ones who will help me make this world just a little bit better."

"You don't strike me as the altruistic type."

Katherine smiled. "I'm not. And I never pretend to be. I said you could have a year with your family and I meant that. But this life here that Michael built, the one you sat on the sidelines observing like some sad puppy for the last ten months? That's over."

Rox wasn't sure how to respond. Michael had made it clear once they rescued Ruby and MJ, he wanted nothing more to do with her. If she had never learned about Emma, she would have acquiesced. But her daughter was evolved and would need someone to teach her how to be safe. Rox had no idea what it meant to be an empath, but she didn't know much about being a healer either. She was learning as she went along. They all were, and being around people who were on a similar journey was vital if they were going to come out on the other side well-adjusted and whole.

"You could all go to Halo after this. Walter and I worked out an agreement that they'll provide safe haven for any evolved ones we come into contact with who need help."

She doubted Walter would have anything to do with her. If she hadn't outright killed Sam, she was responsible for his disappearance. Her body kept reaching out, expecting one of his pulses to greet her and let her know he was OK. Her breath caught at the thought of never feeling him again.

"I can tell by the look on your face that you're thinking about Sam," Katherine said. "You know, he was a father. Sam."

The use of past tense saddened her more than she

thought possible. She hadn't known. There hadn't been time to know. All they had were intense moments where a need to be in physical contact overruled ... everything.

"Nothing worse than losing your kid." There was a small tremor in Katherine's voice that wasn't there before, but when she spoke next, it was with the steadiness of a woman who knew her strength. "I suspect if you can survive that, there's nothing this world can throw at you that you can't hit out of the park."

Rox sat down hard on the edge of the bed. When did her life become so complicated? She had just told Sam she chose him, and now he was gone. Possibly forever. The man she had come here to build a life with wanted nothing do with her any longer, which would suit her eldest daughter just fine. MJ would probably be so irrevocably scarred from this experience that any chance he had at a normal life was gone.

But Emma.

"No doctors," Rox said, as she returned to her feet.

Katherine held her breath like she was considering it as an option, but then shook her head. "You've no more clue about how your ability works than I do. You're a danger to yourself and everyone around – as you just so aptly proved."

"I'm doing just fine," Rox said, and took a step towards her.

"Hmph." Katherine placed her hands on her hips. She looked Rox in the eyes, and in that moment Rox understood how the woman was able to run a global organization that operated on the fringes of legality. "Imagine a woman who could call lightning and send out energy pulses more potent than a concussion grenade. A woman who could steal and give life at will."

Katherine took her own step closer, her finger pointed at Rox and her eyes locked in a challenge. "Right now, sweetheart, no one fears you because you don't know your true potential. Your kids will always be your weakness because you've proven again and again that there's no consequence to crossing you, to taking you off the shelf like you're nothing more than a commodity. You've had your flesh set on fire and your throat sliced open so wide your head was holding on by its tailbone." Katherine chuckled. "Hell, the only thing keeping me from putting you down is the fact that I'm the good guy. And your willingness to work with me."

Rox had never wanted to yank someone's life energy from them with such venom as she did at that moment, to wipe that smug look of superiority off Katherine's face. But the truth of her words held Rox back.

"Right now, you're the least valuable member on my team because you stink of fear." Katherine took a few deep breaths like she was attempting to calm herself. "You'll follow Mika's instructions. You'll save your two children and heal anyone who gets injured." She spun around and walked to the door, but stopped with her hand hovering just above the handle. "And try not to make anyone else disappear this time."

The door closed with a slam that could have easily been explained by well-oiled hinges, but Rox knew it for what it was: a wake-up call. Fresh tears of frustration and humiliation ran down her cheeks. She was tired of feeling so unsure of herself. She had been training everyday with Mika for the last ten months, and she still wasn't good enough to prevent her children from being taken. If it hadn't been for Sam, she could be waking up in one of Tusk's labs again. This time, right next to her children.

But Sam wasn't here to save her this time and Josh had his own son to protect. Besides, she was tired of everyone else saving her, of everyone having so much control over her life and what she did or where she went. First Josh, then Sam and Walter, and now Katherine. She was constantly trading one warden for the next.

Rox didn't like Katherine and trusted her even less. She wanted to believe that Meita cared about her more than a means to an end, but like Katherine said, Meita was two-sided.

As much as Rox craved a normal life, she was beginning to accept that wasn't possible. Not for her or her family. Maybe there was more to her power than healing. Maybe she could control energy. She had learned how to tap into the thunderstorm when they were at Watership Down. What if she could use it to not only heal herself and others, but somehow manipulate it to crack stone? What if she could pull the energy running between the walls and use it to incapacitate?

¿Amor, listo?

Yes, she was finally ready. Ready to get her children back and to live her life on her terms, and lightning was going to strike anyone who got in her way.

~

Survive

5th August, 2:35am (-1 SGT)
Gulf of Thailand

Ruby had been slammed on the mat more times than she could count. It was part of her training, learning how to fall. It was also part of her training to learn how to get back up. Quickly, efficiently, and ready to fight. But there was something wholly different from getting kicked by another kid in your weight class versus being struck by a full-grown adult. The lump on her cheek was not going down easily. Luckily, she was familiar with the pain and knew it would ease, but knowledge didn't stop it from hurting.

A computer screen clicked on somewhere in front of her, and Ruby could see for the first time since being shoved aboard. She had never seen a boat so narrow; it couldn't be more than five meters by two meters. At first, she thought the men were going to drown them, but one of them climbed in too. He tied their hands and knocked Ruby on the face when she wouldn't stop struggling.

Ruby could make out his profile in the screen's light. She didn't remember him being overly tall, but even he had to slouch as he typed something onto the keyboard. He was wearing earphones, the kind that fitted over the head, and he studied the screen for a long moment before he glanced over at her. He gave no indication that he could tell she was awake, and so she didn't move until he looked away.

MJ sat curled in her lap, silent like a cat lost in thought. He held onto her shirt like it was the only thing saving him from tipping overboard. She understood. He was ten and they had just been abducted.

Ruby's sensei always told her to let logic act as her guide through fear, but right now, she was struggling to think. Growing up in Singapore had necessitated that they become good swimmers, but open water was vastly different than a swimming pool. There were no sides to reach for and no bottom to bounce off. The waves would cast them about like flotsam, and she knew there was no way either of them would survive. And that was their goal. To survive.

The attack happened so fast, Ruby simply acted on training. She had never been more grateful for her judo lessons. There was a time when she had wanted to quit, but her mom asked her to give it a year. *Then see how you feel,* her mother had said. But then her mother had died, and Ruby continued the lessons simply because it was what her mother had wanted.

There was a point during the fight when Ruby thought she was going to win, but then she got attacked from behind. Four against one. Not impossible odds, but she realized the mistake in all her years of training: she had always known just how many people would be attacking her. She realized the element of surprise could overtake even the most skilled fighter.

She had no idea why anyone wanted to abduct her and MJ. Her father was famous for the company he created, but there were a lot more people with more wealth. Besides, things like this never happened in Singapore. Everyone knew there was too much surveillance, too many people invested in a peaceful and safe society for anyone to tolerate this kind of violence. This had something to do with Rox and the people who were there because of her.

Fear she didn't want to acknowledge gripped her when she thought back to the Fort Gate. Rox had been struck on the head with a blackjack. Her sensei had brought in a few to class one day and used them for training. Their small size made them easy to conceal, but their weight made them deadly. In the right hands, a blackjack could do far more damage than a handgun at close range.

Ruby had been impressed when she saw Rox get up after a blow to the back of the head. It gave her the boost of adrenaline she needed to keep fighting, but then she saw Rox being struck by lightning. She had never seen a light so bright, and she couldn't help but feel bad for the woman who had showed up out of the blue wanting desperately to be the mother they had all said goodbye to six years ago.

Ruby didn't like Rox. She made no attempt to keep it a secret. Having her show up with the same face but none of the memories was a trip through the past that Ruby wasn't interested in taking. It wasn't that she thought Rox was an imposter – that made no sense because there was very little for her to gain by pretending to be their mother. But building a relationship with her simply required more energy than Ruby was willing to invest in another person. It wasn't her job to help Rox remember the moments she forgot. They were getting on just fine without a mother. Why rock the boat?

But seeing Rox's body paralyzed by the lightning strike gave Ruby a moment to reflect on just how difficult it must have been for her to be driven by instinct, but no memories to help make sense of it. Ruby didn't want Rox dead, she just wanted her gone. She had a responsibility to her younger siblings simply by being the eldest. She couldn't fill her mother's shoes, but she was the one who was going to have to push them out into the real world. She didn't have the option of an international college education. She was going to have to go to university right there in Singapore because she couldn't leave until MJ left. That's what a mother would do, and in the absence of a mother, that's what the eldest sibling did.

Ruby doubted that Rox was alive anyway, which was a shame because it meant MJ and Emma had lost their mother a second time. Their pain would be inconsolable, but the best thing she could do for them would be to leave them to their grief. They would come out of it in their own time. Broken? Yes, but death did that. No one survived without a few cracks. There was never any going back. Forward was the only option. Or perhaps not moving at all.

Wasn't that what her father had done? Buried his head into his work like nothing else existed, leaving Marie to become the parent they needed, even when they didn't want her. Marie had given them stability and created as much normalcy as a domestic worker could under such circumstances. She was the one who dried MJ's tears in the middle of the night and had explained puberty to her. But she wouldn't be there forever. She had her own family to return to, and Marie was counting down the years when her son would be out of school and she wouldn't have any more tuition bills to pay, which meant she could finally go home. She would return to an empty nest, but she would have the satisfaction that she had created a world for him where he would never have to leave his children just to put food on the table.

Poor Marie. She would be beside herself with worry when she realized that MJ was missing. He was her favorite. She didn't mean to have one, but MJ had become a surrogate for her son. It would be her who noticed their absence first, which meant she would have to tell their father. Ruby didn't envy Marie that task, or Emma, who would be grilled about their whereabouts. If Emma were smart, she would keep her mouth shut, but she would talk. Ruby couldn't deny she was grateful that her sister would put concern for them above concern for the punishment she was sure to receive.

By the time their father got involved, she and MJ would be in some other country, high off drugs neither of them wanted but were fed nevertheless to keep them docile. She had read the stories and seen the movies about girls her age who went missing and boys the same age as MJ being sold to twisted old men who didn't care who they hurt or how many lives they ruined in pursuit of the next orgasm.

Ruby was a lot older than her father thought she was. Losing her mother did that. It aged her in a practical sort of way that Ruby believed a mother protected her children from. Ruby understood cause and effect, and that a desired outcome first required hard work. She possessed the mental maturity to remember to clean her room, but where her clothes lay had zero bearing on how she went about her day. It did not keep the lights on or food on the table or magically complete her homework. In fact, now that she thought about it, her messy room reflected her state of mind: complicated, busy, and stressed, yet functioning.

Ruby couldn't remember her exact age or the circumstance, but one time she had asked her mother what she should do if she were ever kidnapped. A dark look had settled on her mother's face and tears had filled her eyes as if her thoughts were preoccupied with something else. Ruby remembered thinking she had somehow annoyed her with that question.

By the time her mother responded, Ruby's mind had wandered on to another topic. At the time, the answer didn't make sense, but Ruby left it, not wanting to annoy her further. But now, with her head banging against the hull as the waves slammed into their boat, her brother huddled so close to her that she wished she could put him inside herself to keep him safe, did she understand where her mother's mind had gone and why her response had been a single, delayed word.

"MJ?" Ruby had to whisper his name twice to break through to wherever his mind had escaped.

"No matter what happens," Ruby said, her voice catching in very much the same way her mother's had. "No matter what happens, you have one job, understand?"

MJ's eyes looked glazed, like his mind was torn between remaining in the happy place he had created for himself and listening to his sister who existed in that place where pain, suffering, and fear were all around him.

"MJ, are you listening?"

He nodded.

"Repeat after me: my job is to survive."

He nodded, but didn't speak.

"Say it!"

Her tone broke through the haze and fresh tears poured down his cheeks. Pain replaced the fear that had encircled Ruby's heart, and she rested her forehead on his, her mother's hesitation becoming clear. "My job is to survive. Say it for me, okay?"

His voice was too small to be heard, but his lips moved to form the right word.

"Survive."

"Survive."

~

Subterfuge

5th August, 3:30am (-1 SGT)
Chiang Rai, Thailand

On a commercial airliner, the flight from Singapore's Changi Airport to Mae Fah Luang-Chiang Rai International Airport would take just over three hours, but when flying on a private carrier, it took half that time.

The fight to get Michael to remain at the hotel had almost turned physical. He didn't trust any of them, not even Rox, to bring his children back home safely. In the end, it was Emma who got him to see reason. She simply told him that she was scared and she needed him. It worked, but Michael made Rox promise she wouldn't return until she found them. It was an easy promise to make.

Before they left the hotel, Meita was able to reach one of her Thai contacts who made a few calls to find someone willing to check out the coordinates she had found on the Mockingbird file while Katherine made a few calls about satellite repositioning.

They were on the plane when Meita's contact phoned and told her the coordinates led to a warehouse, but there had been no activity, no sign of children or people anywhere. Rox's heart dropped, and she almost succumbed to the dangerous thoughts that tended to take flight in the absence of knowledge, but she regained control. Her children needed her thinking, not creating stories. Besides, Ruby would fight. She would hold on until they arrived. One did not contain all that built-up rage for nothing.

Rox looked out the window of the private jet and thought back to a similar night when the weather was equally unforgiving. It hadn't been a year since she jumped out of a helicopter in the middle of a storm, the wind swinging her rope over an ocean indifferent to her plight. She would end up dying that night, but not before she saved Sam's sister. And another woman, too, from room 203. Rox had to learn her name.

The wheels touched the tarmac with such ease she wasn't sure they had made contact with the ground. She would give anything to feel the soft fur of Shaira's coat. She laughed to herself at the thought of feeling more secure with a wolf at her side, but the animal had her back during a time when there was no one else for either of them to trust. How would Shaira feel if she knew Sam was missing? Rox was sure that leaving her behind wasn't easy for him, and she had to acknowledge her own disappointment at Shaira's absence.

The plane began to slow as it taxied to a private hangar away from the main terminal. Mika explained he had two guys waiting for them who would take the lead should they run into "resistance".

Rox assumed that was a euphemism for trouble of the physical nature. She had been training with Mika and was much better than in her Watership Down days, but she doubted her strength would ever lie in hand-to-hand combat. Mika must have realized that early on and that was why he taught her how to disarm, disable, and flee.

She walked down the steps of the plane as a light mist peppered her face. Rain seemed to follow her, but this time she wasn't sure if it was the beginning of a storm or its end. She reached out and kinetic energy flowed over her like it was returning home. It filled her up, repelling any fatigue that the early-morning hour induced. She lifted her hand toward Josh and felt it slip off her fingertips like water being redirected. She pushed more energy toward Mika and the two men who had gotten out of their cars to greet them. One of the engines was still running, and Rox leapt back when the rough edges of its energy scraped its way to her. It clawed up her side like it, too, wanted a domicile. She had never been able to draw from artificial energy, and its weighted, jagged power frightened her.

She took a deep breath to calm herself and the sky rumbled. The air smelled different. It lacked the raw humidity of Singapore and the dry heat of Crossroads. The fumes from burnt plastic floated on the breeze, and Rox turned to study the hangar to the right.

How many airplanes did it have hidden inside? Had MJ and Ruby come this way?

They said no one's been through here today who hasn't logged flight plans at least two days ago, Josh answered her thought.

There was no way Tusk could know he would be able to take her kids a couple of days ago, and she wasn't sure whether to feel relieved or frustrated.

Rox reached out with her energy again to feel for Sam. She didn't expect to feel his familiar pulse, but she was still disappointed when it didn't come.

On the flight, she went to sit by Mika so she could apologize. He told her it wasn't her fault, but she couldn't tell whether his words rang untrue or if it were her own guilt eating away at her.

She glanced over at him to study his profile, still surprised that he and Sam were brothers. They looked nothing alike. While Sam was a younger version of Walter, fair-skinned with a crooked smile, Mika was an inch taller and had broader shoulders. He worked out more, but like Sam, he too was lithe and light on his feet. He had more of his mother's Asian features, the darker hair that wasn't quite black to Sam's fading ginger. Perhaps when she closed her eyes and thought back to some of their training sessions, she could see the same crooked smile on Mika. The left side. It went up while the right remained unmoved.

Her breath caught at that image. She and Sam had only shared two brief kisses, but they were a promise of what was to come. Now she worried they would never have their date or their moments of discovery. Like so much of her life, nothing had gone to plan. She had searched for so long to find her identity, only to discover that half her family didn't want her and probably would have preferred it if she had remained dead to begin with. She was far from the mother she had envisioned being, but if she were honest with herself, she had no more of a clue what it meant to be a mother than she did when she first set out on this journey. Josh had told her to wing it, but how do you wing something so fragile and so devastatingly important?

Then there was Miles. Her heart hurt for him. He had to have been desperate to leave the security of Halo to come look for her. But why? Their interaction had been so brief, and they had been wholly preoccupied with escaping that there hadn't been time to discuss their abilities or life plans or anything other than surviving.

"If Miles is there," Rox said to Meita, interrupting her discussion with one of the women who had gotten out of the car. "We need to save him, too."

Meita nodded and returned to the map they were looking at.

"I'm serious."

"I know," Meita said, and led her a few steps away. "Miles knows about Halo, and we need to find out what he's told Tusk."

Rox was less concerned about what information he shared and far more focused with Miles' mental stability. Perhaps Meita didn't know what it was like to be tied to a chair or strapped to a bed for days on end, gaining consciousness only when someone wanted or only when the pain broke through all manner of sedatives. Rox couldn't leave anyone to suffer through that. She was still haunted by the nightmares. It was the main reason she was happy to remain in the guest cottage off the kitchen of Michael's house. She didn't want her family asking questions about her nightmares and the screams, or the light she couldn't turn off when the dark became too suffocating.

Miles was reliving the worst moments of his young life. Would he have given up hope by now? Was he wishing for death? Would Tusk be that merciful?

Josh's hand rested on her shoulder, and she waited for the peace that always settled when Sam touched her, but it never came. She felt comforted, but it wasn't the same. The *need* for Sam's touch was there, and nothing seemed to alleviate it. Sam had a way of quieting the energy's hum and of silencing those negative thoughts. She hadn't meant to fall for him. She had only meant to ask Halo for help. But then Walter presented her with a deal she couldn't resist. Then she died, and those energy pulses from Sam kept pulling on her until she couldn't ignore them. She had to touch him, and when she did it was like she had discovered where she belonged. Rox was still unsure how a simple touch could create such a safe haven. It defied logic. She was sure it also defied the laws of physics, but it was her reality. It was *their* reality, she reminded herself, because Sam felt the same way.

Mika came over to her with a backpack. He stooped down so that he could show her its contents. "You've got a water bottle, six protein bars—" he passed one to her, and she opened it to take a bite. "—here's a transmitter that's set to the correct frequency, but use your connection to Josh to communicate. This is for emergencies only." Then he took out two batons, their color matte black. "Sam and I decided you'd probably be better off with these than anything else."

They had just started weapons training, and while she had used them a few times with Mika, she was only skilled enough to take out an attacker who was equally inexperienced.

"Did he ask you to train me?" Rox asked. The fact that Sam and Mika had been conferring about her created a lot of questions.

She didn't think he was going to respond by the way he just looked at her, but then he nodded. "You were—you *are* special to him. That makes you special to me. Now, there's a torch in the side pouch, but again that's for emergencies."

"Mika—"

He shook his head and stood up. "Listen, right now we have an objective and it doesn't include Sam. You talking about my brother is a distraction, and if you want me to help you save your kids, then let's focus on them. I know how he feels about you ... I can *smell* how you feel about him, so I get that this is hard for you, for all of us, but

I don't blame you for what happened to him. I was the one who let him go. I was the one who couldn't hold on when he went racing to you. So if you have a need to blame someone, it's me." He passed her the pair of batons. They were about the length of her forearm. They weren't the retractable kind, instead they were one solid piece of metal that felt like they could crack concrete. "Test 'em."

She took them from him and held them as he had taught her. Her stance widened without thought and she twirled her wrists to get a feel for their weight. They weren't heavy despite the strength of the material, and she sliced with her dominant hand while keeping the other in the guard position.

"Relax your shoulders," he instructed. "Remember they're simply an extension of your arms. You've got to strike through your target or else you're only going to injure your wrists."

Rox nodded, and tried a few more times before she returned them to the bag. She had gained the attention of the men from the car, and one of them smiled at her, nodding his approval.

"Who are they?" she asked Mika.

He looked back over his shoulder. "The less you know the better, but one is Thai military, the other one is his acquaintance."

"Do they have names?"

"I'll do the talking, but if something goes sideways, the one in the cap is called Macc."

Meita joined them. "My contact has someone watching the warehouse, but no one's been seen coming or going.

Said a truck stopped there last evening, unloaded a crate, but she doubts it's a person. Said the crate was too small."

"What? You thinking supplies?" Mika asked.

Meita nodded. "Not much else it could be."

"Then they're not there?" Rox was almost too afraid to ask.

Meita sighed. "Look, to be honest with you, no. I don't think they're there, but I think finding out whatever that place is will help lead us to their true location."

Rox swallowed the cry lodged in her throat and lifted her head to the mist. Despite the darkness she could make out dawn on the horizon She wasn't sure how she knew it, but more rain was coming, and with it thunder and lightning.

"Tusk and his men are smart," Meita said softly. "They knew exactly how to get out of Singapore without drawing attention. It was never going to be a quick find. We were always going to have to go on the hunt."

"The men?" Rox had a sudden thought. "The ones who attacked me, did either of them say anything?"

"No." Mika said. "And they won't. Their families will be well compensated for their silence. They won't risk that, Rox."

Of course. Threaten a person's family and you've gained instant compliance.

"My uncle's reaching out through other channels. He'll let us know if anything involving two foreign children comes across their radar. He's sent out a photo of them; he's offering a separate reward. It's not just us out here looking for them."

We're going to find them.

She looked back at the car where Josh was waiting with Meita's contact.

"So what do you think we should do? Go to this warehouse and wait?" Rox asked. "You think they'll come through there?"

Meita shook her head. "No. I doubt they're flying, and if they are, they're staying far away from any international airports. I think they're heading to a facility."

"Then why are we wasting time going to the warehouse?"

Mika placed his hand on her arm, and she wished it was Sam standing beside her. "Because facilities need supplies. Our best bet is to follow the supply trucks."

Meita nodded. "You, Josh, and Mika will take point searching for the kids." She turned to Mika. "You think you can spare one of your guys?"

"They're at your disposal."

"Which one is the most people savvy?"

Mika looked back at his guys and gave it some thought. "Well, that depends. Are we dealing with men or women?"

Meita chuckled. "Most of my contacts near the facility will be women, mothers, but he can't cross the line with them."

"Alright, then you want the guy with the automatic on his back."

"Can we clean him up a bit?"

Mika looked confused. "Like a shower?"

She shook her head. "No, a trim would be nice, though. He's not going to persuade any woman to tell him anything with his hair looking like that."

Rox was too stunned to speak. Her children were missing and they were talking about personal grooming. As much as she wanted to tell them to focus, she realized she was in their world now. A world that was rapidly becoming her own, and she was clueless about how to operate in it. Her best option was to be silent and observe.

Meita motioned to her contact, and the woman jogged over to them. She switched to Thai as she spoke, and then turned back to Mika. "She's going to take him to her brothers, get him ready, and then she'll tell him what he has to do."

Mika nodded as Josh walked over to Rox and wrapped his arms around her. She had never been more grateful for him than now. *You're doing just fine.*

She didn't feel like it. She felt woefully out of her element, and the deeper she got, the more apparent it became. The last time she felt like this was when she was breaking into Watership Down to rescue Val, and that memory triggered her to reach out once more for Sam. She knew he wouldn't respond, but she would settle for a brush of fur around her legs … a low growl even.

"I don't think Shaira likes me," Josh said.

"Did she take a chunk out of your shoulder when she met you?"

Josh chuckled at her first memory of Shaira. "No. She kept her teeth to herself."

"Then you're practically best friends."

~

"When"ever

Date/Time & Location: Unknown

Sam awoke with a sudden jerk that sent pain racing down his side. Dampened daylight broke through the trees overhead and gave him his first good look at his surroundings.

He was definitely in a rainforest. Despite the sharp chill, humidity hung in the air like cobwebs. Rich, vibrantly colored plants sprouted around the base of trees that reminded him of the ones he had seen back in Yosemite Park when he was a boy camping with his father. Bushes and shrubs created pathways that led either deeper into the forest or, hopefully, out.

He tilted his head to the side and listened. The early morning called to him, and for a moment, he just inhaled the sweetness in the air. Shrills from birds he had only ever heard on TV filled the canopy above. His watch wasn't working, so he had no idea of the exact time, but he sensed it was about an hour after sunrise.

Sam had no recollection of falling asleep. He had followed behind the large creature for maybe an hour, but then he had to stop and rest. His boots protected his toes from the many roots and stones he stumbled over, but it was the throbbing of his ribs that had gotten the best of him. He had called out to the animal, and then simply sat down with his back against a tree. He must have fallen asleep straightaway because he couldn't remember anything afterward.

No matter where he was on the planet, one thing was constant, and that was the sun rising from the east, which made it possible for him to calculate north. He put his hands down to push to his feet, but was once again taken by the lushness of the grass. It was damp and thick, like green carpet with an insanely high density. He inhaled its fragrance and tried to identify the scent of the other smells, but everything seemed foreign.

A growl from the bushes just in front stilled him. The branches began to rustle as the head of the creature from last night broke through. With the benefit of daylight, Sam got a better look at the animal pacing before him. Its two curved fangs made him think of prehistoric times, but to be fair, he was no zoologist and he had only ever seen images of one animal with teeth like that, and regardless of *where* he was, that animal shouldn't still exist.

Then Sam's breath caught. He squinted to get a better look at it, trying to find something that would tell him he was wrong. His ability only allowed him to travel forward in time, yet ... He glanced back up at the trees overhead and the richness of the fauna around him.

Surely he hadn't traveled back. That made no sense. He went forward. And only by a few seconds at that.

But then again, he had been standing so close to Rox he could have sworn he actually touched her. Perhaps her ability combined with the lightning somehow impacted how his ability worked. Maybe, when he touched her, instead of moving forward in time, he actually moved backwards?

He didn't need to try to increase his heart rate because it was already beating at an apoplectic rate. He closed his eyes and attempted to slip through time, but nothing happened. His eyes flew open when the animal in front of him chuffed, like it was trying to communicate, but Sam ignored it and tried again to move forward, and again, nothing.

"No." He couldn't be stuck here. He wasn't sure *when* here was, but he needed to get back home.

He was in Singapore when Rox got struck, but nothing about his surroundings was reminiscent of Singapore. Not even one of its smaller, more rural islands like Pulau Ubin had animals like this. This creature was too big, easily one-and-a-half times the size of Shaira. It was an apex predator, which meant it would never be allowed to roam free in a place where humans frequented.

Wherever – or whenever – he had been sent was remote, and now the question was how to get back? Without his ability.

He took a slow step backwards. This couldn't be real. Perhaps he was hallucinating. Maybe he was suffering from a concussion. That made more sense. There was no way he was sent back in time. Surely that was impossible.

But wasn't it also impossible to slip *forward* through time?

Sam opened his mouth, but his mind was struggling to form words. He squeezed his eyes shut for a few seconds. He just needed to calm down. He was definitely *not* back in some prehistoric time. He was in a rainforest. He would find a river. Civilization always existed near a body of water. Water was essential to living. So he just needed to pick a direction.

He glanced back at the canopy. The sun was coming up on his right side, which meant that way was east. He'd head that way. East was as good a direction as any.

But when he looked back down, the creature was still in front of him. Staring. Calm, but ready to strike. Sam couldn't figure out why the animal didn't just attack him. Surely it could sense it was the stronger of the two. Perhaps it knew that Sam would fight back, but without a weapon, a well-placed jab would do little damage against one so muscled. Sam was tempted again to label it a tiger, but his stereotype of large cats were sleek and limber. This animal was stockier, and why was its tail so short? Didn't lions and tigers have longer tails?

The animal snorted, and then turned away. It walked around a tree, then between two bushes before it disappeared from sight. Sam shook his head in frustration. Of course. It was heading west.

A low-pitched moan sounded, and years of working with Shaira taught him that the animal was calling to him. He would have chuckled if he weren't lost. In a rainforest. Located somewhere or some*when* unfamiliar, with an animal he was sure didn't exist, or hadn't existed for a long time.

Sam was growing more and more fond of the idea of hallucinating. In some odd way, it seemed to make more sense. He was injured, wet and had spent the night exposed to the elements. Maybe he had a fever. Or maybe the creature hadn't attacked because it wasn't real. Maybe this entire rainforest was nothing more than a figment of his imagination. The trees and the rain were physical metaphors that represented being lost. He was more than likely lying in some hospital, attached to different machines keeping him alive until he was well enough to awaken.

In fact, Sam stopped following the creature and turned his head to the side so that his ears were facing front. He listened for the steady beep and whirls of a hospital room. What he heard instead confused him. Then recognition filled him.

"Water," he said as he grabbed his ribs and hurried after the animal again.

He pushed low lying branches and leaves the size of pillows out of his path. The ground began to change from lush green to thinner blades of grass that gave way to stones and dirt, and finally water.

It was far too small to be a river, more like a brook, but Sam was thirsty. So thirsty he didn't stop to check his surroundings and ran right to the edge. He scooped a few handfuls into his mouth before he leaned forward and drank straight from the source.

It was cold and tasted like the air, light and sweet. Drinking reminded him he hadn't eaten in a while. He'd have to find some sustenance soon. He knew how to build a fire, so perhaps he would catch fish.

For a moment, he let his thoughts wonder about what it would mean if he had been transported back to some prehistoric time. What if he never got back? What if everyone thought he was dead?

Sam shook his head. Neither Mika nor Walter would accept his death without a body, just like he wouldn't accept theirs without one. No, they'd look for him until they found one. But how would they know to look in a rainforest? And even if they miraculously knew to look in such a remote location, he wasn't sure he was in the right "when" for them to find him.

He thought of Rox and wondered if she would know how to find him. But she didn't know about his ability. He had never shared it with her. There had never been the time to discuss anything more than survival with her. From the moment she trespassed on their property, it had been one thing after another. He had seen her die three times now, and each one of them had been his fault. But he had never witnessed anything like what he saw last night. Or had it been longer than that? How long had he been missing?

Sam squeezed his eyes shut from the memory and sat back against a tree along the water's edge. He let out a hiss when something sharp poked through the thin fabric of his shirt. He spun around and noticed the tree had spikes sticking out of the bark that looked like needles.

What kind of tree had needles sticking out of it? What purpose could that serve?

He leaned in closer to get a better look when the animal growled from behind him. He turned around, but all of a sudden there were two of them. Sam shook his head in confusion.

Two?

He opened his mouth, but it was dry and heavy, which seemed odd given he had just drank. He glanced back at the brook, but it took him a few seconds to make it out.

Sam struggled to his feet and realized he had been poisoned. It took him several tries before he was able to glance over his shoulder and discover he had three spikes sticking out. His arms felt like weights were attached to them as he tried to reach around and pull them out.

His knees gave out and he fell to the rocky bank. His stomach rolled like it was trying to purge something, and then all the water he just drank came rushing back up. With his stomach empty, he thought he was alright, but then his fingers began to curl, like someone had grabbed his fists and were squeezing them close.

Sam struggled to his feet again only to find himself back down on the stones moments later. He'd forgotten about the pain in his ribs because it seemed to be spreading. Now it was in his stomach, his knees, the back of his neck. It alternated between a sharp, shooting pain, and a slow burn, like he was lying too close to an open flame.

He attempted to lift his head to look at the creature, but the muscles along his spine seemed to be atrophying, drawing his body smaller and in onto itself.

He opened his mouth to scream, but all of a sudden he couldn't inhale. Panic set in as he struggled to take his next breath.

The last thing Sam remembered were the curved teeth of the animal lying down beside him.

CHAPTER TEN

~

Youth

5th August, 3:33am
Pak Tha, Laos

"I thought you might still be up," Leona said as she entered his office.

"What time is it?" Tusk looked up from his laptop.

"Late. Early." Leona shrugged. "Listen, I think I got something."

Tusk rubbed his eyes to help them make the adjustment from the brightness of the screen. "Good, because I've got nothing. I thought I located all the genetic markers that gave her her abilities, but when I run the simulation to turn them off, the result is she's left in a vegetative state." Tusk raised his arms over his head into a deep stretch. He'd lost track of how long he had been in front of the computer. "There're just too many variations, and without finding them all … "

"Who you talking about? Dream Weaver?" Leona asked.

"Yes. And I prefer not to create playful nicknames for my patients." He had told her that before. Once they were in his care, it was important they maintained a degree of objectivity, and humans were notorious for naming things and then developing an attachment that could later jeopardize the initial objectives.

She rolled her eyes. "We can't call them all 'patient'. How will we know who we're talking about? I actually like the name Dream Weaver, or—"

"No!" Tusk had been forced to have this same discussion with Harry. Names such as those romanticized his work and was an insult to what he was trying to achieve. "We give them numbers or we refer to them by their specific ability. Use context. It's simple enough to know who I'm speaking of by exercising elementary listening skills."

"Fine!"

Leona tossed her tablet onto his desk and the sound of two metals colliding startled him. Tusk looked at the device with curiosity. It was unlike anything he had ever seen. Its casing was thick, easily about one-and-a-half inches, though its length was only about the distance from his wrist to the tips of his fingers. He picked it up, surprised by its weight. While most of technology had gone smaller and lighter, whoever designed this was more concerned with function than aesthetics. It was clean with rounded angles so as not to aggravate the skin when holding it by the edges, but it was heavy, like the piece of tech inside was robust and wouldn't break with the slightest fumble.

"What is this?"

She shrugged. "A new design one of my friends is making. I said I'd test it out for him."

Had she lost her mind? "Is this connected to the network?"

"Relax." She said putting her hand on her hip. "Not only is he a friend, but he's also legit. I checked it myself."

"Oh, good to know your skills now encompass operating systems, malware, and viral detection?"

"Don't be an ass. Look, I think I found something. You wanna hear it or not?"

"Yes. As soon as you disconnect this from our network and have it forget our settings." He knew if her friend had malicious intent, it was already too late. Disabling it would achieve nothing. But he needed her to understand the work they were doing here was not only secretive, but also highly illegal. Their funding may come from black-book government accounts or appear on the balance sheets of organizations under the expense column for R&D, but no one would ever acknowledge their involvement. Industries could be ruined. Economies could falter, and no one cast blame like a person who was in danger of losing his money, or his status.

Leona snatched the tablet out of his hand and disabled the network connection. Then she rebooted it and typed in her passcode. She tapped the screen, and an image projected upwards, about thirty inches from the actual tablet itself. She tapped an icon he couldn't make out, and the image rotated and zoomed out, but retained its resolution.

Hmph. A holograph. He hadn't been anticipating that.

Tusk leaned forward and ran his fingers through the image. He didn't feel anything – he wasn't expecting to – but the moment his fingers broke the plane, the image vanished.

"Oh, so now you're curious," Leona drawled.

"Well, of course I'm curious. But we can't just go around trusting people on their face value." He was back to thinking she was too inexperienced for this kind of work.

"Would you trust him if I told you I am funding his research and this very prototype? Would he somehow be more trustworthy if I told you that if he betrays me, I've got contingencies in place to ensure he's brought up on charges of sexual misconduct, child pornography, and treason?"

Yes, the needle would swing more towards trustworthy under such a scenario. "Treason seems a bit of an overkill, though."

"It is. The charges would never stick, but the sexual misconduct and child pornography are enough to ruin his life and embark him on a new career in custodial management."

Tusk chuckled. "What did you have to show me?"

She tapped the screen again and an image of a woman appeared. "So, I had a look at everyone who entered Singapore twelve hours before and after that Major Sam dude and Josh Mendez. And everyone checks out—"

"What do you mean 'everyone checks out'?"

"If you don't interrupt, you'll soon find out." She rolled her eyes again. "So, taking out all nationals and residents, everyone coming in is on business trips, holidays – I've got a few backpackers, a handful of guys transiting on their way to Thailand, and a family that recently won the Euro lottery and are on an impromptu visit to Singapore – but my point is their trips were planned in advance so it's an easy trail to follow."

Tusk nodded like he understood, but he didn't.

"But this woman? She didn't win the lottery. She doesn't work for any of the international corporations with offices in Singapore, and she didn't continue on to another destination – not by legal means anyway – and what's even more interesting is that her passport was not entered into the central database for hotel registrations by *any* hotel, upmarket or the backpacker type."

"She could be staying with a friend," Tusk offered, and Leona sucked in an exaggerated breath.

"OK, old man, not sure what I need to do to prove this isn't my first attempt at illegal surveillance, but I'm done trying. Listen. I've checked all possibilities, and the most likely scenario is she's here with that Sam and Josh."

"Let me see."

Leona placed her thumb, fore- and middle finger on the screen and then widened them like she was attempting to stretch a rubber band into the shape of a triangle. The image enlarged, and then she threw her hand up just a few inches to the right of the screen, and the image followed. The picture was far from high res like the previous one, but it was enough to work with.

"I've sent it to a few people I know who can get access to government databases," Leona said, "but so far, they've got nothing."

This was good. Well, it was potentially good. Especially since they knew that Katherine – Harry's replacement

– was also in Singapore. "Did she come before or after Ms Cheung?"

It took a moment for Leona to realize where he was going with that question, but then a broad smile crossed her face. "Before. Why? You thinking she's with GFO?"

Yes, he was thinking that, but without evidence, it was merely a hypothesis. "Send me that image. I'll ask Harry. Maybe he'll recognize her."

"Really?" Leona shook her head in what appeared to be disbelief.

"Yes." Tusk was confounded. "What's so hard to believe about that?"

"Can't send you much of anything now, can I? You know, since you had me disconnect from the network, and I assumed that included turning off bluetooth."

He missed the hell out of Nancy. No backchat, she had more than a modicum of common sense, and she didn't take everything so goddamn literally. He realized that was his problem with young people: they hadn't yet learned how to read between the lines. He was forever wasting his time explaining things, helping them connect the dots.

But Leona had money, and she hadn't been as ineffective as he had initially thought she would be. If it weren't for her, they would have never been able to get hold of Tara's children, which also meant they would have never been this close to getting Tara back. One thing he was certain of, he would even go so far as to bet his entire career on, and that was Tara coming for her children. That motherhood drive was woven into the fabric of their cells much more finitely written than any genetic marker. And it didn't require the act of childbirth. Tara didn't even have her memories, and yet she was still drawn to them.

Tusk had learned from his mistakes, though. He wasn't trading them for her. He was going to get her *and* her children.

"Er, you still want me to send this?"

He had momentarily forgotten Leona was there, and so he nodded.

"How?" she asked

"Figure it out!" What he wouldn't give to be able to resurrect the dead.

~

Spirit House

5th August, 5:34am (-1 SGT)
Wiang Kaen Province, Chiang Rai, Thailand

The scent of burning incense was the first thing Meita noticed when she got out of the car. She located the san phra phum, or spirit house, in the front yard. It was in the corner, far enough from the house as never to be in its shadow regardless of the positioning of the sun. It was mounted upon a dais reaching about chest height and was reminiscent of a miniature-sized Thai temple carved out of auspicious wood and painted a deep, strawberry red. It was strung with marigold garland, and its intricately carved roof, gold trimmed pillars, and elaborate altar were well kept. Inside were the incense sticks she smelled, a bowl of cooked rice, another of mandarin oranges, and a bottle of red Fanta. Meita assumed the burning sticks meant that a recent offering was given, probably for added protection against their arrival.

That only furthered her feelings of unease.

The door opened just as she was about to knock, and a woman slightly shorter stepped back to allow entry. "เชิญค่ะ," she said to Meita.

Meita placed her palms together and gave a slight bow as she returned the standard greeting. She removed her boots with the ease of someone accustomed to slipping out of their shoes before stepping inside someone's home. Rox was sitting at a small table, her leg bouncing in an unconscious way to release stress. She appeared to be holding up well, considering the circumstances. She looked better, too. Mika's training regimen had taken a few inches off her waist and added them to her biceps and quads. She would never be a fighter; Rox had simply started too late for that, but she had learned to hold her own, and with continued practice, she would only get better.

Josh was seated next to her, and neither of them noticed she had entered. They were doing that thing where they didn't use words to speak, and Meita wondered what it would be like to have her mind read or feel a wave of healing energy. Her ability prevented any of that. Instead, she was able to identify evolved ones. She could tell just by looking at them. It wasn't a tingling feeling or a sense of dread, it was simply a certainty that she was staring at an evolved human. There was no way for her to know their ability just by looking at them, but there was also no way for them to use it against her.

She was the great equalizer.

The benefit of her ability was that Josh couldn't invade her thoughts, which had been a good thing given the true purpose of their initial meeting, but the obvious detriment was she didn't have a safety net. If she got injured, Rox couldn't heal her. Meita tried to remind herself that wasn't anything new; after all, she had just met the woman ten months ago, but still ... knowledge changed things.

The fragrance of a fresh pot of noodles being served up filled the small two-bedroom bungalow. The only light came from a single exposed bulb overhead, but its glare was bright and strong. Josh and Rox were seated around the dining table working on their second servings.

Meita's stomach let out a growl, but she ignored it as she tried to work out why she didn't feel entirely good about their situation. Her contact who met them at the airport had taken Mika's guy to help him look more attractive. After they had finished cleaning up his appearance, Meita gave him almost all of her cash, keys to a car, and instructed him to visit as many of the local bars that were still open, and any restaurants and shops later on in the day to see what he could uncover about the warehouse.

Meita leaned back against the wall as the lady who opened the door disappeared into the kitchen. She was fairly certain they weren't going to find the kids at the warehouse. As much as she hated herself for it, finding the children was a secondary objective – a close second, but second nonetheless.

GFO efforts had been largely focused on North American facilities because Katherine was simply unsure of who to trust. While Meita had a few operators on the lookout in Asia and North Africa, the reality was without her continued presence and attention, it was always going to boil down to luck finding one of Tusk's facilities in this hemisphere. But they had gotten lucky, and now she had to do what she could to locate it.

Katherine had tasked Meita with monitoring Rox's field activity: could she hold up under pressure, did she have physical prowess, and how well she followed instructions. Katherine wasn't looking for an excuse to terminate Rox *per se*, but they needed to keep their options open. Neither she nor Katherine could get a read on whether Rox truly intended to hold up her end of the bargain to work with them.

Meita's problem was that she understood Rox's position. Rox hadn't asked for any of this. Not everyone was cut out for this lifestyle and not everyone wanted it. All Rox wanted was to find her family, but with an ability as powerful as hers, she was never going to be left alone. What government could walk away from such an asset? Which scientist wouldn't want to unlock the key to immortality, because if Rox could indeed heal herself and hadn't aged since her abilities began, wasn't that the definition of eternal life?

If Meita hadn't been doing this job for as long as she had, she might have let some of her emotions leak onto her face. But she had learned a long time ago to keep her thoughts in her mind and off her expression.

She was on the fence about Rox, in truth. The woman had grit. She had rescued Val and 203 – Su Kim – from

Watership Down. Then she had gone back for Sam and Walter at great cost to herself, which showed she had a moral compass. But the feelings she and Sam had for one another complicated things. It would be easier to get Michael on board if Rox and he were still together. Michael had an aptitude for programming and networks that only needed fine-tuning, and then he would be a fabulous asset to GFO. The good news was his daughter was an EO, so he was forced to be a part of this world even if he didn't want it. Meita just needed to find out if he could work with them knowing that his wife – soon-to-be ex-wife – was romantically involved with their field lead.

Meita caught herself before her sigh escaped. She didn't even want to think about Sam right now. The fact that he had literally passed through some kind of portal was astounding. The drone footage had answered one question she and Katherine had about his ability, and that was how it *didn't* work. It wasn't linked to speed, but more about jumping into another plane of existence for a few seconds. But where did he go? And if he were there now, wherever *there* was, what state was he in? Meita's instincts were telling her he had been gone much longer than he should have been.

She had developed a soft spot for Sam and Josh. They had worked on two assignments since they joined ten months ago. They were both honorable men, trying to make the world a little more fair for EOs, each with their own strategy until Katherine pulled them together. Once they got used to one another, they would all make a fantastic team; but even then, they would still be far from perfect.

Sam was too old and at the end of his prime. The best they could hope for was that he would train someone younger to take over. Josh lacked the training and expertise that would make him the obvious replacement, but sadly, by the time he got that experience, it would be too late for him and he would be just like Sam.

Neither Sam nor Josh trusted her, but she was alright with that. She didn't need their trust. They were the type of men whose trust was earned, and she knew only time could resolve that.

Meita stifled a yawn. She had been up approaching twenty-four hours, and she wondered how Josh and Mika were doing. Aside from the dark circles under Rox's eyes that had to be signs of stress, Meita wondered if Rox was tired given she had recently woken up, or perhaps "un-died" would be more accurate.

Meita pushed off the wall and was about to join them when a chill ran down her spine. She took a step thinking it was a lack of sleep, but stopped. Something felt wrong, and she hadn't survived as long as she had by ignoring her instincts. For the first time since arriving, she slowed her mind to analyze everything she saw.

The house was nice, just like all the houses that bordered the perimeter of the warehouse. It had a large blue plastic tank at the back that gave the family most, if not all, of its running water. Its floors were tiled as opposed to concrete or earth, and the cinder block walls were painted a pale baby blue and held family photos and a picture of the king. While this type of home was far from uncommon in Thailand, it was more surprising given their distance from the center of Chiang Rai or an equally large employment hub.

Mika came up beside her, and Meita had to admit she hadn't noticed him when she walked in. He inhaled deeply, like he was trying to identify an unrecognizable scent. "Something's off."

She nodded, something was off. People with steady jobs wanted to move closer to their place of work, that made sense. But where were the jobs funding these homes? Her contact said the warehouse only received a few shipments every couple of months, but mostly remained dormant. How does a warehouse that remains largely inactive keep an entire neighborhood in such good condition? There were at least ten families on this side alone. And weren't there two cars in front of the house next door? One on the lawn and another out front.

"Any thoughts?" he asked.

She had a few. A wealthy family member might explain the quality of a house or two, but to have an entire area like this with houses outside of the socio-economic bracket of its peers was alarming.

"Seen the other houses that border this neighborhood?" she asked.

Mika nodded. "Macc drove us around the area for a bit to make sure we weren't followed before he took off."

"Where are these people getting their money from?" It was a rhetorical question because she had her own thoughts. She had seen this before in other parts of the world, and she didn't like the conclusions her mind was drawing.

"They must have supplemental income," she whispered.

Mika inhaled deeply, letting the implications sink in. "Warehouse," he said between clenched teeth.

People were paid to keep their mouths shut. Meita slowly turned back to where Josh and Rox were eating. Josh had dropped his spoon and it took him three tries to pick it up.

The woman came over with two plates of noodles and offered Mika one first. It would be the height of rudeness to reject, and Meita's stomach let out an audible growl, but she had a feeling if she ate those noodles, she might not wake up.

They both accepted their plates, and Mika leaned forward and inhaled. He dropped it to the floor, and that was the only signal she needed. Meita drove the heel of her hand up into the woman's nose. Blood sprayed out, but Meita had her gun out from the back of her trousers before the woman completed her fall backwards.

To her credit, Meita thought, the woman didn't scream. Josh and Rox heard the commotion, but only Rox managed to get to her feet. She swayed like she was about to tumble forward, but then righted herself. Josh was slumped over, his face not quite in his plate, but close enough to indicate something was very wrong with them.

"What's happening?" Rox asked, her mouth sounding dry.

"Poison," Mika said as he came around the table and disappeared into the kitchen. There was an interrupted wail, a loud bang, and then the cook was being hauled out by the back of his shirt. Mika brought him over to where his wife was sitting on her backside still too stunned to realize how she wound up on the floor. Mika kicked the man's shin. It made a sickening pop and he fell down in a fit of screams.

Rox inhaled sharply, and Meita realized she was probably trying to stop herself from healing him. Rox tilted her head to the side and stared off like she was searching for something not visible to anyone else. Thunder rumbled across the sky and the single filament bulb overhead flickered. Meita took a step back and motioned for the woman to get on her knees. When she didn't, Meita released the safety.

"Rox?" Meita called.

"I got it," she said, as if the two of them were finally on the same page.

Rox's eyes slipped closed. At first, she stood rigid, but then slowly her muscles began to relax. Her body swayed like it had just a few moments ago, but again she remained upright. Her arms lifted, one slightly higher than the other, and it made Meita think she was drawing energy from somewhere with one hand and releasing it with the other.

Lightning flashed so strong it brightened the house's interior. Its clash was much closer than anything Meita had ever heard. Josh's head slowly lifted. His body rocked forward a few times, and then everything he had eaten came roaring back out. The color that had drained from his face finally returned.

"I'm under instructions to follow your lead on this," Mika said. "So you wanna kill 'em or what?"

Meita shook her head. "Not yet. I wanna make sure she heals Josh first."

Meita took her attention off Rox for a moment and looked at the woman. "Who told you to poison us?"

The woman pressed her lips sealed.

If that's how she wanted to play this, Meita was game. She reached into her jacket pocket and pulled out a cylinder she began to twist on the muzzle of her weapon.

The woman's eyes grew wide and she opened her mouth as if contemplating whether to say something, but Meita had to prove a point. Most people don't actually follow through with their threats because the overwhelming majority of people use them as a deterrent. There are only a handful of circumstances that would drive someone to actually harm another. The human body physically reacts to the sound of another person in pain. Firstly, with fear, but then humans are hardwired to help, even if it comes in the form of running away to get the help. It takes practice and a certain kind of individual to listen to someone scream in agony for more than a few seconds. It grates at the nerve endings and empties the bowels. It etches itself into the memory, refusing to be exorcised.

But this family was protecting something – more than likely someone. The fact that this woman had been struck *and* had a gun pulled on her, not to mention having her husband's knee dislocated, yet she still chose to keep quiet meant she was more afraid of whoever she was protecting than of Meita, and Meita needed to change that.

The sound of the bullet exiting the chamber was like a

poof of air, the kind you hear when you're having an eye exam. The woman's screams were much louder.

"Meita?" Rox said, her concentration broken.

"Keep healing," Meita said, without taking her attention from the woman who was now lying on her back, clutching her shoulder.

The woman began to plead for her life in rapid Thai, but Meita silenced her by lifting her finger to her lips and mouthing *shh*. Tears slipped down the woman's face and into the back of her hair.

"Who told you to poison us?" Meita asked again.

The woman shook her head. "Please, I have children." As if on cue, two small heads poked out from behind one of the closed doors. They looked to be no older than five or six, but it was hard to tell.

Meita looked at Mika, who only returned her stare, his face giving away no indication of how he felt. Josh managed to get to his feet as he understood what she was about to do. "Meita, you don't have to—" he said, but she tuned him out.

There were moments when Meita hated her job, when her desires had become irrelevant to the greater good. She lifted the gun and pointed it a few millimeters to the left of where the two innocent little heads stuck out. She pulled the trigger twice, piercing two holes into the cinder block and casting its dust and shards into the air.

"No!" the woman screamed, and tried to get up, but Meita pushed her back down. The door slammed shut, and Meita silently prayed for forgiveness as she returned her attention to the woman.

"Who told you to poison us?"

It came out in a mix of Thai and broken English, and Meita had to ask her to repeat it more than once. The stench of consumed food and poison filled the air, but Meita had survived worse.

"So what'd ya wanna do now?" Mika asked.

"I say we pretend like they got us. See who comes to help them get rid of the bodies," Meita said.

"No," the woman shrieked. "No, please. My children."

Josh was surprisingly steady on his feet as he bent down in front of the woman. "You're not the only one with children. We have children, too, and we're trying to get them back."

"Oh, I didn't know!" The woman's face turned sweet with a smile. "I can help you. Tell me, what do they look like?"

Rox moved forward like she was about to provide a description, but Meita shook her head. "She's just trying to save her own skin. You heard her, she doesn't know much. I doubt any of them know anything. They're just getting paid to call a number if anyone comes around asking questions about the warehouse."

Meita kneeled down beside the man. He tried to turn away from the gun she held at the side of his head, the tip of its barrel disappearing beneath the length of his hair. Meita spoke to the wife. "Call whoever is supposed to help you get rid of our bodies. You say anything that might make me think you're trying to warn them, and your husband pays the price."

The woman nodded. Meita almost turned away from the stark fear in the woman's eyes, but she knew if she did, she would lose all the ground she had just gained. Sometimes the only way to show people you were serious was to be serious.

Mika dialed the number and held it to the woman's ear. The conversation was brief, but whoever was coming to alleviate this family of their bodies would arrive in fifteen minutes.

Josh had found a piece of rope, and had tied up the couple with their backs facing one another. The husband moaned quietly through his pain while his wife screamed complaints about her nose and her shoulder, but no one gave either of them an ounce of sympathy.

Rox carefully opened the bedroom door and began to speak to the children in a slow and steady voice. Meita wasn't sure if the kids spoke English, but Rox's demeanor was enough to convey they weren't going to be harmed. She invited them to sit with their parents, but Mika stopped her before Meita could.

At first, Rox appeared like she wanted to protest, but then a hard look settled on her face and she nodded like she understood.

Lightning crashed across the sky, drawing everyone's attention, except Rox's. She kept her eyes focused on the couple tied together on the tiled floor in between their two-seater sofa and the TV. The hair on the nape of Meita's neck rose as the man who had been moaning began to gasp, like he wasn't able to get enough oxygen.

Meita had witnessed this once before, back at the safe house when she had brought Katherine over to meet Rox. It hadn't gone well, but then again, in hindsight it had gone as well as to be expected. But Meita remembered the electrical charge in the air when Rox drew someone's energy from them. It was a frightening thing to witness, but impossible to turn away from.

"Rox." Josh spoke her name softly, like he didn't want to startle her for fear of what she might do. He called her twice more before he broke through, and she released the hold she had on the man's life.

Rox pushed past Josh and Mika and leaned down next to the couple. Meita wasn't sure if Rox had meant to whisper it or if she wanted them all to hear, but the charge in her words drew everyone's attention.

"Anything happens to my children because of what you have done to us, I'll wipe out all of you." It wasn't the words that unsettled Meita. It was the way she rose, the way she held up her fingers and snapped. The bulb overhead blew just as lightning flashed. Shards of glass rained down over the couple, and they screamed, but no one heard them over the thunder.

~

Siblings

5th August, 5:38am (-1 SGT)
Luang Prabang airspace, Laos

Ruby's Chinese marks were always "barely passing" or "just failing". It wasn't that she couldn't speak Mandarin, it was just that she couldn't speak it like it was her mother tongue. Schools in Singapore required all its citizens to be bilingual, and even though Ruby was a permanent resident and not a citizen, the rule still applied to her. It applied to Emma and MJ as well, and no matter how many times her pride hurt when she fumbled through a presentation or an oral exam, she had never been more grateful to know Chinese. The pilot on their small plane spoke to their kidnappers in Mandarin before they took off, and she understood it all.

When they landed, they were going to be taken to the safehouse where one of the men would catch up with his brother who had a job for him. Then later on, they would be taken up the Mekong to Pak Tha by speed boat. Some kind of facility was located there, and instinct was telling Ruby that if these men got them there, there would be no chance again for escape.

MJ squirmed in his seat as the plane dipped. Ruby's ears popped, but she wasn't sure if it had anything to do with the altitude or if it were her eardrums threatening to burst from the twin propeller engines roaring just outside their window.

She shook her brother awake, and he looked up like everything was normal, until he noticed their surroundings. It broke her heart the way he shut down.

"Who's your favorite superhero?"

He hadn't heard her over the engines, so she leaned in closer and asked him again.

He stomped his foot on the floor and threw his back against the seat in frustration. He banged his head on the side of the plane and kicked out like he was trying to run whilst sitting down.

"Stop that!" she screamed. She didn't want to be here anymore than he did. She was trying to develop an escape plan, and a temper tantrum was the last thing she needed. She tried to get hold of him, but she couldn't get the right kind of leverage because of the damn restraints.

He suddenly stilled and his eyes grew much too large for it to be a part of his meltdown, so Ruby looked over her shoulder.

One of the men who had taken them was crouched beside them. "Tell him not to do that again."

Ruby had never actually hated anyone before. She had never wished for anyone's death or for anything ill to happen to someone, not even Rox when she showed up trying to replace their mother. Yes, she had wanted Rox gone in no uncertain terms, but Ruby supposed now that she knew what true hatred felt like, she didn't wish Rox dead, just somewhere else. But the man leaning so close that his arm brushed against her knee? Him, she would kill if given the chance.

MJ stamped his foot again and started to throw himself around the small seat. The plane bucked with the sudden shift of force and weight. The man reached over and tried to grab him, but Ruby used her entire body to push him away before he could make contact.

"You touch my brother and I will kill you." She would never be sure if it was the bass in her voice or the determination in her eyes, but he snorted and returned to his seat near the pilot.

Ruby spun around and pulled MJ in her arms as best as she could with her hands still tied. She rocked him and told him it was going to be OK and that he had to be still now. She reminded him of his single objective, and that they were both going to survive this.

"Emma's going to be so jealous when she finds out that we're going to Luang Prabang," Ruby said. "Remember it's on our family list of places to go."

MJ stopped thrashing about but continued to rock. This was too much for him and there was nothing she could do to get him out of it.

"I want to go home," he said.

Tears ran down her face as she thought about her father. He would know they were missing by now. Either Marie would have discovered them gone or Emma might have confessed. Perhaps someone found Rox's dead body. She doubted any of her friends would have dared to call 999. Maybe no one had noticed she and MJ were gone yet and they were truly on their own.

The sky was brightening, and Ruby could see dawn on the horizon. She should have never brought MJ along with her, but he said he was going to tell if she didn't, and all Ruby had cared about was seeing Lukas. He was the only one who had been in her corner throughout these last ten months; the only one who believed her when she said that Rox wasn't her mother. Just last week they had decided to become exclusive. He had asked her out on a date, and although she hadn't told her father yet, she and Lukas had met at Fort Canning to discuss where they were going to go.

A small hand reached up to wipe away her tears, and that made them fall faster. Their hug was awkward given both their hands were tied, but that somehow made it more comforting. She had to get them out of this. It would have to wait until they landed because there wasn't much escaping they could do on an airplane.

"We're going to be OK, aren't we, Ruby?"

For a long moment, she did nothing more than hold her breath. The truth was, she didn't know. She couldn't know. Was he old enough for the truth? Ruby found herself nodding even though she couldn't back it up with words.

"I'm ready to be brave now." He had to shout to be heard. "What's our plan?"

"Well …" She didn't have one. "When I say run, you have to run. Even if I can't come just yet."

He shook his head. "I won't leave you."

More tears fell, but she put on a smile anyway. "Who's going to call Dad and tell him where we are if at least one of us doesn't get away?"

She could tell he was thinking about that, and that was good. This was the first time he had shown any emotion other than fear since they were shoved in the bottom of the first boat back in Singapore.

"But where do I go? Who do I ask for help?"

Ruby wished she was her mother. She always had answers for things. The truth was, Ruby didn't know where to tell him to go or who to trust. What if they landed in a town filled with evil people like the ones who took them?

"You'll just have to use your judgment, buddy. Look for a police officer and if you can't find one, then look for a kind face." What kind of advice was that? A kind face? "I'm sorry, I just—"

"Good idea. Didn't Emma say she could see the truth by looking at someone's eyes?"

Ruby nodded. She didn't remember Emma ever saying such a thing, but now was not the time to argue.

"I won't leave you unless I have to," he said.

She wouldn't ask him to unless she could find no other way. She didn't like the idea of him being out there on his own. He was just ten, and ten seemed so young to her all of a sudden. "Hey, anytime you want to come sleep in my room when this is over, you just come climb in my bed, okay?" Guilt gnawed at her for all those nights when he awoke from a bad dream and only wanted to sleep with her, but she had turned him away. "I'm so sorry, MJ. I'm so sorry I haven't been a good big sister."

A smile much too bright given their situation flashed across his face. "I'd much rather be stuck in this situation with you. Emma can't even fight."

She burst out laughing at his honesty. Yeah, Emma was more of a pacifist, but she had her strengths. For one, Emma was a good kid and wouldn't have snuck out of the house and brought her younger brother with her. She also knew how to read a situation; she knew just what to say to make someone feel better or how to rip the rug out from under their feet. Emma's strength wasn't physical, it was her wit, her selflessness, and her quiet determination.

Ruby wanted to see her sister again. She wanted to apologize for all the times she had taken advantage of her or bullied her into giving in. She remembered her mother saying to her that Emma only wanted to be like her big sister. Well, not anymore. Now, they mostly fought, kept to their separate rooms and spoke to their separate groups of friends. Her mother had once said that when she was dead and gone, all they would have would be each other. She remembered Emma bawling at the notion of her mother dying, and that had annoyed Ruby, which made her call her little sister stupid.

"I'm glad Emma's safe," she told MJ, and he nodded in agreement.

"I think we're the tough ones, Rubes, and that's why we were taken." His eyes widened much like they had earlier, and she glanced over her shoulder to see if anyone was standing there. "Mom! Remember she was there, too? What do you think happened to her?"

Ruby wasn't sure what to say. Now didn't feel like the right time to tell him what she had witnessed. That would probably freak him out more than he already was, and they both needed a level head if they were going to survive this.

The plane began its descent, and she took his hands in hers. "I think she probably ran off to get help. She probably ran back to Dad, and they're coming for us right now."

MJ looked unconvinced. "I don't think she would have left us. You didn't see the look on her face, Rubes. When she saw me, she was scared. And then that man hit her on the back of the head." He said it like he was piecing together the memories as he spoke. He jumped to his feet. "You don't think she's dead, do you? You don't think he killed her?"

Ruby shook her head and pulled him back to his seat. The plane was small and every time he jumped, it wobbled.

"I seriously doubt it. I believe she's gone back to Dad and told him."

"Or one of those guys who came to the house. Who were they?"

She didn't know who they were. There was a tension in all of them, even the man who had come to train Rox had seemed different when they were all together. "Listen, we can't get separated. We have to fight if they try to take us away from one another."

His bottom lip trembled, but he nodded. "I won't let them take you away from me."

"Me either. But if it happens, you gotta promise me you'll keep trying to escape."

He turned away from her to look out the window. From this altitude, they could see the silver lining around each cloud. Dawn was here and it was beautiful. She wasn't sure what awaited them beneath those clouds, but for now, she sat back in her seat, grabbed her brother's hand and simply enjoyed the sunrise.

"Isn't it beautiful?" MJ said.

She pulled him into her lap and placed a kiss on his head. She would kill anyone who harmed him, or she would die trying.

CHAPTER ELEVEN

~

Awakening

5th August, 6:09am (-1 SGT)
Wiang Kaen Province, Chiang Rai, Thailand

Whoever was in charge of this warehouse didn't do much in the way of maintenance. Dust floated in the daylight that broke through the grime on the windows. Most of the glass panes were still intact, but a few had cracks. Grass sprouted through the fractures in the concrete floor, giving it an urban jungle feel. The paint looked faded from the sun, but otherwise bore no marks of wear and tear. There were no signs or fences to prohibit entrance, but these weren't necessary with a neighborhood watch willing to poison and potentially kill trespassers.

Josh had read the couple's minds with Mika's help, and they were surprisingly light on details. All they knew was that in exchange for reporting anyone asking questions about the warehouse, they would get a bonus on top of the US$200 stipend they received monthly for acting as "concerned citizens". Last night was meant to be a massive payout for them, and Rox couldn't hide her mounting frustration anymore. All she wanted was her two children back, but now, they also had to figure out whether it was Mika's contact or Meita's who had double-crossed them.

Mika half carried, half dragged one of the men who had shown up at the house to collect their bodies. Rox had to concentrate not to heal his ankle, but it wasn't as hard as it used to be.

A square crate a little shorter than waist height sat in the middle of the empty warehouse. A single fan was directed at the box, and Rox assumed it was to keep the contents from overheating, which seemed like a futile exercise given the corrugated tin roof acted like a grill top, roasting whatever was inside.

Mika stopped and inhaled while Josh turned his head to the side like he heard something.

"What?" Meita asked.

"Someone's in there," Mika answered first.

Rox started toward the crate, but Meita pulled her back.

"It could be a trap," Meita explained. Her tone said that should have been fairly obvious, but Meita couldn't feel the energy the way Rox could.

"He's trying to be quiet," Josh said. "Well ... I think. His thoughts are running all over the place."

Mika exhaled sharply through his nose like he was trying to expel something. "And he's not been allowed to use the toilet."

"I think he's a kid. No ..." Josh cocked his head to the side again. "Late teens." He shrugged. "It's hard to pinpoint; he's not thinking about his age."

Rox turned and looked at the man who was grunting in pain. She hadn't really given it much thought before, but now that she found herself in a derelict warehouse, her kids missing, and another victim stuffed inside a crate not large enough to allow them to stretch, she realized that on some subconscious level, she always assumed being a healer meant she was supposed to do no harm. It's why killing Connor Chatsworth back at Watership Down gave her nightmares even though she had won that fight fair and square. It was why she couldn't shake the guilt over stealing energy from a man who lay helpless while she searched for something to aid in her escape after just having her throat slit. It was also why she doubted her ability at everything – every goddamn-thing from being a good healer to being an adequate mother. It was all because she believed she was supposed to be good and pure, and perfect and worthy of such an ability.

But the more she thought about it – when she actually stepped back and looked at her life, or the last five years roughly – the more she realized that there was no such thing as pure and perfect. People weren't worthy of a lot of things. Often they got lucky or they worked hard until luck came their way. She had been thinking about her ability all wrong. She wasn't a healer. She wasn't some kind of benevolent EO sent to heal the world.

Rox?

Her ability interacted with energy, and that energy could heal people, but it could also harm them. And as much as she hated to admit it, Katherine was right. There had to be consequences.

She looked at Meita and then at Mika, who were both staring at her. Good. Let them wonder. She could take Josh's energy and Mika's, leaving them incapacitated, and while Meita was a better fighter, she wouldn't stand a chance against Rox amped up on adrenaline.

Good strategy, but why are we thinking about turning on one another?

Because I'm tired of being afraid. She wasn't sure if she spoke aloud, but she was past caring.

"We're going to find them," Mika said softly, but Rox had lost interest in the conversation.

She felt the hum from the dormant electricity sitting inside the walls of the warehouse just waiting for a switch to be flipped. She felt kinetic energy from everyone's elevated heart rate and the breeze created by a poorly oscillating fan. There was all this power around her, and she had never thought to tap into it.

The storm outside was passing, but she felt the charges in the clouds hop from one to the next, reversing its pattern to reach her. The memory of the lightning strike broke her train of concentration, but then just as quickly she wondered if maybe she could direct it.

"Can we test that hypothesis later?" Josh asked her.

She didn't want to. A parent's right to protect their child superseded everything. Laws were simply there to keep society in check, but they messed with her children, and there were going to be consequences.

She wanted this man who was silently crying, watching her every move, to know the torment of being stuffed inside a box like you didn't matter.

Rox—

She started towards the man who was happy to deliver them up like they were goods at a merchant bazaar. The tips of fingers pulsated as she balled them into a fist and then stretched them out wide again.

Mika stepped in front of her, but she pulled, and he crumbled.

Me estás asustando, mi amor.

Good. He should be scared because she was tired of being the only one.

The man Mika was holding fell, then flipped over on his stomach and attempted to crawl away from her. He was saying something in Thai, but she couldn't understand him, and she didn't care anyway.

When they were back at that couple's house, she felt a sense of clarity settle over her. She had spent so much time trying to figure out her abilities, that she had never once simply surrendered to them to see what would happen. But now ... now, she had been struck by lightning and instead of being dead, she was more powerful.

Instinct told her to lift her hand, and when her fingers snapped, a charge of energy raced across an invisible line and struck the man in the center of his back. His body went rigid, his scream paused.

"Rox!" Meita's voice was insistent, and for some reason that made Rox feel good.

She lifted her hand again, but something slammed down on her thoughts that prevented her from connecting her fingertips.

"Babe, listen to me, okay." Josh slowly walked around

until he was within her peripheral vision, and then moved even slower until he was in her full line of sight. His hands were up and the look on his face said he was concentrating hard on stopping her from snapping her fingers. "You're kinda scaring us right now. Mika was on our side. He's one of the good guys, remember."

A small part of Rox wanted to listen to him, but the energy she had built up was itching to be used. "There've got to be consequences," she said between clenched teeth.

"And there will be," Meita said. "But we're not cold-blooded killers."

"They took my children."

Josh groaned from the effort it was taking to hold her, and she smiled. "That lightning made me stronger."

No shit.

Let me go.

There was a moment of silence where she knew he was weighing up his options.

Rox, you know I'd never hurt you.

Then let me go.

You're the only mom Jay has. Please don't do this.

Stop using kids against me like they're a fucking weapon. It's cheap and it's getting old.

It's the only one I've got left, amor. Sweat was dripping down his face from the effort it was taking to keep her two fingers apart.

She hated him. She hated him for the myriad of emotions he had made her feel since waking up. Tears of frustration threatened to fall, but she was so damn tired of crying. It seemed like all she did was cry, or fret over this, fight through that.

How 'bout this, I'll let you fry the guy after you wake Mika up. Hmm?

Josh was opening his mind to her, allowing her to see things from his perspective, sharing his concern over her actions. It hurt him that she thought she hated him, but he was mostly trying to get her to focus on their shared objective: saving her children. He would stop at nothing to get them back. He felt he owed her that much. She had given herself up for Jay, and he thought he would never be able to repay that, but now was his chance.

"You don't owe me anything, Josh. I would have done it even if you hadn't wanted me to."

She put her arm down and the hold on her mind eased.

"We good?" he asked.

Rox looked back at Meita, whose weapon was drawn and pointing directly at her. If Josh hadn't talked her down, there was no question that Meita would have pulled the trigger.

It's not like you can't heal. C'mon. You had us freaking out.

No, but it's good to know where she stands.

Meita didn't survive this long by wishful thinking.

Rox's eyebrow raised. *Oh, since when did you become a* Meita *fan?*

Josh rolled his eyes. "Go wake him up." *Hey, any idea what his ability is?*

Rox shook her head as she leaned over Mika. *But he moves with such grace. He's not someone you ever wanna have to face.*

Yeah, I meant to tell you you're looking good. He's helped move some of the weight from there, he pointed to her thighs and midsection, *to up here.* He was referring to her shoulders and arms.

"You know, I might only have about five years' worth of memories, but even I know you never talk about a woman's weight."

Josh chuckled as Mika's eyes flew open. He grabbed his head and attempted to sit up. "What happened?"

"You tripped," Josh teased.

"Rox?" It came from inside the box, and everyone stilled.

Rox reached out with her energy and a familiar wave rushed back to her.

"Oh my god." Miles!

~

Anger-related

5th August, 5:37pm (-1 SGT)
Wiang Kaen Province, Chiang Rai, Thailand

The truck rumbling into the warehouse had long since given up on living, but its owner had different ideas. It was a patchwork of repairs and mismatched paint jobs. One of its tires was new while the others looked like they were desperate for retirement. It was early evening, so the headlights were on, but one kept flickering like it was giving advance notice of an imminent shutdown.

The man on the passenger side got out first, his weapon drawn as he gave the place a quick once over. He walked to the crate and looked inside, where Rox pretended to be a scared Miles. It was an easy role to play because she was petrified. Josh, Meita, and Miles were lying face down on the warehouse floor, pretending to be unconscious beside the man with a broken ankle, who didn't need to pretend.

The truck's passenger shouted something in Thai, and the driver got out, but left the engine running. He walked to the back of the truck, lifted the tarpaulin, and two more men climbed out, their weapons drawn.

Mika says there's a total of four. Three armed. Josh said.

I count the same, Rox told him as she peered through the crate's small breathing holes. *How do we play this?*

Sec, let me ask Mika.

Rox's thoughts were tempted to drift to Sam. He would have an idea about how to handle this situation, but she couldn't let her mind get away from her. Sam wasn't here. She hoped he was safe and that he was trying to make his way back to her. To all of them.

"มานี่แล้วช่วยฉันยกหน่อย," the passenger shouted to the driver, as he swung his rifle strap over his shoulder.

The driver hopped out and walked over to his companion. Neither one of them looked at Rox as they lifted the crate. They could see that someone was inside, but they didn't appear bothered or even surprised by it.

Mika's going to get their attention. Be ready in three ... two ...

"วางปืนลง," Mika shouted from somewhere behind the metal girders at the back of the warehouse.

The two from the back of the truck raised their weapons, pointing in the direction of his voice. All of a sudden Rox felt herself dropping, and then the crate crashed onto the floor. Wood splintered and dug into her hands and side, and she cried out, but Josh told her to remain still.

One of the men shouted, "นั่นใครน่ะ? เดินมานี่ซิ."

"โอกาสสุดท้ายแล้วนะที่จะวางลง," Mika warned.

She had no idea what they were saying, but could see from the look on their faces they were about to fire.

Shoot! Tell him to shoot!

Two rapid gunshots fired, both of them taking out their intended targets. Meita and Josh were on their feet, the weapons they had been concealing by lying on them now aimed at the driver and the passenger.

Rox kicked the side of the crate and it collapsed. She stood up and looked at the two guards from the back of the truck, both thankfully dead. She breathed a sigh of relief, just as she realized she was standing far too close to them.

"Shit!" She turned to run away, but death's energy slammed into her like an invisible force from behind, knocking her forward onto her knees.

The need to exorcise the energy was there, but unlike previous times, she didn't feel the urge to do sit-ups. She pushed to her feet as a tingling sensation raced up her back and around her waist to coalesce in the center of her chest. Death's energy had never done that before. It was attempting to merge with her natural energy, and she knew the moment their frequencies aligned because her muscles twitched, like she had touched an exposed wire, but instead of the raw pain she expected, it felt like a colony of ants marching underneath her skin. She wanted to scratch, but when she looked down at her hands, an arc of orange light jumped from one fingertip to the next.

Rox didn't think it was possible for her heart to beat any faster. "Did you see that?"

She spun around, but Josh was helping a visibly unstable Miles to his feet. Mika was tossing the guards' weapons in the back of the truck, and Meita kept her attention (and her weapon) on the driver and passenger.

"See what?" Josh asked without looking at her.

"You think anyone heard the gunshots?" Meita asked.

"I'd rather not wait to find out," Mika said.

"Holy shit," said Josh.

Everyone turned to witness brilliant sparks of orange energy hopping from one finger to the next. Rox pointed her hand at the far wall, and a ray of light as thin as a strand of thread snaked its way into an explosion on the far side of the warehouse. A jagged hole punched through the cinder blocks, and the evening's fading light seeped in through the dust and debris.

Rox's breath caught as she looked at Josh. Did she just shoot a beam of energy and create a hole in the wall? A concrete wall?

"Can you control that?" Mika asked.

Rox wasn't sure she understood his question. "What?"

"Do you have any control over that? Or are you going to be blowing holes in things involuntarily?" Meita elaborated.

How was she supposed to know? This was the first time anything like that had ever happened. "I don't think so, why?"

Meita sighed. "Josh, find out what they know. Mika will

translate for you." Then she turned her attention to Rox. "Because if they didn't hear the gunshots, they definitely heard the huge hole you just made."

"Please don't leave me again," Miles said. He was standing off to the side, shaking from adrenaline and fear. He limped his way over to Rox, but she met him halfway.

So many emotions played across his face as she allowed her energy to heal him.

"You're OK now." She had no idea what he had been through or how he had gotten in that crate, but she knew it had to have been traumatic. No one wound up in a box in a derelict warehouse in a foreign country without a story containing horrors.

For a while, she just stood there letting him cling to her while he hiccupped through his tears. When he grew quiet, she lifted her head so that she could see his face. "Why did you run?" she asked.

"You block the emotions," he said too quietly for anyone else to hear.

She didn't know what that meant, but then he continued. "Everyone's feelings are so intense. Fear and anger or sadness, and you just make them go away so I can …" he shrugged, "so I can just feel what *I'm* feeling."

"How'd they get you?" Meita interrupted.

Miles gave Rox a look that asked if it were OK to answer, so she nodded. He stepped out of her embrace and turned to Meita, but then cocked his head to the side as if studying her. "I can't feel you." He took a tentative step closer, then shook his head. "Nothing."

Meita smiled, and then placed her hand on his shoulder. "Do you think you can help us? Can you tell us how you wound up in the box?"

He nodded. "They jumped me in the bathroom at the park. I felt them before I saw them, but there were three of them, and one of them injected me with something. It was pretty strong because the next time I woke up, they were taking me off some boat and putting me on a plane."

"Did anyone talk to you? Tell you where you were going?"

He shook his head. "Not long after I was put on the plane, I passed back out. The next time I woke up, I was inside that." He pointed to the pieces of the crate, and then looked down to the front of his trousers.

Rox's anger grew at the thought of not letting another human relieve himself. When was the last time he ate? Drank? Was the same thing happening to her children now?

Rox held up her hands, and for a moment, everything was covered in an orange tint. She felt Josh roaming in her head and looked at him, but he was busy staring at her. They all were.

Babe, I think you need to calm down. This might be anger-related. It's definitely an emotional response.

The orange tint that covered everything faded as Rox wrapped her arms around Miles. She pulled him in and rocked him like she had Emma. "You're safe now," she said softly.

"I hate to break this up, but we need to move," Mika said.

Twenty minutes later, the driver was back in the driver's seat and Mika was in the passenger's. Rox, Josh, Meita, and Miles were in the back underneath the tarpaulin, attempting to hold on as they veered towards the border between Laos and Thailand. Destination, Pak Tha.

~

My own hero

5th August, 6:43pm (-1 SGT)
Luang Prabang, Laos

MJ screamed just like Ruby told him to, not too loud so they attracted the attention of others, but alarming enough to bring the guard.

It worked. A chair scratched against the hardwood floors, followed by urgent footsteps approaching.

The bathroom door swung open, and Ruby threw a basket of used toilet paper she had filled with water in the guard's face. He cried out like it had been scalding hot, but that was just his mind playing tricks.

She followed the guard as he backstepped out of the bathroom and bumped into the round table behind him. He lost his footing, and for a moment he forgot about the wet paper stuck to his forehead as his arms swung out in an attempt to regain his balance.

The look on his face as he righted himself scared Ruby into action. She ran up to him, planted her left foot and drove her right knee up into his groin. Pain like nothing she'd experienced ricocheted down her shin, and for a moment she thought all was lost because she might have dislocated something, but when she placed her foot back on the floor, it could bear her weight. Not a lot, but enough.

Her training kicked in and she knew just because an attacker was brought to his knees, didn't mean he wasn't dangerous. Before he could rise, she grabbed him by the ears and slammed his head onto the edge of the table he had just stumbled into. A loud crack echoed around the room as a section of it splintered off.

The guard was disorientated, but still conscious. Ruby performed a side kick, aiming for his head which was now about waist height. But the pain in her knee threw off her balance, causing her foot to slip perfectly in between the space just below his jaw and above his shoulders, dislocating two of his seven cervical vertebrae. His body slumped forward onto the floor, creating an awkward silence around the room.

Ruby stumbled back, and it was MJ who kept her upright. She didn't think she had the strength to do that to a grown man. Not as large and as muscular as this one. He was as tall as her dad, and definitely wider. This man worked out, and she was just a sixteen-year-old girl who took judo lessons twice, sometimes three times a week. She hadn't meant to kill him. But hadn't she threatened to do just that if he touched her brother?

Ruby clasped her hand over her mouth as she stared at the guard.

"Is he dead?" There was fear in MJ's voice, like he knew they had done something that could get them into trouble. But then again, what could be worse than the trouble they were already in?

Ruby tried to think through her fear. They needed to

find a way out before anyone came to check on them, or came looking for the cause of the ruckus.

"We should check his pockets," Ruby said as they approached the guard slowly like he could jump up at any minute and grab them. But he didn't. He couldn't.

Ruby's heart soared when MJ passed her a mobile phone that was lying on the floor near the broken edge of the table. "Please ..." she prayed, hoping there was sufficient battery to call her father. There was, but the phone was locked.

"Try 1, 2, 3, 4, 5, 6," MJ suggested. But that didn't work, and neither did six zeroes, six ones, or six nines.

Ruby groaned in frustration when the screen said the phone was disabled for six minutes. She felt like throwing it across the room, but remembered they needed to be quiet. This wasn't the time to give in her to her anger. Or her fear.

She looked around the small room to see if there was something she could use to defend them, but it was sadly bare. A dirty, stained mattress was pushed up against the wall in one corner and an equally-used wood laminate dresser with half its drawers missing were the room's only other items besides the broken table and its single chair.

An intense feeling of fatigue settled over Ruby, and for the briefest of moments she thought about lying down to take a nap. They had been through so much already, and now she had to orchestrate their escape. Where was her father? Why hadn't he sent someone to get them by now? Did he even know where they were?

"What's this?" MJ pressed a button and a blade sprung free. He hissed as it nicked the palm of his hand.

Protection, Ruby thought as a boost of adrenaline renewed her hope. It was too small to do much damage, but it would give them the element of surprise if someone tried to stop them.

"It's just a scratch," he said and licked the small cut.

Ruby was grateful because she doubted this room had much in the way of antiseptic. "I'll carry it." She closed the blade as they both crept to the door. Ruby put her ear against it while MJ came up behind her and laid on the floor to peer though the crack underneath. He shook his head when he got up.

She hated what had to come next, but the only alternative was to cower and wait, so she took a deep breath and twisted the knob as slowly as possible until the door creaked open wide enough for her to take a look.

The hallway was clear. The door across from them blessedly closed.

She took MJ's hand and they crept down the stairs with their backs pressed against the wall. They were halfway down when she realized their clothes were making a soft rustling sound, and so she told him to walk down the center. The stairs were impossibly noisy, and by the time they got to the landing beneath them, Ruby's hands were shaking so badly she put the switchblade in her pocket for fear of dropping it.

There were two doors facing one another on the next floor, just like on the floor above. It would be so much easier if she knew there was someone on the other side willing to help them. They were only kids. Who did this to children?

Ruby swallowed her sob as she looked back at her younger brother. He was frightened, too, but he looked up at her with such confidence and belief that she had no choice but to be brave and figure things out. They had to keep moving and trust that luck would find them.

She turned the next corner and stopped. The front door was at the base of the stairs. It was open, and the late evening breeze from outside carried the acrid scent of cigarette and rain. One of the men who had taken them was sitting on the porch talking to someone she couldn't see. For a moment, she simply froze, too afraid to move. She slowly stepped back into MJ, who immediately understood they weren't going to escape via the front. They went halfway back up the stairs and waited. Five seconds. Fifteen seconds. After about a minute, Ruby breathed a small sigh of relief. They hadn't been seen. But now what?

MJ pointed to the two doors they had passed, and she nodded. They didn't have any other choice. Ruby went to the one nearest them on the left and quietly tried to open it, but it was locked.

Hot tears burned her eyes as she realized she was going to have to step back into the opening of the landing to try the other door. She signaled for MJ to stay where he was as she took another deep breath and tiptoed over to the second door. If the men sitting outside turned around, they'd see her standing at the top of the stairs, so she kept her movements slow and light. She twisted the knob and it squealed. She stopped and waited a few seconds before she continued.

It was dark inside the room except for the intermittent light coming from the TV. It took a moment for Ruby's eyes to adjust, but when they did, she saw a woman lying on the bed, her light snores competing with the volume and the tick-tick-ticking of the oscillating fan near the bed.

Ruby didn't know what to do. If they woke her to ask for help, she might call the men downstairs. If they went into the hall, they risked being seen. If they went back upstairs to the room they had just left—

No, they weren't going back.

Ruby was thinking about trying the door opposite them again when she spotted a window. Its sheer curtains billowing out and then back in as the breeze from outside shifted. She placed her hands over her mouth to smother her cry of joy when she realized she had found their means of escape. She turned back to MJ and waved him in with one hand, and the other signaling for him to be silent.

She pushed the door closed slowly, and when she turned back around to MJ, he was already over at the window. He eased it up a few more inches so that they could fit through, and Ruby crept over to gauge how far the drop would be.

The window looked out onto a narrow alley that separated the house they were in from the neighbor's. Down the alley and to the right was the front of the house, but to the left she thought she could make out a small road. She tilted her head to the side and listened for the distinctive sounds of motorbikes. It was too dark and the rain prevented her from seeing far, but her instincts were telling her that once they were out, they should go left.

She looked down at the broken alley just underneath the window. It was a big jump. Two stories. She couldn't tell if the ground was concrete or dirt, but it didn't really matter.

Ruby pulled MJ so close that when she whispered, she felt his ear brush against her lips. "You cannot make a sound. When you drop down, quickly move to the back of the house because I'm coming down right after you."

Sirens blared from the TV, and they both froze. They looked back at the woman to see if she would turn over or give any indication that her sleep had been disturbed, but when she didn't, Ruby pushed MJ to go.

He placed one leg out of the window followed by another, then he spun around with his legs dangling and his stomach resting on the bottom of the window frame. He used his upper body strength to lower himself from the window as far as his arms would stretch, and then he let go.

Ruby stuck her head out and looked down after him. He had landed quietly and was up and moving like nothing was broken. She turned back and looked at the woman once more before she followed after her brother. She landed on her feet, and pain ran down her knee through to her shins. She thought of the man she had just killed—

"C'mon!" MJ grabbed her hand and pulled her down the alley to the back of the house. It opened up onto a narrow street. Motorcycles whizzed by just like they did in Phuket where their family often went. The sidewalks had been inconsistent there, and she thought it might be the same here. They would have to watch their steps. Neither of them could risk getting injured.

"Where do we go now?" MJ asked her.

"We need to find a phone. One that's not locked."

"You think someone will let us use their phone?"

She was too afraid to ask anyone if she were honest. Without knowing who to trust, she felt like everyone was the enemy.

Ruby took his hand and they walked down the street, both of them taking turns to look over their shoulders. It was rainy season, which meant that most of the shops had shortened hours or were closed altogether.

Twenty minutes later, they passed a motorbike with a gas-cylinder stove attached to it underneath a portable canopy. A woman was stirring ingredients in a wok, and the food smelled so good Ruby contemplated grabbing a few handfuls and running off. But the woman looked up, and Ruby blushed with embarrassment. The woman picked up a thin stick and skewered several pieces of barbecued meat onto it before passing it to MJ.

"F-O-C," she said. "You take."

MJ's eyes lit up. He took a big bite that reduced the portion to half, but then he passed the remainder to Ruby. "It's so good, Rubes." He smiled at the lady. "Thank you. We were starving."

The lady nodded and then turned her attention back to the contents of her wok.

Ruby mumbled a thank you, too embarrassed by the stranger's generosity to say more as they continued down the uneven pavement. Most of the tourist shops they passed were closed, but a few were still open selling things that once upon a time Ruby would have given anything to go in to see, but now, held no interest to her. She needed to find a way to contact her dad. To do that, she needed to find someone she could trust.

"We gotta get a bit further away from this area," she said to MJ. "We don't know who those guys were working with, but it makes sense they would be known in this neighborhood."

"So where do we go?"

She had no clue, so they walked in the opposite direction of the house, lost and jumping at any loud sound or the many stray dogs that crossed their paths. Ruby wasn't sure how far they had walked, but it was night now and everything was closed except the bars and a few late-night restaurants.

MJ said he needed a break, so they huddled underneath the awning of a 24-hour bookshop that was situated down a narrow alley off the main road. It was mostly dark, but a few of the lights were still on inside and it looked empty.

Instinct told Ruby they needed to stay away from the rowdier establishments, but where could they stay that was warm, dry, and safe?

Two girls with beautifully embroidered handbags slung over their shoulders looked down at them as they exited the bookshop. They were only a few years older than Ruby, and they were speaking about the bargains to be had during rainy season. But what Ruby found most interesting about their conversation was the fact that they were conversing in Chinese.

Ruby jumped to her feet. "对不起，你能帮个忙吗？"

The girls turned and looked surprised to hear their mother tongue from someone who was obviously not Chinese asking for help.

Ruby took their moment of hesitation to continue on. She told them that she and her brother had their passports stolen, and then she asked if she could borrow their phone to call her father who was wondering what had happened to them.

Ruby hated lying, but she wasn't sure if she told them the truth about being kidnapped they would want to get involved.

The girls eyed her carefully, and Ruby wondered for the first time how she must look to a stranger. Was her hair disheveled? Her clothes stained and rumpled? She probably didn't look like someone you should pass your phone to, even if it were only for a minute. But then they turned to MJ.

"你好," he waved with a big smile.

The girl who looked to be the eldest smiled back, and then reached into her bag. She ran her fingers across the screen in a specific pattern to unlock it. "Can you read Chinese?" she asked.

"Oh, you speak English?" Ruby asked with relief. Of course they spoke English!

The girl smiled as she passed her the phone. "Yes. You can call your Dad now."

Ruby pressed the plus sign, followed by 6 and 5, and then dialed home.

He answered on the second ring.

"Daddy?"

CHAPTER TWELVE

~

So close

5th August, 7:05pm
The Mekong, Thailand

The driver took them to Wat Huai Luek and parked in a space adjacent to the temple. Rox had no memories of being in Thailand, but Michael had told her they often vacationed there. He had showed her a digital photo album of them backpacking their way across northern Thailand, down to Bangkok where, on a whim, he said, they took a sleeper train to Penang, Malaysia. It all sounded romantic and adventurous, but even now, when she would give anything to remember a sliver of information about this country that could help her find her children, her mind came up empty.

The tarpaulin lifted and Mika motioned them out. "We're crossing here."

"Crossing?" Rox asked as she climbed out. It was surprisingly dark. The clouds blocked out any light from the sky and the few kiosks set up around the temple were closed, leaving the only visibility coming from the truck's high beams.

"The Mekong."

"Doesn't look like there's border patrol," Meita said when she stepped down.

Forget border patrol. Where was the actual border? Rox expected some kind of building or at least a hut to signify anything vaguely representing immigration.

"Driver said someone meets him here to take the goods across," Mika said.

"You trust him?" Meita asked.

Mika shrugged. "Don't trust anyone, really."

Meita nodded like she agreed with him. "Anything I need to know?"

"No. Just be on your guard."

"You think he'll try something?" Rox asked.

"He'd be an idiot not to," Meita said. "He's the last man standing and he's got no reason to think we'll let him go."

Would they let him go? They had left the passenger from the truck tied next to the two guys Mika had killed and the man Rox had struck with her energy back at the warehouse. The lady and her husband who poisoned them were also still alive, as were their two children. But Meita had separated them, putting the woman in the bathroom with her hands and feet tied together behind her back, and the husband bound to one of the dining table chairs. She had given the kids two glasses of water and then locked them inside their bedroom. Mika had taken the added precaution of removing the SIM cards from their phones and breaking them in half. He said he was sure someone would find them; he was just hoping for a head start.

Truthfully, Rox was torn about whether to kill the

driver. He had played a role in the kidnapping of Miles. If not directly, then indirectly. Miles would still be in the box if they hadn't turned up, about to be put on a boat and ferried across the Mekong like he meant nothing.

"He say how long he has to wait?" Meita asked.

"Five minutes, though it could be as long as twenty before the boatman arrives. Says it depends on the rain."

It was rainy season, and that meant rain was never too far away. The river would be swollen, making a crossing difficult, even with a boat.

Half an hour later, a man approached, calling out a greeting in Thai. Meita and Mika reacted first, drawing their weapons but keeping them lowered. The man slowed and began to back up, but Meita told him to stop.

"Do you speak English?" she asked.

He looked at the driver and then back at Meita before he nodded. "Yes, a little."

"Good. From now on, you will speak in English. Only in English. Even to him," Meita used her gun to point at the driver.

"OK." What else could he say? They were all dressed in black and two of them were armed. They didn't look like the negotiating types.

"We need to get across the river," Meita said. "Now."

The boatman nodded.

Mika asked him what would happen after they crossed. He began to respond in Thai, but Meita cast him a look that said it was in his best interest to switch. So he explained in English that once they crossed, there would be another truck waiting to pick up the supplies.

"And from there?" Mika asked.

"I don't know," the boatman answered.

"Is he telling the truth?" Meita asked Josh.

Josh tilted his head to the side for a moment. "Yes. As far as I can tell."

They followed the boatman to where he was moored, and Mika stepped aboard first so he could help Miles.

The boat was not what Rox was expecting. It looked old, much like the truck. Instead of a mounted seat, there was a metal stool and two white buckets that had been turned upside down as seats for the passengers. Over the steering wheel was a gray tarpaulin secured to what looked like four garden parasol poles. One side sloped down at the back as the yellow twine securing it needed re-knotting.

Rox looked around and concern for this next leg of their journey gripped her. There were no life jackets and nothing for them to hold on to except the side of the boat. Miles was meant to be transported in this? Inside a crate? He would have been drenched, possibly drowned, by the time he reached his destination.

"You try anything and he shoots your friend here," Meita pointed first to Mika, and then the driver. "And then I shoot you."

"OK."

This was not how Rox envisioned the rescue of her children, but then again, she was wholly unprepared to do battle with a man like Tusk. The connections, the money, the network he had established was simply beyond anything she could imagine.

Heavier clouds gathered overhead, gobbling up what little light there was and the rain began to fall in earnest.

The boatman unwound the rope that kept them from drifting away from the planks, switched on the front lights, and looked at Meita before he started the engine. Its roar killed the silence as he backed them out onto the choppy waters of the Mekong.

"How long does this take?" Rox shouted to be heard over the rain and the motor.

"Two hours. Sometimes more," the boatman said, and as if to prove his point, water splashed up out of the river and into the boat, wetting everyone on port side.

Ruby and MJ had been officially abducted for almost twenty-four hours. Would they be at the facility by now or were they still in transit like Miles? Were they hurt?

Can't think like that.

She knew Josh was right, but it was hard not to when there was so much beyond her control.

Josh placed his hand on her shoulder and some of the tension eased. *Meita knows what she's doing.*

Rox looked at Meita where she sat just behind the driver and to his left. She had gotten sprayed with the river, but hadn't flinched, her gun never wavered.

I don't know what to think about her. Rox admitted. *I want to trust her, but then again, instinct is telling me not to.*

Always follow your instincts, mi amor.

They cruised for two hours, going faster at times while at others progressing at a snail's pace. It was too dark to make out anything except for the small cone of visibility provided by the boat's light, so Rox alternated between reaching out with her energy and allowing her thoughts to run free.

She didn't envy Michael for having to remain at the hotel. He would have preferred to be here with them – what parent wouldn't – but it was good that he hadn't come because if things took a turn for the worst, Emma would still have her father. Rox was beginning to realize that her dreams of creating a family were just that, dreams. If she knew ten months ago what she knew now, would she have ever come back? They were doing fine without her, but then Emma would have grown up without the support of an evolved parent, and Rox was determined to be there for her daughter so she didn't have to learn about her ability in secret.

A little over three hours after they boarded, the boat eased up next to a wooden pier that disappeared each time a wave swept by. The boatman reached up and turned off the light, and Meita lifted her gun.

"No-no," he said, holding up one of his hands while he continued to steer with the other. "There are people staying in those rooms. We don't want the light to wake them."

Meita nodded, but didn't lower her weapon.

Mika grabbed the truck driver and they alighted first.

When Rox stepped out of the boat, she had to fight the temptation to scream. She wasn't sure what she was expecting, but a sleepy river community was not it. Houses constructed out of nothing more than driftwood and elevated on stilts sat about fifty meters from the river's edge. There were no outside lights and she assumed it was too late for anyone on the inside to be awake. Even without the rain, it was the remoteness of their new location that caused her despair. If Ruby and MJ managed to escape, where could they go? Who would help them? How would they get back to civilization?

Rox's boots disappeared beneath the waves as they walked up the embankment. They stopped in front of a small hut tucked behind the houses about seven hundred meters from the river. Its roof was made of dried grass or perhaps banana leaves, Rox wasn't sure, but when they entered, another man was seated at a desk. The smile he wore was quickly replaced by a look of terror when he saw them.

He, too, spoke English, which was helpful because it meant Rox didn't need to rely on Mika or Meita to translate. He explained that he usually waited up until the supplies arrived, then he would drive them to the facility at first light.

"Not tonight," Meita said. But then her phone vibrated. Everyone fell silent.

Rox wasn't sure what made her reach into Meita's pocket for the phone, but something about the vibrations made her think she could interact with it.

Don't. Let me get it.

No, I actually think I can do this. But then the ringing stopped, and Rox thought she had broken it, but then the screen flashed bright with a missed call alert. Caller ID blocked.

"I missed it," Rox said, but felt a moment of joy that she had interacted with her first piece of electronics since waking up five years ago.

"They'll call back. Just hang on to it for me."

The man who had been sitting inside the hut led them to the top of the hill where a truck, not too dissimilar to the one they had abandoned back at the temple, was wedged in between two other vehicles.

Mika handed his weapon to Josh and used the keys the man had given him to start the engine. It rattled to life on the second attempt, and Mika eased it out far enough for everyone to get in.

Rox was about to step up into the back cabin when Meita's phone vibrated again.

It was Katherine. Ruby had called.

Rox's hands were shaking so badly she almost dropped the phone, but she felt Josh probing her thoughts as she listened to Katherine's update.

"What?" Meita asked.

Josh explained.

Meita swore, and that caught Rox's attention. Did something happen? Was she upset?

"How long ago was this?" Meita asked.

Josh waited until Rox had asked the question and Katherine had answered before he told Meita four hours ago.

"Whoever took them would have noticed by now," Meita said. "Please tell me they're not with the police."

Mika got out of the truck and took his weapon back from Josh. "What's up?"

"Ruby and MJ escaped. They're in Luang Prabang," Josh said.

Mika sighed, too, like their escape was somehow an inconvenience.

"What is wrong with you people?" Rox took the phone away from her ear. "They got away! How is that a bad thing?"

"Give me the phone," Meita said.

"No." Rox wasn't giving her anything. Why wasn't Meita as happy about this as she was? Didn't they see this was a good thing?

"Rox," Meita said softly, "Luang Prabang is a five-hour speedboat ride from here. In this weather, it could easily turn into seven, and we don't have a speedboat. The nearest airport is back at Chiang Rai."

"There's Huay Xia about an hour up the road," the man from the hut supplied. "But it's been closed for renovations going on five years now."

The realization of what they were up against threatened to shatter what little resolve Rox had left. They were so close.

"What about a helicopter?" Josh asked.

"Nearest place we could *possibly* get that is in Huay Xia," Meita said. "But that kind of transportation requires planning."

"What do you mean?" Rox shouted. "We got this far without planning!"

Meita looked at the three men they were holding hostage before she turned her attention back to Rox. "We don't have enough cash to pay for the fuel?"

"Money? You're worried about money at a time like this?" Rox lifted the phone back to her ear. "Katherine, we need you to transfer some money." Rox looked back at Meita. "She said what's the account number."

"Rox, these people don't have bank accounts," Meita

said. "Look around you. People operate off of barter and cash. And even if they did have an account, no one would have a helicopter that can fly in this kind of weather, especially across that kind of distance. Most of the helicopters these people have are decades old, meant for fifteen to thirty-minute tour rides on a circuit."

Rox shook her head. There had to be another way. Her children had escaped, dammit. They had done more than their part. Was Meita proposing just leaving them there?

She's not talking about leaving them. Let's just hear her out first.

"What if we, we just booked a flight from this Why-Zeeya place?" Rox suggested, her tears mixing in with the rain.

"It's closed for renovations, remember? And even if it wasn't, Luang Prabang's airport isn't open twenty-four hours."

Rox forgot she had the phone in her hand as she spun away from them. She didn't even hear it hit the ground over the sound of her heartbeat. She knew Ruby would fight back, and she did. She had saved herself and her little brother. She had somehow found a phone and managed to call home. Rox couldn't accept they were in the same goddamn country, but there was just no way to get to them other than a seven-hour boat ride!

She hadn't meant to scream. Making that kind of noise drew attention, but it came out of nowhere, and it felt good, so she did it again, and again. When she looked up next, everything was tinted in orange and the urge to snap her fingers was almost unbearable. Everyone had taken a step away from her, everyone except Meita who had picked up the phone and was talking with Katherine.

"Book them into the most expensive hotel. Instruct them not to open the door for anyone, not even room service," Meita said, and then paused while she listened to Katherine. "OK, good. Then see if they can get a room at that ... It's rainy season! How are they fully booked?"

Another long moment of silence.

"OK, so what do we know about the Chinese ladies they're with?"

What Chinese ladies?

Meita massaged the space between her eyebrows with the heel of her palm as she repeated a litany of okays and yeses. "They'll have to leave if the two ladies don't want them to stay ... OK, find another place they can go to if that happens. They shouldn't leave where they are unless it's absolutely imperative ... Six, seven, maybe eight hours ... It's rainy season, Katherine, even a speedboat can't compete with that ... OK. Call me back if anything changes. Yeah, I'll do the same."

Meita put the phone back in her pocket and lifted her gun to the man who had been in the hut. "We need two containers of petrol."

The man hesitated as he looked back and forth between Rox and Meita.

"Or, I'll let her electrocute this entire village," Meita said. "Starting with you."

~

Neo

Date/Time & Location: Unkown

Sam slammed back into consciousness with a deep breath. He inhaled twice before he even considered moving. His eyes were already opened, and staring back at him was the animal with the two saber teeth. Its head was so close he could see the line separating its lips. He was surprised by how far the opening of its mouth stretched back into its jaw. Its fur was thick upon closer inspection and the color of honey, manuka, with lighter spots sprinkled throughout.

It groaned at Sam, and he once again wondered why it hadn't kill him. He wasn't sure how long he had been unconscious, but that would have been the most opportune time to attack. He was beginning to wonder if the animal wanted companionship. Perhaps it was just as lost as he was and wasn't capable of finding its way back home. Or, perhaps, it wasn't real to begin with.

The bottom of Sam's left eyelid began to twitch as he rolled onto his back and looked up at the treetops. For a while, he laid there simply grateful he had control of his limbs again. Despite the chill on the ground, it was comfortable. This close to the brook, everything held a pristine look. Untouched.

A breeze blew through and the rustling of the leaves quieted the birds for a moment. Overhead, he saw something with a bright yellow tail fly from one tree to the next before disappearing.

He should feel more afraid, but for this one moment, he only wanted to enjoy the view. He had survived. He was alive, and that was enough for now. He would figure a way back home later. How? He wasn't certain. If his fears were right, then touching Rox had transported him back in time. How far, he wasn't sure, but far enough to see a creature that shouldn't exist in any time frame he could contemplate.

He moaned through the pain in his ribs as he sat up and flexed his fingers, widening them so he could get circulation back to the tips. The joints along his knuckles ached each time he curled them, and he wondered how long it would take the poison from the tree spikes to clear his system.

He stared up at the sun and realized that it hadn't moved far since he lost consciousness. Had he only been out a few minutes? Luckily, he hadn't stopped breathing.

Sam crawled his way back to the brook and on shaking arms, lowered his head down to drink once again. The frigid temperature helped to clear the fog, and when he was finished, his stomach reminded him that he still hadn't eaten.

A chuff came from further up the brook, and Sam looked in that direction. His companion was trying to get his attention. It must be time to move on.

Sam smiled to himself as he pushed to his feet. Maybe the animal would catch some food for them later, in addition to acting as his personal guide.

They followed the river upstream. The rhythmic flow of the water trickling over the rocks was hypnotic. Its constant ripple kept them at a steady pace, and every now and again, Sam would pick up a flint to test its sharpness before slipping it into his pocket with the others. At some point later on, he was going to have to make a fire. He would also have to find something portable he could use for shelter when it rained. He glanced back up at the sky. There were clouds on the horizon, but thankfully heading in the opposite direction.

Much later when the sun began to slip, Sam whistled to his guide that he was stopping. In scouts when he was just a kid, he learned how to craft a fishing rod with a long stick, his shoelace, and a sharp, sturdy twig. But this time, he decided it would be easier to build a dam using twigs and branches. He dug a small waterway beside it and added dead worms and crushed snails he had dug up. It took longer than he would've liked, but he caught three fish just large enough to make a single meal.

By the time he used his sharpest flint as a knife to gut the fish, it was almost dark and he had to hurry to gather kindling for the fire. The canopy above was completely shrouded in black when the first spark lit. Sam's guide growled and stepped back to watch from a safer distance.

It took a while before the flames were steady, but when they were, Sam chuckled. His father would have built a treehouse and had several large trout already hanging from a rack he had also constructed. He would have either found civilization or had discovered a way back to it by now.

Sam held the fish close to the flames as the fire crackled.

The reality of his situation began to settle in and with it the struggle not to panic. His ability wasn't working, which meant he had no way of getting home; and if he had somehow managed to slip back in time, there was no way for anyone to find him, let alone rescue him.

It circled the fire, its nose twitching as the night breeze picked up the smells from the fish oils and cast them about.

Sam hadn't seen his personal guide eat today, but even if it had eaten, there was no way it would turn away from more food.

"Hungry?" Sam asked as he speared the second small fish on his stick. He was hoping the sound of his voice would distract it long enough for him to finish cooking.

Sam was willing to share, but he knew sharing was a concept that took humans thousands of years to understand. If he gave in and allowed the animal to eat everything, then Sam would certainly starve to death because it would always take his food. But if Sam held his ground, then there was a high probability that the animal would attack, and there was no way he would survive that.

Sam quickly added more branches to the fire until it was roaring. He was wasting wood and the fire would go out well before sunrise, but right now that wasn't his main concern. Right now, he had to keep the animal back so he could eat his fish, and then only after he had finished would he give the animal its portion. Anything else, any sign of weakness he showed, and Sam would be facing an animal in its territory with fire as his only weapon.

Sam moved closer to the flames and immediately began to sweat despite the chill in the night air. When his two pieces were done, he ate quickly. He was certain he was swallowing a few bones, but his guide had started to circle, flicking its tongue over its curved teeth and hissing like it was calculating the odds.

When Sam had only two bites left, he stood with the remaining fish on the stick, and slowly crept toward the animal. It stopped its pacing and gave a low growl. Sam held up his last bites and made it watch as he put them in his mouth. It crouched, its muscle taut and ready to pounce, but then Sam tossed the remaining fish on the ground between them.

It would have been easier to throw the fish farther away, but Sam was trying to establish the initial bonds of trust. The animal's hiss was louder than he had ever heard, but when Sam didn't move, it carefully placed first one paw out in front. A few seconds later, it lunged for the fish with a speed Sam knew he was incapable of evading. It devoured it, and a piece of the stick, in a single bite much like Shaira would have.

Thinking of his wolf made him think of home. He thought back to his captivity training. He had been told to think in terms of small, achievable goals because panic would create its own form of sabotage. "Routine is important," his instructor had bellowed. "It becomes crucial to survival." He had been told to get up, to exercise, to talk to himself if necessary, but to talk about the good times, and to laugh out loud. A lot. The key was to make sure he heard another human's voice, even if it were his own.

When the animal was finished licking the grass where the fish landed, Sam sat down. "I'm going to give you a name."

The animal cocked its head to the side and watched him with those sparkling eyes.

"I know that look," Sam said. "I haven't got any more food."

The creature remained silent as Sam began peeling the first layer of bark off one of the large sticks he had picked up earlier and was hoping to test as a weapon.

"I have a friend who sports the same kind of look every now and again. I think you'd like her." He gave his comment some thought and then shook his head. "Well, I think you'd like her if she didn't try to attack you first. She's not one for strangers, I must admit."

The animal chuffed, but maintained its distance from the fire.

"My name's Sam." He pointed at himself with the flint he'd been using to raise the bark off the stick. "And unless you're willing to tell me your name, I'm going to have to give you one."

The animal turned as if it were going to leave, but then it stopped and circled before lying down, it's head resting on its paws.

"What'd you think about Rufus?"

Silence.

"Me, too. Rufus doesn't exactly scream intelligence. More of a junkyard dog kinda name."

Sam peeled another stretch of bark from the heavy stick and tossed it into the pile with the others he was keeping for kindling.

"How about Neo?" He looked up for a sign that it approved, but the animal just continued to stare at him.

"Yeah, I agree. It *is* a bit progressive considering the time, but I think it suits you."

It felt good to talk after spending the entire day in his head, even if the dialogue was a bit one-sided.

"You gotta girl waiting for you, Neo?"

Silence.

"Yeah, me, too. Wait … " Sam squinted into the darkness as he tried to check out Neo's genitalia. "You're male, right? I made that mistake once a long time ago, and I swear she still holds it against me." Sam chuckled. "A bit of free advice: never mistake a female wolf for a male. They go ab-so-lute-ly batshit over a thing like that."

Neo moaned softly, and Sam smiled. He was going to get through this. He would simply take it a day at a time. He looked up at just the right moment to see an orange streak of lightning flash across the sky. There was no thunder and it was too dark to make out if the storm had changed direction, but he took it as a sign that the woman he loved would wait for his return. Not even a lightning's strike could keep them apart. Not for long, he hoped.

～

The will

6th August, 7:30am (-1 SGT)
Luang Prabang, Laos

Morning had breached the horizon, but the sun was still trapped behind heavy clouds when their boat docked. The ride had been dangerous and a few times they almost capsized, but the boatman was experienced and kept them right-side-up despite the currents.

The pier was busy with activity as they slipped into an empty space beside a long, blue boat with yellow plastic chairs lined up like in a cinema. Men with broad shoulders and bare feet ducked and then disappeared with the boxes they carried into the steering room at the back of the boat.

Rox looked back up to the warehouse where crates were loaded onto trollies and then wheeled down to the pier where even more men waited to carry them aboard the other docked boats. No two vessels looked alike; instead, they spanned the spectrum from rusting relics to sleek and shiny.

Most workers slowed and stared at them. Meita and Mika had concealed their weapons, but Rox wondered if people could tell they were holding three men against their will. Either way, it didn't matter. She wasn't there to make friends.

The plan was that Mika and Rox would alight first and then find a taxi to the Hôtel Sofitel where MJ and Ruby had stayed the night. Apparently, despite it being rainy season, the hotel was fully booked because over half of the rooms were undergoing renovations.

Josh, Meita, and Miles would catch up with them later after the appropriate authorities arrived to take custody of the truck driver, the boatman, and the man who was inside the hut. Meita said chances were nothing would happen to them. There was very little in the way of evidence, and Miles was in no state to testify. Their best chances for preventing this from happening again was to shut down the source, which meant finding Tusk and shutting down the facility.

Mika took the lead and Rox followed him along the pier and up into the lot with the trucks. They sidestepped the puddles and potholes until they reached the sidewalk.

Mika explained that normally the street would be lined with taxis, but given the time of year, they were far and few between. Rox wanted to scream in frustration at how difficult everything had been since returning to her family. It seemed like everywhere she turned, things were stacked against her and she first needed to overcome this challenge or solve that problem. Right now, she could use a win. She *needed* one.

Mika reached for her hand and pulled her close. "If you look like a desperate woman, people will know they can take advantage of you."

She *was* a desperate woman. Desperate to get to her children. They had escaped over twelve hours ago and were relying on the generosity of literal strangers. But Rox did as Mika instructed and took a deep, calming breath before putting her arm around his waist. They were just a couple with reservations at the Sofitel, anxious to get the next leg of their holiday started.

She was surprised when he leaned in close like he was about to kiss her, but instead brushed his lips against her ear. "There's an SUV with four men over there. No, don't look. Your three o'clock."

"Let me guess, you don't think they're waiting to offer us a tour or something?"

He smiled like she had said something funny. "Doubt it.

The driver's the only one awake and he's got a coffee in his hand. Everyone else here is busy doing something, setting up their stall, unloading, or prepping their boat."

"You think they're with Tusk?"

Mika shrugged. "No clue, but I'm more worried they're meant to watch the pier for the kids."

Anger surged through her, but she wasn't sure how to react when he started to massage the nape of her neck. "Calm down," he said with another fake smile. "You don't want to go all orange on me."

She looked at him in confusion.

"Well, you don't actually turn orange so much as you get this distant look in your eyes and your fingertips, they definitely go orange."

Rox reached up and ran her hand over her wet head. A chill raced down her spine because she had forgotten how short her hair was now. It didn't matter who they pretended to be because there was no hiding just how bedraggled they looked. Their appearance alone was enough to draw attention.

"Let's start walking."

They crossed the road to where a few coffee shops were still closed. During the height of tourist season, these shops would be open, but during the rainy season, they operated a smaller shift and worked fewer hours.

Mika spun around and walked backwards, like he was talking to her about something, but she knew he was checking to see if anyone followed them. "Are you ready?" he asked her.

"For what?"

"I think we've picked up a tail. The two who were sleeping are now up and coming this way. The driver's gone down to the pier." He reached into his pocket and pulled out his phone. "You've got incoming," he said a few seconds later. "Tall, blue T-shirt, black jeans, and black workman boots."

They walked for thirty minutes, turning left and then right, like they were a couple exploring without a care in the world. The scent of baking bread was heavy in the air, and it felt wrong to have something smell so divine when her children were running for their lives.

"The hotel's down there on your left," Mika said. "You remember the room number?"

As if she would ever forget.

"Good," he said. "We don't have another choice but to lead them to the hotel. You head to the room, and I'll intercept them in the lobby so they don't follow you."

"And how do we get everyone out of here?" she asked. "None of us have passports."

"Katherine's working on that."

Rox walked into the hotel and stopped so abruptly, Mika almost bumped into her. She was surprised at its beauty. Brown and white marble tiled floors and bright yellow and red flowered plants were strategically placed around the lobby to extend the outdoor feel to inside. Dark woods and exquisite artwork added the finishing touches to what appeared to be a high-end hotel.

A receptionist greeted them with a slight nod of her head and the palms of her hands pressed together. Her make-up was far too fresh to have been applied last night, which meant the woman was part of the day shift. She introduced herself as Anna, and asked if Rox had a reservation. It wasn't until then that Rox realized she had been expecting a hostel or some run-down hotel with brown, peeling paint and stained linoleum flooring.

"Actually, I'm here to see my children. They gave me their room number, so I was hoping I could surprise them."

Anna stuttered like there was protocol against letting non-guests roam the halls, but Rox had pulled the mom card, and that had stumped the receptionist.

"They're in room 17. We just got in on a private boat from Chiang Rai, and I can't wait to see them. Do you mind showing me the way?"

The offer of an escort seemed to appease Anna, and she told Rox to wait a moment. She went behind the desk and picked up a transistor radio. She spoke in Lao so Rox didn't understand, but she assumed she was calling for someone to come to the front desk.

A few minutes later, a sleepy-looking young man about the same age as the receptionist appeared. He performed the same greeting, and Anna told him to lead her to room 17. "And the gentleman?" She pointed towards Mika with an open palm.

"Oh, he'll wait here," Rox said.

It took more self-control than Rox thought she was capable of not to shove the young guy escorting her out of her way and just run full tilt in search of room 17. Their names were stuck in her throat, like she wanted to yell out to them, but knew she needed to keep up appearances.

The young man attempted to make small talk, asking

if this was her first time in Luang Prabang and then explaining how most people don't come during this time of the year. He informed her that if she didn't mind the rain, however, she could enjoy the same quality rooms at much cheaper prices.

He might as well have been talking to himself for as much as she retained, but he finally quieted as they reached the room. He knocked twice for her, and then pressed the palms of his hands together and nodded his goodbye.

"请问你是谁?" The voice on the other side of the door was feminine, but didn't belong to Ruby.

Rox remembered that the women they were staying with were Chinese. "Ugh … " Would her children recognize her as Rox? "It's Ruby's and MJ's mom?" Why had she said it like it was a question. She *was* their mom.

She heard voices from behind the door. They were still speaking in Chinese.

"What's the password?"

For a moment Rox was stuck. Password? Then she remembered what Michael had said back when they were looking for them at Fort Canning.

God, that seemed a lifetime ago.

"There's no hoverboard until you've saved up half the money." Her voice caught at the end, and she had to repeat herself.

Rox heard MJ's squeal and the locks turning. The door swung back and MJ launched himself into her arms. Nothing, absolutely nothing in her life would ever feel this good. His little legs wrapped around her waist as she exhaled a breath she had no idea she had been holding.

She stepped inside the room with him in her arms and looked for Ruby.

The sixteen-year-old was standing by the lounge chair, looking as uncertain and as vulnerable as a child in her predicament would feel. But beneath that was steel, a steel Rox recognized and admired.

"Get on my back," Rox said to MJ, and he climbed around her like he was a monkey. She crossed the room and pulled her eldest daughter in her arms and squeezed her hard like somehow a hug could communicate the depth of her emotions.

Ruby remained rigid, her arms not returning the hug at first, but then the dam broke and she fell into her mother's embrace. "You … you're alive," Ruby said. "But I saw you … you were struck—"

"Shh … *you* survived, baby. Nothing else matters." Rox placed a rain of kisses on her daughter's face. She laughed through blinding tears as they stood there, holding one another like a family should.

"You shaved your head?" MJ asked from her back, and Rox laughed.

"Yeah. It was time for a new look."

Without letting go of Ruby, Rox turned to the two ladies who had helped her children. Her voice broke as she tried to say thank you, but they understood and came in for one massive group hug.

There was a knock on the door, and everyone froze. "Ruby, take your brother." There was no peephole, so Rox asked who it was. When she didn't get an answer, she grabbed the lounge chair and pulled it in front of the door. Whoever it was could still get in, but the chair would slow them.

Rox threw open the curtains, ready to get everyone out through the patio doors, but a man was squatting on the other side of the glass. She heard the moment the lock disengaged, his pick a success. She didn't hesitate, and neither did he. He slid the door open with such force it slammed into the wall, coming off its rails and crashing to the floor. Large chunks of glass broke off, but luckily didn't shatter.

Rox drew, and his eyes rolled to the back of his head. She stepped back out of his way as he fell face-first onto the beautifully maintained wooden floors. She continued to draw even though a little voice inside told her to stop, that she had taken enough, but she didn't want to. This man was hunting her children, and there would be consequences.

Death's energy slammed into her just as the front door clicked open like someone had used the room key.

The two ladies screamed, and thankfully, Ruby and MJ stepped back. Rox raised her hand as an arc of orange energy flew across the room and slammed into the chest of the other man who was following them.

"C'mon," Rox said.

Ruby and MJ immediately followed, but the other two ladies hesitated, so Rox turned to them. "Listen, it's not safe here anymore. They're going to think you're with us." Then she remembered they had answered the door in Chinese. "Do you speak English?"

The eldest one nodded.

"Then let's go." Rox turned to Ruby. "Hold his hand. No matter what happens, don't let go."

"Wait!" The other young lady ran to the closet where she opened the door and quickly entered a code to the safe. She retrieved their passports and wallets. "OK," she said.

Rox grabbed MJ's hand and told him to hold onto Ruby's.

"Don't let go."

Rox led them out through the shattered balcony door, past the pool and back to the front desk where Mika was lounging near the front door.

"I think they're hanging back," he said when he saw them approaching.

"No, they're back at the room."

Anna's radio jumped to life behind the desk, and the voice on the other end echoed throughout the lobby.

"Let's go," Rox said and led them all out of the hotel.

Mika pulled out his phone and called Meita. "We've got them. Where are you?"

There was a moment of silence. "OK. Plus two more ... yes, I know, but you're going to have to make it work. I doubt she would have brought them if she didn't have to."

"We're not leaving them," Rox shouted, hoping Meita heard. These two young women saved her children. They helped when they didn't have to and as a consequence, they were now in danger. She owed them more than she would ever be able to repay. The least she could do now was save them. Or die trying.

She was half running, half dragging MJ and Ruby after her. Mika was following last to protect them from the rear. "Turn left," he said to her, and she did, right into the chest of a man who was about a good head taller than her.

Rox was just about to apologize when she heard Ruby suck in a deep breath of fear. That was all she needed to know. Rox dropped her son's hand and sucker punched the man standing in their path. It was sloppy and she was sure she hurt her hand more than his jaw.

His comeback was much more powerful than hers. He picked her up and slammed her into the side of the building, the concrete corner eating into her back, but she didn't let that distract her. She sucked his energy from him and then used it against him. She dropped into a crouch and aimed for his stomach. He buckled under her blow and she brought her hands together up over her head and slammed them down across his back. He was down, possibly unconscious, but Rox continued to take his energy. She knew the moment he was nothing more than a corpse because the urge to snap her fingers was making her palms itch.

"Let's go," she said.

"Left, right, and second left," Mika shouted, still on the phone with Meita.

The sound of wheels screeching to a stop from behind made them all look over their shoulders.

"Run," Mika shouted.

A van had turned around and was now barreling down the narrow side street after them. They needed to make it to the main road up ahead or they would be run over.

Rox glanced over her shoulder and saw that Mika was urging the two girls into a sprint.

Rox called the kinetic energy from the storm clouds around her. Adrenaline washed over, and with it came the will to stop running, to turn around, and fight.

She took a left onto the main straight and then instructed MJ and Ruby to keep running. She sensed Mika's and the girls' energy coming around the corner, and she easily sidestepped out of their way.

"What are you doing? Run!" Mika grabbed her arm to pull her after him, but then let go when he felt the live current coursing through her.

The hair on her arms rose and everything faded into that orange tint. The van came careening around the corner just as Rox snapped her fingers.

Lightning the color of a perfect sunset slammed down into the front of the van, flipping it over. Shards of glass and bits of broken metal flew through the air towards them like bomb fragments.

Rox threw up her hands and a shimmering orange wall of energy formed, absorbing most of the blast, but not enough to neutralize it. She flew back through a shop window, skidding across the tops of tables until she crashed to the floor.

Air flew out of her lungs, and for a moment she wondered if she were still alive. But the high-pitched whining in her ears assured her that she was still breathing. Tiny splinters of glass sunk into her palms when she pushed to her feet, and blood from a cut on her forehead ran into her right eye, but she had to keep moving. Ruby and MJ wouldn't be safe until she had gotten them far from this place.

"Ruby?" she shouted as she staggered back out onto the street.

Mika was helping everyone to their feet, trying to keep them moving in the direction that Meita had instructed. He spun around, but stopped short when he saw her. "Don't take it out," he said.

Take what out?

Rox looked down to where a large, triangular piece of glass was sticking out from her lower abdomen, just below the compression vest that protected the upper part of her chest.

She would have collapsed if Mika hadn't caught her. She gripped the shard of glass, and Mika slapped her hand away. But he didn't understand that her body was already healing itself. If he left it in, she would simply heal around it, thus cutting herself a second time when she pulled it free.

Rox gathered her strength and pushed away from him as she yanked out the glass. Her knees buckled and everything grew dark. She remembered that energy was all around her, and so she called it to her. The first to respond was the storm's, followed by the thousands of wires running from the telephone poles and across the rooftops. It raced down her chest and gathered around her open wound. She lifted her head and screamed in pain. She felt the wound closing, like thousands of tiny red ants attempting to suture her from the inside out.

Mika hauled her to her feet and began dragging her

down the sidewalk. People came out of their shops to watch them as they passed. Someone shouted at Mika to lay Rox down because she was bleeding, but then Meita appeared driving a cream-colored van with flashing lights. Its wheels locked and the van skidded to a stop. The side door opened automatically, but a lot slower than anyone expected.

Ruby grabbed MJ's hand and took a step back.

"Get in," Mika shouted, but Ruby looked at Rox for confirmation and Rox nodded her approval.

You're covered in blood. Josh's thoughts penetrated her mind.

"Yeah, but you should see the other guys."

"Mom?" It was MJ. His eyes were wide with fright as the door slowly closed and Meita reversed them back down the street. She fishtailed into an intersection and put the van in drive.

"I'm OK, I promise," Rox said, once the van stopped rocking.

"But you're bleeding," he said softly.

Rox felt more energy flow into her, and she groaned at the final bits of healing. She took deep breaths through the pain as everyone watched her, everyone except Meita.

When she could breathe normally again, she sat up slowly. Ruby and MJ stared at her as if they had never seen her before. She wanted that closeness they had in the hotel room back. She wanted their arms wrapped around her and hers around them.

"How'd you do that?" MJ asked. "How'd you make that van explode?"

She wasn't sure how to respond. Simply saying that she was a healer no longer felt accurate. She laid her head against the back of the seat. "I'm not sure how to explain it, buddy."

It felt surprisingly good to tell them the truth.

EPILOGUE

~

Around the bend

6th August, 8:00pm (-1 SGT)
Suvarnabhumi Airport Bangkok, Thailand

The drive from Luang Prabang to Vientiane took over seven hours, and from there Katherine had arranged flights for them to Bangkok. They flew on diplomatic passes on a commercial airliner. When they landed, the two young Chinese ladies, whose names were Dawn and Summer, met both sets of their parents at the gate. Rox discovered that the girls were aged nineteen and twenty, and weren't sisters but best friends from childhood.

Katherine had somehow managed to get their parents through to the gate without boarding passes, which shouldn't have been surprising. The parents spoke very little English, but Mika translated their heartfelt gratitude.

Meita passed a business card to both sets of parents and told them to give the number a call if they had any questions. Ruby and MJ gave Dawn and Summer a hug, and thanked them for their help. They said one last tearful goodbye as security escorted them through the airport to their gate where they would await their flight home.

Another two security guards escorted Rox, Meita, Josh, Mika, Miles, Ruby, and MJ to a private airfield adjacent to the airport. A private jet was waiting for them. "This will take you to London, Heathrow."

Heathrow? "But Emma's—"

Meita sighed, and for the first time, Rox noticed the circles under her eyes. How long had she been up strategizing, organizing, and ultimately executing the rescue of Miles and her children?

"Don't worry," Meita said. "Emma and Michael will be waiting for you when you arrive."

There was an awkward moment of silence as Rox tried finding the right words to express her gratitude. In the end, all she could think to say was thank you.

Meita gave her a sad smile. "In an indirect way, I should be thanking your kids. Because of them, we now know there's a facility in Laos. I don't know how many people are there, and Tusk definitely knows we're on to him, but we've got to try and save as many as we can."

Rox had forgotten about the facility. She forgot about the people who were being held captive and the experiments they would be forced to endure.

"Josh and I will catch up with you in a few days," Meita said. "We've gotta track somebody down." Her eyes narrowed in a way that showed more emotions on her face than Rox had ever seen.

"Who?"

Meita explained that she believed one of Mika's contacts had turned on them. "He's got a lot of my money, and if it weren't for you, things would not have gone as smoothly as they did."

There was another awkward moment of silence before Rox extended her hand. "I'll never be able to repay you for what you've done for me and my family."

Meita's smile was small. "We're a team now, Rox. I'm sure you'll return the favor soon enough."

Rox had mixed feelings about being a part of their team. She wasn't cut out for the type of life they led. There were too many moving parts to manage, too many people to manipulate, and all too often death was waiting just around the bend.

Josh came up to her and that's when the weight of the last two days came crashing down on her. "What would I do without you?"

"Oh, I don't know," he said. "Make all sorts of bad decisions that involve running away, jumping out of helicopters, rescuing people who later lead the bad guys directly to you … hell, you might even die a time or two."

She pulled him into her arms and held him tight. He squeezed her back until he had lifted her off her feet. She was going to miss him. All of a sudden, two months felt like such a long time.

You won't spend a second thinking about me. You'll be too busy learning about your new abilities. I think I might have to call you—

"Rox works just fine."

He cupped her cheek in his palm and rubbed a tear away with his thumb. He leaned in and pressed a kiss on her lips. She wasn't expecting it and didn't have the opportunity to pull away, but then again, she wasn't sure she wanted to. Everything was so mixed up now, she needed space. Some time to think things through. To heal.

Te quiero.

I love you, too.

~

Keenan

6th August, 6:30pm
Goring Heath, England

Rox slept the majority of the flight from Bangkok to London. When they got off the plane, a reinforced SUV much like the one they took from Crossroads was waiting for them. She reached out with her energy for Sam, but his familiar pulse didn't return. She wondered if he were injured and trying to make his way back. Or maybe he was in a better place, a place where people didn't experiment on EOs. Maybe his wife and child were there, too. Silent tears fell at the thought of never seeing him again. Their time together had been so brief. She wasn't ready to say goodbye.

"Sam." It was nothing more than a whisper, but she sent it out into the universe anyway, trusting that it would find him, and he would find his way back. To her.

"When are we going to see Dad?" MJ asked.

Truthfully, Rox didn't know. Meita said that Michael and Emma would be waiting for them, and Rox had assumed she meant at the airport. "Soon," she said, and hoped she was telling the truth.

The ride from Heathrow was bucolic. She had only been to London once, with Josh, to see a play. London was a beautiful city, vibrant and diverse, and full of history. Now, they drove down small country lanes that cut through fields where great big bales of hay were stacked one on top of another.

The screen that separated the front of the SUV from the back slid down exactly one hour and twenty minutes after the start of their journey. A man with a heavy British accent announced they had arrived. They turned right onto a narrow lane with a thicket of dense trees beginning to change colors on either side.

"Straight on is the Almshouses, but you'll be staying over here." The SUV took a narrow lane leading off to the right and followed it to a massive three-story home.

"Wow," said MJ as he stared out his window.

"Is Dad here?" Ruby asked seconds before the front door opened and Michael rushed out to meet them.

Ruby opened the door before they came to a full stop and jumped into her father's arms. MJ was only a second behind her. Katherine stepped out of the house dressed in riding pants, boots, and an oversized sweater.

Rox looked up as she got out of the SUV and stared at the sky. Thick white clouds jetted by, making her wonder if rain was imminent. A howl pierced her consciousness and she spun around. She caught sight of a bright white ball of fur racing its way towards her. She hadn't realized she was running until the wolf launched itself over the ditch separating the house from the thicket. They both tumbled to the ground where Rox happily lay on her back and let Shaira lick her face. When the wolf was done, Rox sat up and buried herself into the softness of Shaira's coat. How quickly her joy turned to sadness. "I'm sorry, girl. I couldn't bring him back with me."

Shaira lifted her head and howled, and they sat there for a moment, just happy to be in one another's presence. She noticed Walter when she got to her feet. He had just released his son, Mika, from an embrace. He walked over to her, and in truth Rox didn't know what to expect. They had gotten off to a rocky start when they first met, and she wasn't sure how much had been repaired by time and distance.

She opened her mouth to say something, but nothing seemed appropriate. She cleared her throat and tried again, but he pulled her into his arms. "It ain't your fault." But it was. If only she had better control of her abilities, if only she hadn't been struck by lightning, if only … "And he ain't dead. Not till I see a body."

"I chose him." She blurted it out before she knew what she was saying. "I mean … well, I mean, I know that … "

Walter threw back his head and laughed. "Good to see you're still a mess." He wrapped his arm around her shoulder and led her around the house toward the backyard. They walked slowly, both lost in their thoughts and struggling to say something, but unsure of how to say it.

Freshly cut grass as green and as smooth as carpet covered an area far wider than anything Rox had been expecting. Beautiful, colored flowers decorated the borders of the house as well as the center of the grounds, and it made Rox think of simpler times.

Whoever owned this property was wealthy, and not like Michael's wealth that was derived from recent innovation. This was old money. Money that languished in the past and had been passed down through the generations.

"You know I've met your husband, Michael," Walter said, and Rox sucked in her breath, not sure what to say. "Nice young man. Very good looking, too. Much better looking than my son."

She stopped and turned to face him. She wasn't sure what he was getting at, but she wanted – no – needed him to know. "I chose Sam."

Walter gave her a sad smile, like he knew something she didn't. "I know you did. I know you did."

Katherine walked over. "Good job," she said to Rox. "Meita told me you've managed to get yourself some new abilities. Well, it's about damn time. Was beginning to think I was never going to be able to introduce you to Keenan."

Rox looked to where Katherine was pointing. Just looking at him was like touching a live wire. Her energy flowed into him like they were old mates. Then, just as suddenly as it left, it returned, along with his, and she knew immediately that she was in the presence of another healer.

"Don't let his looks fool you," Katherine said. "He's older than all of us put together." She winked at Walter. "Including you, you old codger."

Keenan walked over to them with the grace of a gazelle. He was tall, but not overly. His dark brown skin and tight, short curls were a stark contrast to the pale blue shirt he wore. "So you are the one I have been hearing so much about." He spoke with an accent from somewhere in Northern Africa. He lifted the back of her hand to his lips, and for a moment, she was tempted to pull away. He couldn't be older than twenty, maybe twenty-five. "You are thrown by my appearance, are you not?"

It wasn't every day she met a man who spoke like he was Walter's age, but looked closer to Jay's. Speaking of, she turned to look for him.

"He is out taking a walk with Ian, the warden," Walter said, as if reading her mind. "Said he wants to get the lay of the land if you will be staying here for a few nights."

Rox couldn't hide her disappointment.

"You will see him soon enough." Walter patted her shoulder and then looked at Keenan. "That food ready? You know in America, we tell people to show up to a barbecue when the food is almost done, not when it's just touching the grill."

Keenan laughed. "Then it is a good thing we are not in America, my friend." He waited for Walter to get a sufficient distance away before he turned back to her. "You have an interesting story, Rox. Or do you go by Tara now?"

"Rox." It felt right.

"Rox it is." They both stared at the people mingling around. Most of them she knew, but there were a few she didn't.

"Katherine showed up at my doorstep yesterday and I must admit I almost killed her." He said it like they were doing nothing more than exchanging polite conversation.

Rox wasn't sure what to say at first, but then she laughed as she thought back to when she met the head of GFO. "She has that effect on people."

He joined in with her laughter. The sound was deep, like it came from his gut.

"What was she withholding from you?" Rox asked.

"Katherine and I have a complicated relationship. But she told me she had found another healer, and for a moment, I almost did not believe her."

"What changed your mind?"

"The wind."

Rox cast him a sideways glance that said she wasn't buying it.

"Energy is in everything, Rox. The sooner you realize that, the more powerful you will become."

"I'm not interested in power," she said as she watched MJ atop his father's shoulders. He was far too big to be up there, but she understood his need, and Michael's desire to hold him. She turned around and looked for Emma.

"Your other daughter is in the house. I am afraid she is still growing accustomed to her abilities. Too many potent emotions flying around for her to deal with at the moment."

Rox wasn't sure how much she appreciated Keenan knowing so much about her. "Well, it's been a pleasure to meet you—"

"Rox?"

She turned to Keenan and he snapped his fingers. A strong breeze came in from above and began to swirl around them, blocking everyone else from sight.

"What are you doing?"

"Offering you an opportunity." His voice sounded as if he were closer to her than he actually was. "Katherine said you awoke to your abilities almost five years ago. I know how confusing they can be. I know that with them comes memory loss. Confusion. Sorrow. I can help you."

She was taken aback by his proposal. She wanted to ask his age, but fear of his response made her pause. Did she want to confront the possibility that she was going to outlive everyone she knew? Was she ready for that? But then curiosity prodded her. "How old are you?"

"Is it not rude to ask someone their age?"

"Only a woman. And you don't look like a woman to me."

He threw back his head with laughter. "Let us just say that I have been on both sides of an empire. I have helped them rise and I have died many times as they crumbled."

Rox wasn't sure what to say about that, partly because she wasn't sure how to fit "empire" into a modern context. The fact that he had lived through so much history was just a little too much for her to process.

"You will not age." His voice had gone soft. "You will watch the people you love grow old, and it will play tricks with your mind. I cannot take the pain of their deaths away, but I can teach you ways to get through it."

"How do you get through watching your children die?"

"By learning to be at peace with your ability."

Rox spun around and looked at the tunnel of wind that was circling them. She attempted to step through the clouds, but Keenan blocked her. Then she attempted to draw from the kinetic energy created by the swirling vortex, but he reached out to stop her. "If we combine our abilities, it would create a funnel of electricity, and once the wind dispersed, your electrical charges would go with it. We could injure people for hundreds of kilometers around us."

How did he know that? How many other healers did he know?

"Your strength is with lightning. Electricity. Mine is the wind."

"Are there more like us?"

Keenan tilted his head to the side like he had to think about it. "I do not think so. But it is hard to tell. Evolved ones have existed for as long as humanity, but there have only ever been a few of us."

"Why?"

Keenan shrugged. "I do not know exactly. I assume to maintain balance. Imagine what we could do if there were five of us? Ten of us?"

She had never thought about it that way because she had never been interested in world domination. She wasn't sure how much she was interested in saving the world from domination either.

"Your eldest, Ruby, she is evolved as well."

Rox looked up in surprise.

"But not like you think. Our abilities will not work on her. Just like there are only a few of us, there, too, are always a few of them."

How did he know that? She had so many questions for him, she didn't know where to start.

If her evolved abilities didn't work on Ruby, then she was like Meita, which meant Ruby would've known that Rox was evolved, or if not evolved, just not her mother.

"How is it that you know so much about my life and we're just meeting for the first time?"

Keenan smiled like he was genuinely embarrassed. "My apologies, but I required all the information Katherine could give me before I decided whether or not to train you."

"I haven't decided whether I want your training."

"I saw the footage," Keenan said.

"What footage?" She knew what footage.

"I have never met a man like Sam before, but I have heard of his kind. Rumors say their origins began in the Scandinavian Mountains and that they could transport themselves in time."

She wasn't sure what that meant. Did that mean Sam was alive, just transported somewhere else? Her mouth opened like she was about to ask, but then closed. Was she ready to handle it if he said no? Was hope better than the truth when the truth had the potential to be devastating?

"Would you like to learn how to harness your ability?"

She wanted to know how to protect her family. How to call lightning at will. And she wanted to know how to build an effective energy shield, one that could withstand a blast and not send her hurtling back through shop windows.

But it would come at a cost. Everything always did.

"What do you want?" she asked.

"You to stay in the fight." He began to walk, and she

had no choice but to walk with him or get swept up by his wind tunnel. "I have lived long enough to see the world suffer great consequences when our kind prefer to live on the sidelines."

"And if I don't want to?"

"I do not do threats, Rox. I either do or I do not."

They walked for some time in silence. They left the landscaped backyard and went across the grounds of the Almshouse. He explained that the local elderly who were still too young for a nursing home lived in the different units onsite. Ian, the warden was responsible for checking on them each morning and night and seeing to their basic repairs when needed.

Rox wasn't sure why he was telling her this, but she listened as he explained the local history to her. He dispersed the wind tunnel a little later and led them down a path that ran through the pastures at the back. For the first time since Josh and Meita showed up, she felt herself calming. The tension in her shoulders dissipated and the lines on her forehead softened. Cows lifted their heads and watched them pass in silence. As did the horses and the pheasants, who ran a respectably safe distance away before turning to watch them.

Rox allowed herself to feel the beauty and the peace. Nothing else mattered at that moment. Just this.

"How long will it take?" she asked.

"That depends on you, I am afraid."

"A ballpark? A month or are we talking years?"

"I have never met anyone who could master anything in a single month."

Of course not. There would have to be a comparable sacrifice, and what could be more valuable than time with her family?

"I don't want to stay here, away from my family for years. If it's going to take years, then I'm not interested. I'll have to learn as I go."

He nodded like her response was reasonable. "Give me six months and then you can come every year for one month."

She thought about that. Six months and then one month per year. It seemed reasonable, especially since he was willing to teach her about her ability. But there had to be a catch. There always was.

"What's it going to cost me?"

He nodded like he was pleased with her question. "Time."

She chuckled. "If you're anything to go by, then I've got quite a lot of that."

His smile wasn't as wide or as bright as before. "Yes. You do. But they do not."

They had returned to the backyard where everyone was now eating around the table. Jay was back and he sat nearest Shaira, his hand absently running through her fur.

She missed him. He was her son just as much as MJ. She didn't care if no one understood. There was enough love in her heart for them both, for all of them, Ruby, Emma, and Miles too.

"I'm not sure Katherine will agree to me missing six months."

Keenan's hearty laugh returned. "My dear, Katherine only controls what you allow her to control."

She looked at him in confusion, but then he nodded towards the food. "Go. Eat. Be with your family. Our ability requires a lot of sustenance. Go. Get yours."

Rox wanted to stay and talk to him. Find out more about what it meant to be a healer, but he had been right. Her family didn't have all the time she did. They were going to grow old. The thought of losing them all over again, so soon after she'd just found them stole her breath.

"We start your training tomorrow," Keenan said.

"Tomorrow? I just got knocked on my ass by an exploding van."

"Then perhaps we need to start sooner."

Author's Note

I hope you enjoyed reading *Sacrifice* as much as I did writing it. I have to admit there were some twists I didn't see coming until I was in front of my laptop, writing them down.

Sacrifice is meant to be a fun, fast-paced thriller that grips you until the very end, and I sincerely hope I have achieved that as the author. The story, for me, is about the sacrifices we make to achieve our goals and the questions we ask ourselves along the way. Rox fought hard to reunite with her family, and now that she has everything she wanted, will she be able to settle into her new reality?

And where in the world is Sam? Is he still on the same planet? An alternate reality? Thrown back in time? Cast far into the future? Book Three will answer all of these questions, but what I can tell you now is that life is not picture-perfect and our happily ever after rarely resembles a fairy tale. Happiness is a choice. The question is, will Sam and Rox be brave enough to choose it?

Join Rox, Sam, Walter, Shaira, Josh, Katherine, and Meita as they continue fighting for the rights of evolved ones. Everywhere.

From the final book in this trilogy:

The Evolved Ones: Acceptance
(Book 3)

"Pops, set a timer," Danny said. "Eleven minutes to find out why we're short one white dot."

"Right. I don't hear from you by then, I'm sending Curtis," Walter replied.

Curtis was parked three blocks over in a sleek new, silver minivan that blended into their surroundings. He was their lookout and would provide support if anything went wrong. He was a former police detective whose wife went missing ten years ago. They had never found the body or any clues leading to her disappearance. It was a cold case, and if it weren't for Halo taking him in, he would have never survived. He owed Sam his life, but now that Sam was gone, he stayed with Halo just to piss off Walter.

Rox followed Danny to the edge of the trees where they crept along in the shadows until they were up against the fence separating the two houses. She wondered about the lives of the people living in these carbon copy homes. Were they aware they had an EO neighbor? If they were, did they care?

Someone had discovered that the Andersen family was evolved, or at least had an evolved member because the mother had been abducted on her way home from the grocery store three months ago. She had been blindfolded and couldn't make out anything about her kidnappers except the anti-EO rhetoric they had shouted at her. Her escape had been the result of dumb luck, or kidnapper-incompetence, the police report concluded.

Danny remained in a crouched position as he hugged the fence of the house until they were parallel to the back door. He stepped out onto the grass without hesitation and walked up to the house like he was the homeowner. He positioned himself off to the side so that Rox could take the lead.

This was the moment of truth for the Andersen family. Were they really going to pick up and leave all their worldly possessions behind?

Rox knocked on the door and stepped to the other side across from Danny.

Fear would be at irrational levels, Walter counseled, and no matter how much society had progressed, women remained the safer of the two gender options, so females always made first contact.

Walter's second rule of extraction: always remember you can lead a horse to water, but you can't make it drink.

Rox was about to knock again when a timid voice replied. "Hot dog?"

"With mustard," Rox said.

The locks disengaged and the door slowly opened.

"Are you Halo?" It was the husband, Glen, who opened

the door, but it was his wife, Tessa, who spoke. She stood in the hallway leading from the kitchen to the rest of the house.

"Yes, may we come in?" Rox said, and reached out with her energy once more for the missing fourth dot.

Glen stepped back, and Rox stepped inside and out of the way so that Danny could enter. Danny was a third generation army brat. He had dedicated his life to his country, working in special ops, and finally on unclassified assignments that had no visible chain of command, just phone calls, drop sites, and rendezvous meetings. He joined Halo eighteen months ago after an assignment ended his career. He had been lucky to make it out alive, but he was broken, struggling to find a reason to get up in the morning, and so Mcita recruited him.

Danny entered the kitchen at six-foot-one, but it was his girth that was impressive. It was clear he took care of his body. Just by looking at him, you knew where you stood. Rox had been training with him for over a year, and one thing was certain: she would never best him without the use of her ability, and even then, she found him hard to take down.

"This is my partner," Rox said, with a smile. "He's here in case we run into any problems."

The Evolved Ones trilogy:

The Evolved Ones: Awakening
(Book 1)

The Evolved Ones: Sacrifice
(Book 2)

Acknowledgements

I want to thank my beta-readers, Karen Hugg, author of *The Forgetting Flower*, and Tara S, Alex D, Kate C, Katri R, and Kece H for always being in my corner, regardless of where we are situated around the globe.

A special thanks to Xris Koh Schlingensiepen for reviewing my Chinese (OK, for translating my English into Chinese). I miss you and our hawker moments; I will treasure them always. Natalia Zarate for reviewing my Spanish and helping to make Josh's colloquialisms more appropriate given his mixed heritage. Num Punpeng for assisting me with Thai and Magali Finet for your unwavering support and friendship – and Meita's French.

I would also like to thank Anita for her kind and gentle approach to book editing. She remains an invaluable guide and a trusted friend.

My acknowledgements wouldn't be complete if I did not thank you, my reader, for spending your free moments with my characters. With so many options from which to choose, I feel beyond grateful that you are following Rox's journey. I hope you continue to follow her as she explores her new life in a world where evolved ones have only one choice remaining, and that's to step out into the light.

If you liked *Sacrifice*, leave a 5-star review from wherever you purchased this book. Bookstore purchases can be reviewed on GoodReads.com. Your positive reviews make it possible to reach more readers.

Follow my blog, NatashaOliver.com to get the latest updates about my book (perhaps some sneak peeks about what I'm working on) and my general musings on life.

I love receiving emails from readers, and so don't be shy, reach out to me at natashaoliverauthor@gmail.com or follow me on Instagram at *natasha_oliver_author* for my Monday round of #Motivation on being your own hero. I'm also on Facebook at *natashaoliverauthor* and Twitter at *natashaoliver.*

About the Author

Born in South Carolina, Natasha Oliver has lived in NYC, Boston, DC, Tokyo, England, and Singapore, and has spent 15 years working in North and South Asia. She earned a Master of Fine Arts in Creative Writing at Goddard College and a Bachelor of Science in Marketing at Lehigh University. Natasha enjoys writing strong, mature female characters in fantasy settings.